# Jumping over Fire

# JUMPING OVER FIRE

## Nahid Rachlin

CITY LIGHTS BOOKS
San Francisco

Editor: Nancy J. Peters
Cover design: Yolanda Montijo
Typography: Harvest Graphics

Library of Congress Cataloging-in-Publication Data

Rachlin, Nahid.
  Jumping over fire / Nahid Rachlin.
    p.    cm.
  ISBN 0-87286-452-9
    1. Refugees—Iran—Fiction.    2. Iranians—United States—Fiction.
3. Brothers and sisters—Fiction.    4. Incest—Fiction.    5. Ethnic
relations—Fiction.    6. Iran—Fiction.    I. Title.
  PS3568.A244J86  2006
813'.54—dc22

                                                        2005029778

CITY LIGHTS BOOKS are edited by Lawrence Ferlinghetti and
Nancy J. Peters and published at the City Lights Bookstore,
261 Columbus Avenue, San Francisco CA 94133.

For Howard, Leila, Greg, Ethan, with love

# ACKNOWLEDGMENTS

Thanks and love to my editor Nancy J. Peters for her warm encouragement and brilliant insights into this novel. I am deeply grateful to Stacey Lewis, Mitra Ganley Walker, Sabina Langer, Bob Sharrard, Lawrence Ferlinghetti, Garry Morris, and Karen Zanger for their belief in this book and their assistance. My love and gratitude to my family and friends for their inspiring interest and endless patience.

# Part One

# 1

Soon after Maman and Baba took Jahan from the orphanage in Shiraz and brought him to our home in Masjid-e-Suleiman, she got pregnant with me. Jahan was only a year older than me, and as we were growing up he was always at my side. He was ahead of me in his development and always took the lead. He taught me new words, held my hand, and helped me walk. We spent hours playing together in our spacious house in the Iranian American Oil Company compound. We had a courtyard, a swimming pool and a finished basement. Our parents' bedroom was on the first floor. Jahan's and mine was on the second floor and we were able to break rules, indulge in mischief without always being noticed. We stayed up late and made a tent of sheets and blankets spread over chairs and played house inside it. We lay on one of our beds and, through the window, watched fireflies shining on tree branches, the moon sailing across the sky, numerous stars winking. We made up stories about what could be going on inside the moon and the stars, those distant lights. We wondered if the moon was really looking at us. Was there a magical ladder on which we could climb to the stars? We fell asleep on each other's beds with our clothes still on. When I woke at dawn I went to the window and looked at the courtyard, damp with dew. There was something nebulous and soft about those early mornings, full of the scent of honeysuckle that grew in abundance there. I woke up Jahan and asked him to look out with me. In the early hours of the morning a sweet, languorous feeling came over me, being with him, breathing the same scents, looking at the same sights. He called me Noor, meaning light, a word closest to Nora, the name chosen for me by our American mother with our Iranian father's consent.

In our childhood photographs we are almost always together, standing or sitting with our arms around each other. In one we are in a carriage, a blanket covering us up to our necks, giving the appearance of two heads: one light, one dark, springing out of one body. I took my coloring from Maman, Jahan from Baba. In another photograph he is wearing pants and a shirt and I a full-skirted dress, but we are embracing so tightly that again we look like two parts of the same person.

A girl had little freedom in Masjid-e-Suleiman (in spite of the Shah's attempts at Westernization) and as we grew older Jahan became my source of freedom as well as my protector. With him I could explore different neighborhoods, go to cafés and restaurants, come home late. Our interdependency was all-innocent at first.

We had no idea he was adopted until he was fifteen and I fourteen. I clearly remember the afternoon when we were led to that amazing discovery. It started out in an ordinary way, with me waiting by the door of my high school for him to pick me up. His boys' school was close to my girls' school and it was easy for him to accompany me home and back. He had started doing that when we were still in elementary school to make sure that the tough boys from other neighborhoods who came to our area wouldn't harm me. His instinct to protect me was reinforced by a general attitude that a girl needed protection.

Other students, all in the required uniforms, gray with white collars, were also waiting to be picked up or were getting into cars to be driven home. The relentless heat that had seized the town for the last six months hadn't quite subsided. The air smelled of gas discharged from the refinery and the underground petroleum deposits. Flames coming out of the refinery towers, visible from almost every area of the town, glowed like an advertisement for the inferno. Trees were withered and dusty.

Jahan was late and I looked up and down the street anxiously. Then I saw him coming, wearing what his school required: gray pants, a white shirt, a navy blue jacket, well-shined shoes.

"Jahan, I was worried."

"I'm sorry Noor, I was held up talking to Bijan."

Even though it was hot we decided to walk around for a while before going home. We passed through the square that divided the old town from the new town, where the Americans and Iranians working in the oil business lived. Around the square were teahouses, restaurants, and shops. Some vendors were selling their merchandise from carts — leather handbags, belts, watches. One vendor had piled chunks of gum that looked like white soap on a cloth spread in front of him on the ground.

We came out of the square onto a narrow, winding street, lined with jewelry shops. Customers, mainly women, were looking in the shop windows at displays of gold rings, earrings, bracelets, and necklaces, studded with sapphires, rubies, and other precious stones. Some were inside haggling with the shopkeepers.

Then we came into the old town's residential section. The streets in this quarter were winding and narrow, flanked by baked mud-brick houses so close together that they formed high walls along the street. They had flat roofs, small doors, and there were no windows overlooking the streets. Instead, they faced inward, into courtyards and gardens. This was to protect women from the eyes of passersby. Jahan thought the houses were beautiful and liked this part of town more than I did. He was a boy and could play freely in these streets with his friends, some of whom lived here, while people always stared at me because I looked like an American girl. The majority of women in this neighborhood wore headscarves or *chadors*, even though covering up was optional at that time, during the Shah's regime. The ultra-conservative Muslims who lived here resented the presence of Americans and the English, because they were a constant reminder of the Shah's embrace of what they considered to be materialistic and immoral. They thought that these foreigners, *farangis*, were spreading vice and that the Shah collaborated with them. Soon I became aware of critical glances for not covering my hair. A bearded man wearing a turban approached us. He stared at me and then said to Jahan, "Who is she to you?"

Jahan ignored him but when the man repeated his question, he took my hand. "Let's get out of here," he said.

We took the quickest way home. When we reached Elm Avenue, an employee of the Christopher Cinema was putting up a poster for the movie *A Place in the Sun*. I was excited that another American movie was coming there. The films they showed were usually decades old but still they transported me away from Masjid-e-Suleiman, which I found more and more stifling as I grew older. I saw some movies more than once, usually with Jahan. He was willing to go if the movie had Farsi subtitles. His English wasn't as good as mine because he didn't try to speak in English with Maman as I did. He stayed with Farsi.

Then we entered the wide, palm-lined Washington Avenue, where our two–story house stood among other grand Tudor style houses, all set back in courtyards — their only Muslim feature. The compound was a classic colonial enclave. Our house was provided by the oil refinery's hospital, where our mother had once worked as a nurse and our father was still employed as a radiologist.

Once home, we immediately put on our bathing suits and dove into the large swimming pool to cool off. When we got out, drops of water like pearls covered our skin. Then we lay in the hammock, which was suspended between two trees behind some dense bushes. It was shaded and secluded there. Lizards scuttled beneath the bushes. Hawks flew above us, their wings spread. We could hear the loud shriek of the parrot, Sabz (Farsi for green), on the porch. "Salaam, halet chetoreh," he squawked the greeting Jahan had taught him. Crows that had built a nest on the top of a tall palm tree, excited by Sabz's voice, flew out, cawed, and wheeled around frantically. Petals from flowering bushes drifted over our faces and into the water, their perfume enveloping us. White-yellow butterflies danced around honeysuckle flowers.

"Jahan, do you know how butterflies are born?"

"From caterpillars. They have a thin, yellow string wrapped around them and the string forms the cocoons. Butterflies grow inside them. Then they tear the cocoons open and fly away."

After a while we dressed and went into the basement to do our homework. It was cool there, well insulated by stone walls. There was a comfortable sofa to sit on. A large filing cabinet and many boxes stood against one of the walls. One box was filled with items left from our early childhood—rattles, toy cars, dolls. A closet contained splendid, formal clothes that Maman and Baba had worn on special occasions—parties given for the refinery employees, an elaborate wedding or Norooz party. After we were finished with homework I took out a shimmering satin dress and put it on. Jahan put on a velvet vest. We took those clothes off and put on others, making up stories, playing different parts. Jahan loved adventure tales, identifying with princes and heroes of the times of Cyrus, Darius, and Xerxes. He'd choose a story from *Shahnameh*, the epic poem by the tenth-century poet, Ferdowsi, and we'd act it out. This afternoon I was Princess Noor, disowned by my family, and Jahan was the prince who comes to my rescue.

Then my eyes went to a locked filing cabinet. "Why is that always locked?" I asked.

"Let me see if I can open it," Jahan said.

I hesitated. "Maybe there's a reason they keep it locked. They wouldn't like it if they found out we opened it."

"We won't tell them," he said.

He began to pull the drawer in different ways but it didn't open. He took a wire hanger from the closet, straightened it, and then hesitated before he pushed the wire into the space between the lock and the upper part of the drawer. He pulled on the drawer and this time it opened. There were several files in it with labels on them: HOUSE, INVESTMENTS, TRAVEL.

"Look at this one," he exclaimed, pointing to a file all the way in the back. It was labeled JAHAN.

We looked at each other, puzzled. He pulled out the folder and we sat with it on the sofa. We found several sheets of paper with signatures and stamps on them. We read every passage slowly, some several times. The technical language was hard to understand. We were utterly silent as we read.

> In the name of Allah. At the Surrogate court, held in Shiraz, the province of Fars. April 18 1960.

> On the petition of Dr. Cyrus Ellahi and Moira Ellahi, his wife, adults, said parties having been examined by me, as required by the law, and the said parties having presented to me an agreement to adopt and treat the minor, Jahan, two months old, presently residing at Bacheh Khaneh Orphanage, as their own lawful child. A statement of the date and place of birth of the person to be adopted, as nearly the same can be ascertained to the change of name proposed and that there has been compliance with all applicable laws. On motion of J. Ali Molavi, attorney for the petitioners, herein, it is ordered that the petition of Dr. Cyrus Ellahi and Moira Ellahi for the pre-adoption of Jahan (the last name is kept confidential), a minor, be permitted. The Child, Jahan, had been found on the steps of Jamei Mosque by a man who had been going there to pray. He brought the infant, who later was established to be fifteen days old, to the Bacheh Khaneh orphanage. Then, soon after the infant was brought to the said orphanage, the mother came in, revealed her identity (kept confidential) and put him up for adoption in accordance with the law.

Another sheet listed our parents' names, incomes, places of birth, occupations, religions (Maman a Christian, Baba a Muslim). And there was the actual adoption paper.

> In the name of Allah. At the Surrogate Court held in Shiraz, Province of Fars, in the Civic Center in the said province, June 21, 1960.

> On the petition of Dr. Cyrus Ellahi and Moira Ellahi, his wife, adults, duly verified before me the day of May 30, 1960, and the

affidavit of J. Ali Molavi, Esq. Duly sworn before me the day of May 30, 1960 and the above named parties having appeared before me together several times with Jahan (last name withheld), a minor under the age of fourteen, and said parties constituting all the parties required to appear before me, and said parties having presented to me an instrument containing substantially the consents required by said law, an agreement on the part of the adoptive parents to adopt and treat the minor as their own lawful child, and a settlement of the date and place of the person to be adopted, as nearly as the same can be ascertained, the religious faith of the parents and of the child, the manner in which the adoptive parents obtained the child, and the said instrument having been duly signed, verified and acknowledged as required by law by each person whose consent is necessary to the adoption. The adoption of the infant, Jahan, would be in the best interests of said infant; and it appearing to my satisfaction that the moral and temporal interests of the infant, Jahan, will be promoted by granting the petition of said Cyrus Ellahi and Moira Ellahi, his wife, and approving the adoption; and it appearing to my satisfaction that there is no reasonable objection. It is ordered that the petition be granted. It is further ordered that the minor Jahan born on February 12 of 1960 in Shiraz, Iran, shall be henceforth regarded and treated in all respects as the child of said Cyrus Ellahi and Moira Ellahi, his wife, and be known and called by the name of Jahan Ellahi.

The whole world was spinning around me. The words themselves were frightening, seemed to be hiding things in that convoluted, strange language.

Finally I said, "I can't believe it. You look just like Baba." Jahan — with an inception of beard on his face, and standing 5'9", five inches taller than I was — looked much like our father.

"Why did they hide it from us?"

"Yes, why?"

"They lied to us," Jahan said. It was hard for me to tell if he was more angry or hurt.

"Yes," I said. "They lied."

# 2

We waited in the living room, hoping our parents would return home early, something they rarely did. Baba usually left for work right after breakfast and returned at about nine in the evening. In the morning, Maman went shopping for things that she couldn't get at the American Club store. She took Golpar, our maid, along with her. Sometimes they walked to the market, at other times the chauffeur took them. Maman liked to go with Golpar because she felt more comfortable when being accompanied outside of the compound, if not by a man, then by someone like Golpar who wore a *chador*. Also Golpar managed to bring down the prices of everything by half with her haggling, and this was a ritual that Maman always enjoyed. Then Maman would leave for the club. Often our parents ate out, either at the club or at their favorite *chelo kebab* restaurant, sometimes with friends. After dinner they'd go to concerts of Iranian classical music, which Baba loved and Maman had cultivated a taste for. Golpar came early in the morning and left late in the evening six days a week and usually served meals to Jahan and me.

So much love flowed between Maman and Baba that little of it ever seemed to come in my or Jahan's direction. They wanted us to turn out well, according to their own visions, but most of the time they ignored us. After our discovery I wanted to say to Jahan that he and I weren't so different, even though he was adopted, because our parents were just as remote from me as they were from him. But we sat in silence, swept up in our separate thoughts. I stared at the blue Nain carpet on the floor, trying to escape into its colors, its intricate designs of birds, flowers, and rectangles surrounding the medallion in the center. Jahan kept pacing around the room. Then we heard the front door.

"Is anyone home?" It was Maman's voice from the hallway.

As soon as she came in, Jahan said in a shaky voice, "Look what we found."

"What?" Maman asked, coming to a stop. She took off the straw hat she wore when she went outside during the day. Her long blond hair flowed over her shoulders.

"What does this mean?" Jahan asked, his face reddening. He gave her the folder. "Why didn't you tell me?" His eyes were filled with tears, but I could tell he was trying not to cry.

Maman gave a start at the sight of the folder. As if to give herself time, she said, "The fan is so low." She went to the switch and turned the fan higher. "It smells of mosquito repellent in here. Ahmad shouldn't have sprayed so much of it inside." Then, in an admonishing tone, she asked, "Why were you messing around with that cabinet?" Her Farsi, the language she used most of the time with Baba and Jahan, was more accented because she was upset, the blue of her eyes denser. "Wasn't it locked?"

"We broke it," Jahan said, looking away.

Maman sighed. "Your father and I were waiting for the right time to tell you." She went over to him and put her arms around him. "We love you as our own son, you *are* our son." She put a quick kiss on his cheek.

"Why do I look so much like Baba then?" Jahan asked in an earnest tone.

"Just a lucky stroke," she said. "We loved you as soon as we laid eyes on you. Here you were, a miniature version of your father. You already had a pile of curly hair and your eyes were the same shade of brown as his." Her voice became wistful. "I still remember the blue outfit you wore that day we went to get you. The nurse put a blue woolen hat on your head and wrapped you up in a checkered white and blue blanket before putting you in my arms."

"Why did my . . . why was I put in an orphanage?"

"The woman who gave birth to you had no way of giving you

all she wished to," Maman said. "I'm sure she hoped someone else would provide better for you. That only shows how much she cared for you. But I'm your mother now. You love me like a mother, don't you, as I love you as my son?"

Jahan nodded but clearly he was still upset. "Does everyone know?"

"No one. Honey, we didn't see the point of telling anyone. We thought it was better that way. People could take things the wrong way."

"Even Uncle Jamshid and Uncle Kaveh?"

"Your father's family didn't visit in those days. They were young and getting settled—your aunts giving birth to one child after another, your uncles traveling because of the jewelry business. My parents never visited either. They were both ill and stayed close to home. You don't have to tell anyone if it's easier for you. We'll keep it as our secret."

"Why is it written like that?" I finally managed to say something.

"Legal documents have their own language."

Jahan turned around and started to climb the stairs.

"We'll talk more about it later, darling," Maman said to him. "You can discuss it with your father too, any time."

Jahan didn't respond. I followed him up the stairs but he went into his room and shut the door. So I went to my room. I tried to do more homework but my mind was on what we had discovered. It was amazing that all our lives we had no hints about it, our parents had kept it hidden so well. It was incredible that Jahan had another mother who had abandoned him, that he had been put in an orphanage.

Baba and Maman must have eaten out, perhaps had an engagement they couldn't break, otherwise wouldn't they have wanted to be with us that evening, after what we had discovered? Golpar hadn't been there either, it being her day off. I slept through dinner and woke several times from dreams that left me uneasy, though I didn't recall their content. Then it was dawn, and rays of morning light were shining into the room. It was odd that Jahan hadn't tried to wake me. He must be very upset. His room was quiet now, its door closed, so I went downstairs by myself. Golpar was back and had spread her prayer rug in her room, adjacent to the dining room, and had a *chador* on. She genuflected, touching her forehead to a *mohr*, a clay tablet from the holy city of Karbala. She rose and intoned, "There is no God but Allah, and Mohammad is his prophet."

She was the only one in our household who prayed. Even though Baba and Maman were strict with me, neither of them practiced religion. Baba came from Muslim parents. My grandmother on Maman's side had been an observant Catholic. My grandfather on her side was a Protestant, who first converted to Catholicism and then finally abandoned religion altogether. Maman said she took after her father. Her mother used to force Maman to go to church with her, but Maman couldn't wait until she didn't have to. Both she and Baba said religion only created factions, that bloody wars were fought in its name. Occasionally she and some of her American friends went to the foothills surrounding our town and prayed together, but she explained, "It isn't religion, it's something more spiritual than church. The mountains have a calming effect." Our parents were certainly full of contradictions — Baba as well as Maman. Baba insisted on my following traditional rules of conduct, for instance, even though in many ways he had disappointed his family's expectations. I often resented Maman's going along with his rules for me. When I complained she said, "We live in this country, it's best to do things the Iranian way." And now I was mistrustful and angry with them, for hiding something so important from Jahan and me.

Golpar had finished praying and came in and served me breakfast — Nescafe, hard-boiled eggs, toast and marmalade. I had selected the instant coffee and marmalade from the American Club store myself. Her *chador* was off, displaying her long, henna-red braids. Her colorful peasant clothes and the braids made her look like a doll, an aged doll, her face all wrinkled. "Did Jahan have his breakfast?" I asked.

"No, *azizam*. He hasn't come down yet." Exuding a warmth and concern that I never felt from our parents, she asked, "What's wrong?"

I shrugged. "Nothing."

"Don't worry, Allah will fix everything. He is compassionate, merciful."

As I ate, Golpar carried on a stream of one-sided talk. "My aunt took her child to Hajrat Fatemeh's shrine and, ever since then, the child can walk. . . In this modern kitchen the food doesn't come out as good as on the old stoves. . . Men have all the power." She chronicled all the suffering "inflicted by men" on her female relatives. Her voice became bitterer as she said, "My poor cousin, her husband doesn't do anything to help her, he goes out and pleases himself. What can we women do but obey? Allah gave them more than us. But Allah must have his reasons which are beyond our comprehension."

Jahan was coming down the stairs and Golpar got up and ran into her room, adjacent to the kitchen, to put her *chador* on. She had started covering up in front of Jahan since he turned fourteen and had become a man in her eyes. She came back and said to him in a deferential tone, "Sit down, let me make you your eggs the way you like them. Two or three? You're a big man, *mashala*."

"Two please, Golpar *joon*." His school clothes were meticulously ironed. Golpar was so painstaking with her tasks, particularly in what she did for Jahan and Baba. She both feared and resented men, which made her deferential toward them in a way she wasn't with Maman or me. But she was so kind and tender that I never felt resentment toward her.

She served Jahan and went back into the kitchen.

After we finished eating, Jahan and I left the house together so he could drop me off at my school as usual. But something was very different, in him, between us.

"Baba came to my room late last night. He said the same thing as Maman—that they were waiting to tell us when we were older. I bet anything that they wouldn't have. I'm already fifteen." Jahan looked unhappy.

"I know you're right."

After a moment he said, "I was abandoned by my real mother."

I thought, poor Jahan, but I didn't say it. He always wanted to be—or to appear to be—strong. Instead I said, "Maman is your mother now. And I love you so much. We have each other, don't we?"

His face brightened a little. "Yes, that's what really matters."

We had reached my school and I was sorry we had to separate. There was so much that I wanted to say and that I knew he, too, wanted to say. In the school's courtyard, girls had clustered under palm trees or stood in shady doorways. Some walked in pairs, arm in arm, talking to each other. The bell rang and we lined up in front of the classrooms facing the courtyard. The school catered to the more conservative segment of the town's 150,000 inhabitants and we were carefully watched to observe proper conduct. Today was "inspection" day and truant officers looked closely at our uniforms to see if they weren't too light a gray or too short, at our faces to make sure we weren't wearing make-up. The truant officer, inspecting the students in my line, was a thin, tall woman, with a surly expression. She pulled out the girl behind me and said, "Go to the principal's office. Your *rupush* is too short."

Then it was my turn. She brushed my lips with her fingers, saying, "Are you wearing lipstick?"

"No."

She looked at her fingers and, finding nothing there, went to the next student. When the inspection was over, the principal, a stern, heavyset woman, stood on the porch and gave a little "rules of conduct" lecture. "Don't ever soften and give in to the pleas from the boys who want to have secret meetings with you. Do you know what the future is for a girl who disgraces herself?" After a pause she said, "Abandonment. A man, if he gets what he wants from a girl, will then disapprove of her for enticing him." Her eyes focusing on one face and then another, she added emphatically, "Men are predators. You can open up to men after you are married. Before that you can trust only men in your family—fathers, uncles, brothers." Her lecture over at last, she left the porch. The bell rang again and we started singing the national anthem. "Oh, Iran, the land of jewels, the land of glory. Long live our king of kings."

Another ring and we all went to our classes, me to History. A portrait of the Shah with Queen Farah hung on one wall. Some of the students were shifting in their seats, looking out of the window, very few paying attention to the lecture. I was no less restless than anyone else, but I didn't feel united with them. Their restlessness mostly came from lack of interest in school. They were waiting for suitable husbands arranged by their parents—for the start of real life, which for them was when they became wives and mothers. But I wanted to lead a life like the American girls I saw in the movies. Those girls asserted themselves, made their own decisions. They fell in love, married men they chose themselves. Desire wasn't forbidden to them, wasn't punished. They said to a boy, "I love you," or, "I've fallen in love with you," and then kissed him passionately. I dreamed of going to college in America, where I could be free, and so I took school seriously. Today though, more than anything else, I was preoccupied with Jahan. So he isn't my real brother. I love him even more, but he's suddenly different.

The history teacher was lecturing dogmatically, "We won the war with the Greeks. We drove them to the sea." According to him we had won every war in the history of civilization. When Jahan talked about history it was different. He told wonderful stories that made it all come alive. He could make me feel I was right there under the giant winged bulls at the ruins of ancient Persepolis. He could immediately take me back in time into a past world of art and beauty. But at school, even though I got top grades, I hated history, having to memorize all the names and dates of the Sassanids, the Arabs, the Turks and the Mongols, the Safavids, the Qajar and all the other dynasties through thousands of years.

Other classes followed. At lunch I bought a chicken sandwich and a bottle of *doogh* at the counter in the school's small cafeteria and went to a secluded corner in the back to eat alone, pulled inward by my thoughts about Jahan. But Simin, my best friend that year, came and joined me. I liked her because she wasn't so focused on the idea of getting married as soon as a suitable husband came along.

"What's the matter?" she asked. "You look so grave."

"Nothing."

"You can tell me."

"I'm just tired."

"Come on, tell me."

"Nothing to tell."

She saw I didn't want to talk to her and abruptly turned on me. "We can never be best friends, you're a *do range*." Half and half. "Your mother is a foreigner, a *farangi*."

I must have looked stunned. She said, "Oh, I'm sorry Nora, it's just that you're acting so unfriendly." She squeezed my hand affectionately, but it didn't reverse the hurt.

I was glad when the bell rang announcing the end of lunch. After school, when Jahan and I started to walk home, I waited for him to bring up what we had found out. But he didn't. So I kept quiet, thinking it would only upset him if I brought up the subject. When we reached our house, all he said was that he had a chemistry project back at school. He got his bicycle from the garage and rode off.

# 3

In my room I tried to drown myself in work. I began to write something for my composition course. After a while I got up and went into Jahan's room. I liked being there, among his belongings. Comics, adventure books in Farsi or Farsi translations, records, and puzzles, lined the shelves. The little clay statues he had made and painted, some for his art class and some for pleasure, stood in a row on a shelf. On another shelf stood a soccer trophy he had received that year. He had hung an enlarged photograph of Pele scoring a goal on one wall. He liked all sports, but soccer was the one he loved the most and he excelled in it.

I went to the window and watched people coming and going on the street. I wanted to see Jahan coming back. American women went by in casual clothes—jeans, cotton skirts and T-shirts, sandals. They wore make-up and their hair was set in different styles. Two American girls, about my age, went by on bicycles, something I wasn't allowed to do. How lucky they are, I thought. Vendors from the old town, carrying merchandise in trays they held on their heads, came into the street. They shouted, "I have the fattest and juiciest mulberries you can imagine," "I have the best chives at the lowest prices." The knife sharpener passed by too, shouting, "Your knife will be as good as new." The vendors' threadbare clothes and tired, weather beaten faces made me sad.

"Jahan, come back, come back." Then I saw him on his bicycle, as if brought back magically by the force of my desire to see him.

"Jahan, Jahan," I called.

He looked up and smiled. When he came into the room we started talking the way we usually did, about teachers, students, his soccer team, but I was still aware of that change in him and between us, intangible, but there.

"Do you want to read my composition?" I asked, sitting at the edge of his bed.

He sat next to me and began to read it. "It's good, but so sad," he said after finishing it.

It was about twin sisters. One of them drowns. The other, grief stricken, tries to kill herself. "That's how it came out," I said, surprised myself at what came out when I put pen to paper.

"Life can be sad," he said. "I went to the library this afternoon and looked up orphanages. They're bad places."

"At least no one thinks of you as a *do range*, you look completely Iranian. Today Simin called me a *do range*."

"She was probably teasing you." He paused for a moment and then blurted out, "Let's not tell anyone about it. What we found out."

"I promise I won't tell anyone." I put my arm around his waist. But I was conscious, and I sensed he was too, of our touching, of a new current flowing between us.

Baba didn't return at dinnertime. Neither did Maman. Jahan and I ate what Golpar had prepared during the day. We didn't talk much. We were on guard as if we had entered a dangerous zone where an alarm could go off at any moment.

Our parents now attempted to pay more attention to Jahan. They went to see him play soccer and took me along too. Baba cheered for him, and when the game was over Maman told him what a wonderful and talented boy he was. Our town was in the Zagros foothills, and knowing how much Jahan liked to hike, Baba asked if he'd go hiking with him. They'd go early in the mornings before it got hot. Maman took him on a shopping spree and bought him new clothes. If they said anything more to him about the adoption he didn't tell me, and I didn't ask.

Jahan began spending a lot of time in his room, making sculptures. He cut pieces of glass with a little wheel on a stick, broke the pieces off and glued them together into prisms and boxes. He bent wires into complex shapes. He was also painting—vivid scenes of animals, birds, trees, mountains. He replaced the Superman poster on the wall of his room with a large calligraphic print from *Shahnameh* about the legendary hero, Rustam, who fought dragons, witches, and Arab invaders. Even with his heroic achievements, he suffered tragically when he mistakenly killed his own son, Sohrab.

> Alas, what sorrow and heart-rending loss
> No mother near, heart pierced by father's blade.

Did Jahan see something of himself in the murdered son, with no mother?

No longer did he and I splash water at each other in the pool, chase each other around the courtyard, from room to room, throw clothing, pillows at each other. A mood of sober shyness grew between us.

On a Friday (the Sabbath in Iran), Jahan went out with his friends. I sat in my room full of vague longings as I read a novel, *Manikin*. It was just a trashy paperback but I was totally absorbed in it. It was about a young girl who comes to New York City from a small town for a career in fashion modeling and succeeds—I had already looked at the ending. I was distracted by a warm liquid trickling down my thighs. I looked and I saw blood. I had been having cramps all day. It was my period, I knew. Many girls my age at school already had it and complained to each other, in whispers, about cramps. Sadness swept over me. This meant being old enough to marry. Even if I went to the university, I would still have to marry when the "right" man came along and then everyone would expect me to devote myself to domesticity.

Two tall mirrors, facing each other, hung on the closet doors in my room. As I stood between them, the sunlight coming from behind me gave a touch of pink to my skin, a shine to my hair. My breasts, my hips, which had been gradually becoming fuller, looked even more so in that light, the curves more pronounced. I saw multiple images of myself, not quite fitting together. I am a half-American, half-Iranian girl, I thought, and the two halves don't seem to make a whole. There is a split somewhere in my existence that is hard to mend. I was actually born in America. Maman had been warned that she would have to have a Cesarean since I was lying sideways in her womb. She'd gone to stay with her parents to give birth to me in a hospital in Ohio; she didn't feel the obstetrics were as good in Iran. Baba couldn't leave the refinery hospital, so he stayed on in Iran with Jahan, who was taken care of by a nursemaid, under his supervision. Maman returned to Iran when I was a month old.

Jahan was changing too, growing taller, more muscular, his voice becoming lower. I watched him shaving in front of the bathroom mirror. He often had a musky scent about him now of after-shave lotion. But even his new knowledge of having been adopted, which had changed him and made him more introspective, didn't seem to make him feel as fragmented as I did. Maybe it was his looking all-Iranian, his freedom as a boy. I felt a pang of envy. Then, without warning, a surge of strong, irresistible desire for him flooded me. I wanted to hold him and kiss him like the movie stars did in the American movies. What was wrong with me? It was all so painful and confusing that tears collected in my eyes and streamed down my face.

No one was home except Maman. She was in her bedroom. I went over and knocked on the door.

"Come in." She was sitting on the bed in her silk blue bathrobe, her hair pulled back in a knot. A thick illustrated book on Persian rugs was open on her lap and she was studying it. It was filled with photographs of rugs—paisleys, rectangles, medallions, palmettos, birds, and flowers. Next to each photograph was the description of the unique feature of the rug—the tightness of the weave, the knots, the dyes used for coloring. She already knew a lot about Iranian rugs and could identify what city each one came from.

"These are real works of art," she said, indicating the rugs shown in the book.

"Maman, I think I'm having a period. I'm bleeding."

"Oh darling, you're a grown woman now." She took me to the bathroom and gave me a box of Tampax and showed me what to do. "You can get these at the American Club store whenever you need to. You should start wearing a bra. They have them at the store too."

She went back to her room, and I joined her after a while. I stared at the photograph of her parents on the bureau. My grandmother was wearing shorts and a casual blouse, and was smiling into the camera. My grandfather had on jeans and a T-shirt. They were young then, and standing outdoors with their arms around each other. They seemed full of life. Maman's mother had come to America from Ireland when she was twenty. My grandfather was born in America. They had lived near Columbus on a small dairy farm. They both died before I had a chance to know them.

"Maman, I'm so miserable in Masjid-e-Suleiman. Why can't I at least be like the other American girls here?" I sat on a chair, hoping to have a real conversation with her. "I hate all the rules. I can't wear this or that, I can't ride a bicycle. It makes me feel like a prisoner."

"Honey, those girls have American fathers and soon will be returning to America. Your father is Iranian and we live here. Nora, look at me. Don't act like a weird teenager."

"Why can't we go and live in America?"

"This is your father's country and he wants to live here. I married him knowing that. Anyway, you have it good here. Do you think girls your age in America have all the luxury you have? I had to work every minute after school to pay for things I needed. I worked, slept, worked, that was my life when I was your age. Girls there have plenty of problems—loneliness, aimlessness, drugs, alcohol. They get pregnant. They are confused and miserable. There's so much competition, so much pressure. We give you everything you need and you still complain."

It was true that our family had a great deal of luxury because of Baba's position. In addition to Golpar, who did the cooking and cleaning, Ali, the gardener, regularly attended to the courtyard. He planted flowers for every season and he had put in shade trees as well as a variety of fruit trees. Khar zahreh plants were scattered throughout. Their bright red flowers and dark thick spiky green leaves supposedly killed mosquitoes. We had someone to take care of the pool, and another man, Ahmad, did odd jobs—fixing things that went out of order, spraying mosquito repellent. A chauffeur-driven dark blue Mercedes limousine was at our service to take us wherever we wanted. A small airplane, holding twenty or so passengers, was available to us once a week free of charge to fly us to Ahvaz, a larger city nearby, twenty minutes by plane. Jahan and I sometimes used it to spend the day there. But none of that compensated for the feelings of imprisonment I had. Anger at Maman, dark and thick, enveloped me.

"I'm in a gilded cage," I said.

"Where did you get that pretentious phrase, gilded cage? You have a lovely home, parents who love each other and you, a wonderful brother, what else do you want?"

But I couldn't trust anything she said. It was always like she was wearing an impenetrable mask, hiding her true self behind it. I looked like her and talked to her in English. When I was little she read English children's books to me. I always helped her set up a Christmas tree (which we observed as well as Norooz, the main Iranian holiday). Yet something was missing between us. She wasn't a mother a girl could confide in. It was true for Jahan too; although she praised him more she wasn't any closer to him. In fact maybe less, since he didn't try to seek out what remained American about her. She did love Baba, that was clear. And he loved her. Yes, they only love each other, I thought. Jahan and I are superfluous.

The phone began to ring. She reached over and got it. "I'll be there soon, Mary," she said.

Next to Baba, she spent the most time with Mary. Jahan and I were a distant third, I thought grudgingly. She and Mary had a lot in common. Like her, Mary was a non-practicing Catholic, Irish American, married to an Iranian doctor. They shared an interest in antique Persian rugs. The intricately woven silk rug on the floor with a complex forest-like pattern was one they had bought together. One day the two of them came home with it, talking excitedly about finding such an exquisite Isfahan rug at an astonishingly low price in a shop in the old town.

She got out of bed and started to dress. "I'm meeting Mary at the club, why don't you come with me?"

"I don't like the club. It's as restrictive as everywhere else in this town." I had liked going there with Jahan when we were children and could swim together in the same pool but now he had to go to the men's section. Because of all the conservative pressure, the first floor was divided into two parts, one for men, one for women. Each part had its own indoor swimming pool, indoor tennis court and ping-pong tables, a common room and other facilities. Only the library on the second floor and the dining room were open to both men and women.

"Come on, honey, maybe you'll meet someone your age you like. Just don't go into the water while you're bleeding."

It felt lonely at home in Jahan's absence, so I agreed to go.

# 4

It was a cool day for October and it was easy enough for Maman and me to walk the eight blocks rather than having the chauffeur take us.

Flames from the refinery refuse burners were always in view as we walked, but in this section the smell of petroleum was disguised by the scent of honeysuckles and *konars*, tall, twisted trees with red flowers, that grew along the sidewalks. American and European cars raced by on Lincoln Avenue. A woman drove by with the top of her convertible down, her hair blowing in the wind like those actresses in the movies. I liked the foreign cars better than the Iranian-made Paykans driven by most people in the old section.

I thought wistfully of our two vacations in America. Maman's parents had already passed away and on both trips we had stayed for a few days with her aunt and uncle who lived near where she grew up, then we traveled on our own to different places. My memories were filled with images of cities full of variety and things to do, museums, plays, and of the beautiful countryside with vast green fields, vast skies.

"Can't we go to America for a vacation?"

"I have no one left there to visit and your father can't take so much time off from work."

"You could go with me and Jahan and we could stay in hotels," I persisted.

"Frankly, it's difficult right now," she said evasively. "Maybe we'll go one day."

"Don't you miss it?"

"Not really. I have sad memories of growing up. I was so lonely.

I had no sisters or brothers and there were no children nearby. My parents were older when I was born. My mother used to be talkative but my father was quiet and she gradually became quiet too. They rarely left the farm. They didn't even come to our wedding. Your father offered to pay for their tickets but they never came. Of course my mother had just been diagnosed with diabetes, but still . . . . "

"You just left one day and came to Iran?" I asked, knowing the story but wanting to hear her tell it again.

"I used to read books like the *Arabian Nights* and dreamed of places like Iran. Then when I was a nurse in the hospital in Columbus, someone from a team sent by the Shah came to recruit nurses for the hospital here, and I said yes immediately. It was a dream come true. Cyrus was recruited from Tehran in the same way."

"You and Baba always did what you wanted, but you have so many rules for me."

"Nora darling, I was twenty-seven when I met Cyrus, old enough to know what I was doing. Besides it doesn't always work to go against what's expected of you. It just happened to work out with your father and me."

After a moment I asked, "Don't you ever miss nursing?"

"I went into it to be practical, so I'd always find work. But the minute I quit, I knew it had been a totally wrong profession for me."

"Aren't you bored doing nothing?"

"Nora, I was much more bored working as a nurse," she said impatiently. "Now I do what I like with my days."

We passed the church, its stained glass windows gleaming in sunlight, and soon we were at the club. The large, two-story structure extended for several blocks.

On one wall of the entrance hall hung the portrait of the Shah, mandatory in public and even some private places. Maman went to the common room to join a group of women, Mary among them. The women were sitting at a table, playing cards and sipping drinks from tall, gold-rimmed glasses. Mary waved at Maman and me and greeted us loudly. All the women were acting a little giddy, laughing. I had heard Maman telling Baba that some of them mixed alcohol with their lemonades and sodas, something she said she didn't approve of, particularly during the day. They reminded her of her drunken relatives. But I suspected that she also drank with the women. Once when Mary was visiting our house the two of them painted circular designs on each other's wrists with henna, bracelets that would wash off after several showers. They both looked drunk then, judging by their hysterical laughter and loud way of talking.

I went to the pool area, my regular clothes still on, and sat on a chair under an awning. There were only two young girls there, sisters, about my age, sitting close to each other at the edge of the pool and talking, oblivious of others. The women sitting in groups on chairs on both sides of me were gossiping. Among them I saw Mrs. Farhangi, one of Maman's Iranian friends, married to an Iranian man who worked with Baba at the refinery. She noticed me and said, "Nora, what a surprise to see you here, did you come with your mother?"

"Yes, she's inside playing cards with Mary and others."

"I should go in then," she said getting up to join them. There was a little rivalry between her and Mary for Maman's attention. I wasn't fond of her, the way I was of Mary. She was soft-spoken but relentless in trying to teach Maman Iranian ways. She taught her how to set up the Haft Sinn table the right way at Norooz holidays, corrected her accent and grammar, even more than Baba did. She gave me warnings. "You have to be so careful, a pretty girl like you."

I listened to snatches of conversation around me. "Look, look, she leaves her child alone in the pool. She's hoping someone will watch over her," one Iranian woman said to another.

"Her bathing suit is so brief, you can see her breasts," the other woman said.

One American woman was saying to another, "She acts so arrogant, who does she think she is?"

The other woman said, "She wears all her expensive jewelry to the pool."

"She wears a polka-dot dress when she walks her Dalmatian!"

The American women married to American men wore shorts and sundresses, shirts with low necklines, bikinis. The ones married to Iranian men, Maman included, wore more sedate, conservative clothes. The differences also applied to the children. The ones whose parents were both American were freer, informal and casual. We half-Iranian children were forced to be more formal, polite, dress sedately like the all-Iranian children. I, like Maman, wore my hair pulled back.

The club wasn't helping me feel less restless. I left the pool area, went to the club library and looked aimlessly through magazines I found on a rack. Then I went to the store, around the corner from the main building and open on Fridays. The shop was filled with American cosmetics, skinny California-style bathing suits, all sorts of other American-made clothes, and some practical items. I tried on some bras and bought a few. I also bought Tampax and some ordinary American food that I liked—Jell-o, chocolate milk, canned tuna. When I was finished shopping I went over to Maman and told her I was going back home. I was allowed to walk alone from there, because it was so close.

Passing a house on Liberty Avenue, I was startled to see, through a window, a young American girl in an embrace with a boy, most likely American too, kissing. A curtain covered the window, but only partially. The voice of a man singing in English blared out.

> It's very clear our love is here to stay; not for a year but
> forever and a day . . . .
> Oh, our love is here to stay.

No one was home and I went to my room. Then I heard the outside door opening and Jahan's footsteps coming up the stairs. I was feeling even more self- conscious at the thought of being with him because of my period and because such strong feelings of desire were swirling through me. I quickly shut the door of my room. In a moment I heard a soft knock on it. "Noor *joonam*," he called.

I didn't answer. I lay in bed, my eyes filling with tears again.

Late one evening I waited in the living room for Maman and Baba. I had an idea for getting out of my school. Its conservative atmosphere was more and more oppressive to me. And then there was the loneliness of having no close friends. I was drifting away from Simin, ever since she had become so impatient with me, and other friendships I started didn't last long. My brief friendship with Trinka, for example. Her father was Iranian Muslim and her mother Dutch, a Christian originally like Maman, but she'd converted to her husband's religion. For a while we hung out together, went to one of our houses during the long lunch breaks. But then she began to act cool toward me and found excuses not to meet me.

"What's wrong?" I asked her. She looked embarrassed as she explained that her father objected. "Your friend doesn't pray or wear a head scarf," he'd said.

It would have helped if there had been girls my age on our street I could be friends with. But our closest neighbors on either side were Iranian couples; the fact that Maman was American created a distance between our families. The two houses across the street were given temporarily to foreigners with short appointments at the refinery, no more than a few weeks. Most of them came to Iran without their children.

For Jahan it was easier. Even if the boys in his school or our district came from different backgrounds, they all had things to share — sports and other outdoor activities.

Finally Baba and Maman walked in at eleven o'clock, talking about a singer they had just heard at a nightclub. "She certainly manages to get away with expressing physical longing," Maman was saying.

"Yes, Googhoush is very daring," Baba said. Noticing me on the sofa, holding an open novel, he remarked, "You're up so late."

"I have a request."

"What?"

"I want to transfer to the American School."

"You mean the Henry Knox D'Arcy School?" Baba asked.

"Everyone calls it the American School," I said.

"Without D'Arcy we wouldn't even be living here. It was his discovery of the first Iranian oil field in Masjid-e-Suleiman back in 1908 that began the Anglo-Iranian Oil Company." Baba went on excitedly, "When they first hit oil here the workers heard the dramatic rumbling of the earth and then saw oil gushing beyond their wildest expectation, more than fifteen feet high. The beginning of the oil industry. But D'Arcy, now, was English, not American . . . . "

"Doesn't matter, English or American," I interrupted, my voice rising, hoping to prevent Baba from getting farther off the subject I wanted to talk about.

"You don't have to shout," Maman said.

"It matters because there's a lot of turbulence in that school," Baba said. "There are 500 English in this town and 3,000 Americans. The Americans control everything now, even the name of the school. The English resent it."

"Anyway that school is overflowing with students," Maman said, taking off her high-heeled shoes and putting them by the door of their bedroom.

As if following her cue, Baba took off his light jacket. He hung it carefully on the back of a chair and said, "All the courses offered there are in American history, a few in English history, American or English geography. So limited." He kept rubbing his cheek as if puzzled by the whole matter.

"I don't mind. I'm an American."

"What are you talking about? You were only born in America," Baba said. "This is your country. Anyway the Henry Knox D'Arcy School is coeducational."

"So what? In Tehran a lot of Iranian girls go to coeducational schools," I said.

"Tehran is a big city, they can get away with it. Here everyone minds everyone else's business," Maman said.

"Coeducational schools are too distracting," Baba said.

"I want to go to college in America, become someone. I wish we would move there."

"End of discussion," Baba said and the two of them turned around and went into their bedroom.

I was beset by surges of anger, not only at Baba, but at Maman too for not coming to my side. They had total control over me. A daughter had to get her father's written permission to obtain a passport and visa to go to another country. Even going to another city in Iran would present huge problems. A girl couldn't live alone, get a job. They said she would end up becoming a prostitute, a main theme in Iranian movies. A young girl who has left home is seduced by a man, he abandons her, she has a child, has to give up the child, and then becomes a prostitute. It was always the same story we heard from the principal at school too.

I ran upstairs. Jahan was still awake. His door was partially open and I could hear faint music coming from his room. My frustration blew away the self-consciousness I was feeling with him lately and I went in. He was sitting in bed with the top of his pajamas off, reading *Sports Weekly*. His skin was golden tan.

"Jahan, don't you wish we could both go to the American school?"

"I don't know. I'd miss my friends, my courses, my art teacher. Mr. Yabi has been really encouraging. He thinks I have talent and a good understanding of art. I showed him my sculpture of a man with a cane and he really liked it."

"But then we'd be together."

"Anyway Baba said no. I heard you talking to them."

I closed the door to make sure our parents wouldn't hear us and then said, "I wish they would listen to me once in a while."

"They wouldn't listen to me either if I asked them for something they don't approve of."

"What do you talk about with Baba when you go out with him?"

"He's trying to get me to become a doctor like him."

"Has he convinced you?"

"I want to be an artist. Maybe an architect."

"I wish Baba would want me to have a profession too."

"Noor, I want you to become anything you want."

"Thanks Jahan *joon*. You're the only one I have in the whole world. I don't have any other close friends."

"Noor *joonam*, you're the only one I have in the whole world too."

His words filled me with a mixture of desire and anxiety so intense that I could no longer bear being in close proximity with him. "I'd better go and get some sleep," I said, leaving his room.

# 5

It was May, the last month of school, and the final exams were approaching. The ceiling fans in every classroom weren't enough to alleviate the heat. At breaks we all drifted into the large student lounge. It was cooler there than in the harshly sunlit courtyard or any of the classrooms. I tried to spend that time studying for exams but the girls' conversations were distracting. "I'm engaged now, yes, to the engineer." "I'll be engaged soon too, he's a colonel. I'll never have to look at a book again." I tried to concentrate, focusing on how much I wanted to go to college. At home, too, I studied for long hours.

When the semester ended I went to school to get my grades, which were posted in Ketabi Hall. I saw Miss Sheibani, my home-room teacher, standing by the door of her office talking to Mr. Dashti, the history teacher. I looked at my posted grades. I had gotten twenties—perfect scores—and only one nineteen. With my excitement over the good grades went sadness, because I was so afraid I'd never be able to put my studies to any use. I'd just have to fight until Baba and Maman softened and let me go to college, if not in America, then in Masjid-e-Suleiman.

As soon as Mr. Dashti walked away, Miss Sheibani said to me, "You've been doing very well, I wish more girls would keep their minds on work." As she turned around to leave, she said, "By the way we're introducing new courses in English at Iran Dohkt. We're hoping to attract American and English girls, but the courses will be open to all."

"That's wonderful." I was amazed that they actually wanted American and English students here. What about all the conservative Iranian parents who wouldn't like what those girls might bring to the school? Before I could ask questions she disappeared into her office. Just outside her door I came across a pile of Iran Dohkt newsletters. I picked one up and right on the front page I saw an article, confirming what Miss Sheibani had said: "Iran Dohkt School is proud to announce that we will be offering all the afternoon classes in English."

I couldn't believe my luck. Part of the American School was coming to Iran Dohkt. What was going on? I could register in all the English courses, make new friends with the American and English girls who might transfer there. Outside, our chauffeur, Asghar, drove me back—he picked me up on the rare occasions when Jahan couldn't.

Later that day, alone with Jahan in the living room, I told him about the new courses, my good grades. He put his arm around me and said, "I'm so proud of you," and kissed me hard on the top of my head and then on one cheek after another. "My grades were pretty good but nothing like yours. I had nineteen in chemistry and eighteen in math. I did the best in art and history, I got twenty in both," he said.

We sat there and talked for a while and then finally went to our separate rooms.

When the second semester started, I could immediately sense there were many changes for the better at school. The volleyball net that had stood sagging was erect now, and a new ping-pong table was set up. The new girls rode to school on bicycles, and some wore make-up. I chose to take as many English courses as possible. Some of them were taught by American or English teachers, and others by Iranians who had been educated abroad. I liked these new teachers better because they allowed students to ask questions.

In my class, Introduction to World Books, I sat next to one of the new students and introduced myself. She said her name was Helen and she was English.

"It's ridiculous that they call this town Little London. There's no resemblance," she said.

"The nickname is from a long time ago, when there were more English here."

"In London we have wide boulevards, beautiful parks, museums, theaters."

"Why did you transfer to Iran Dohkt?"

"My parents think I can concentrate better in this school with no boys around. I have a boyfriend in London, so I don't care."

She invited me to her house for the following afternoon. I accepted though I knew I had to ask my parents for permission.

In the evening I asked Baba. He wanted to know how far away Helen lived, if she had any brothers hanging around her house.

"She lives in the English section. She didn't mention a brother."

He finally said, "Okay, that's close, you can go, but come back before it gets dark."

Helen's family chauffeur drove us to her house. Her mother was in the living room when we arrived and Helen introduced us. Her mother shook my hand, smiling. "Helen has told me so much about you." She was dressed in a miniskirt and a short-sleeved blouse with a low neckline.

Helen got us cokes and biscuits and then led me to her room. The furniture, all modern, was provided by the refinery for temporary employees. On her bureau stood a pile of lipsticks, rouge, eyeliners. Next to them was a framed photograph of a boy about her own age.

"That's my boyfriend." She brought over the photograph. "Doesn't he have the bluest eyes?"

I took the photo and looked at it, envious that she was allowed to have a boyfriend. Why didn't Maman act like an American mother with me, I thought, my anger at her stirring.

On the back of the photo was written, "To my darling Helen."

"Very good looking," I said.

"I miss him," she said. "We spent every minute we could with each other."

"Are you going to marry him?"

She shrugged. "I don't know. My parents say we're too young to think that way. Is that boy who picks you up from school your brother?"

"Yes."

"He's so handsome."

I felt blood racing to my face. I was glad that she went on to another subject.

"Do you want to dance?" she asked.

"I don't know how."

"I'll teach you, it's easy." She scrutinized my face and said, "But first loosen those braids."

I took off the barrettes at the bottom of the braids and loosened the plaits. My hair flowed over my shoulders.

"You look so pretty with your hair down," she said. "You should always wear it like that." She picked a record from a stack and put it on her phonograph. "They're old movie soundtracks." Songs filled the room.

> Without Love you're only living an imitation,
> an imitation of life.
> Would the moon be as bright above.
> without the one you love
> Lips that you kiss tell you clearly
> without this our lives are merely an imitation,
> an imitation of life.

"I saw the movie this song comes from," I said. "I see everything they show at Christopher Cinema."

Taking my hand and holding my waist with her other hand, she showed me some steps. We went around and around dancing until we were both exhausted.

It was beginning to get dark and I had to leave. Their chauffeur wasn't there yet and anyway my house was only ten blocks away. I walked rapidly in case by chance Baba and Maman were home already. But neither of them was there. Golpar was getting dinner ready. After greeting her I went to my room to drop off my school bag and take off my school uniform. Through the window I saw Jahan in the courtyard with his friends, the tall, good-looking Parviz, and the talkative Bijan. They were flying kites in the shapes of a butterfly, a bird, a lantern. I listened to their voices, their laughter ringing in the air. Now a kite has gotten caught in the tree branches and they're trying to dislodge it. Now they're flying another kite. They have quieted down. His friends are about to leave. It is 7:15, 7:20. They are leaving. Jahan is seeing them to the outside door. Jahan is coming up the steps.

I opened the door of my room. He looked at me closely and said, "You're wearing your hair down."

"Which way do you like better?"

"I like you both ways."

"Isn't this even a little better?"

He came inside. "Yes, it's beautiful, like a gold waterfall."

"Touch it."

He caressed my hair. Blood rushed to my face. He looked flushed too. Our interaction was no longer just playful. Something else was mixed with everything we said and did—excitement, an inexplicable fear. We were both under the same spell.

Then Golpar was calling, "Dinner is ready." We immediately raced down the stairway and took our seats at the dining table.

Helen and I were spending more and more time with each other. She showed me new dance steps, and we went skating at the English club. Sometimes we had lunch there on Fridays when there was no school. We went to the movies at the Christopher Cinema or the King Cinema in the English compound. The English movies were a little different from the American ones, more serious. I liked them just as much—again, the young women portrayed in them had an independence you never saw in Iranian movies.

For my fifteenth birthday in March, my parents were taking us to the American Club restaurant for dinner and I invited Helen to come along. A dozen colored balloons floated near the ceiling above our booth. As we ate, Baba asked Helen questions: "Do you miss home?" "Do you like Iran?" "How long will you be here?" Helen answered everything politely. She kept turning to Jahan, tried to talk to him, but she barely knew Farsi and he knew little English. Was he eager to talk to her, did he feel excitement in her presence? He was just being normally polite. Ashamed of my possessiveness, I started translating what she asked him and his answers—all ordinary matters, but heightened in my mind.

Frank Sinatra was singing in the background: "When I'm close to you dear, the stars fill the sky, so in love with you am I, I'm yours till I die."

Baba complained about the volume, got up impatiently, and went to the manager in front to ask him to turn it down.

The waiter brought over the birthday cake. It said, "Happy Birthday Nora," in English, as I had requested. On Jahan's birthdays his name on the cake was always written in Farsi. That is Jahan, and this is me, I thought.

After the restaurant we all went to our house. Helen and I went to my room. Soon after I had finished opening my presents, her family's chauffeur came to take her home.

Later that night Jahan came to my room and said, "Let's go to Ahvaz tomorrow and rent a boat."

"Great," I said. I loved boat rides on the Karoon River, which flowed south through town to join the Tigris and Euphrates at the Persian Gulf. It could be so beautiful on days when the water was clean—free of the dark streaks of oil that often leaked into it from the refineries.

The next day the little plane that was available to us wasn't operating, so Asghar drove us to Ahvaz. The ride went fast for me because I was with Jahan. I was never bored or restless when with him. I was wearing a yellow dress with a pleated skirt. Close to the neckline I had pinned the ceramic brooch in the shape and bright coloring of a butterfly that Jahan had made and given to me for my birthday, and my hand kept going to it.

Asghar dropped us off by the river. We rented a boat from a thin, young Arab boy—probably an Iraqi immigrant, among many who crossed the border to find jobs. I asked the boy to take a picture of Jahan and me together, handing him my camera. The photograph captures Jahan in full. His back is arched, his head is lowered looking at the water, and a tangle of hair is hanging over his forehead. He looks sensitive, thoughtful.

Jahan rowed the boat across the river. On the right bank we got out, tied the boat to the pier, and went into a park in the modern residential area for foreigners working in the oil business. After wandering a while we sat in the park café that overlooked the river and had lunch, watching boats gliding by and listening to the murmur of the water rushing away. The sky was ablaze with deep gold sunlight. A confused longing flooded through me.

We returned in time for Asghar to drive us back. At home I asked Jahan to come to my room and I put on the record Helen had given me as my birthday present.

> Without Love you're only living an imitation,
> an imitation of life.
> Would the moon be as bright above, without the one you love
> Lips that you kiss tell you clearly
> Without this our lives are merely an imitation,
> an imitation of life.

"Let's dance. I'll show you the steps Helen taught me." It was one of the rare occasions when I was teaching him something.

My breasts pressed against his chest, my thighs against his. I could feel the muscles of his arms. Desire was taking over, out of my control. I held my face to him and said, "Kiss me." He kissed me hard on my lips. The inception of beard on his face rubbed against my skin.

A picture of the two of us as children playing in the courtyard came to me. We had built a house with pieces of cardboard. He said, "I'm the husband and you're my wife," then he leaned over and kissed me on my lips. Maman walked into the courtyard and said, "You should never kiss on the lips. Do you understand, not on the lips."

Jahan's voice brought me to the present. "We shouldn't. You're my sister."

But we just lingered there. I wanted to grab his arm, ask him to dance more, hold me longer, kiss again, stay the night. We looked into each other's eyes and saw excitement, confusion. In a moment he stroked my arm and then left the room.

I went to bed, full of longing. Crickets and frogs were making a din but my mind dwelled on his saying, "We shouldn't, you're my sister." Am I really his sister? Not by blood. He has another mother and father.

Finally, when I fell asleep, Jahan was in my dreams all night. In one we were lying on the hammock, both naked—we didn't even have our bathing suits on. We were looking upward at birds hovering around a paper kite floating in the sky as Jahan caressed my hair, my breasts. In another dream we were wearing elaborate wedding clothes and were surrounded by guests dressed up in beautiful clothes. Our parents were there too. Maman stared at me, and then leaned over and whispered something in my ear that frightened me.

I got out of bed, put on a bathrobe, and tiptoed to the window. In the courtyard the cluster of bird-of-paradise flowers, the hibiscus bushes and the poinsettia plants, were vivid in the pearly light. They looked different today, full of an inner energy, life.

Alas, a little later as Jahan and I had breakfast together, a wall of reticence stood between us. When we walked to school and then back he went into long descriptions about his friends, his courses, anything, it seemed, to avoid what had started between us.

# 6

The summer heat came early that year. The cool breeze from the mountains that usually blew all through spring was blocked by a heat wave from Shatt al-Arab, the tidal river at the Iraqi border, a marshy channel of brown water contaminated with oil. The muggy heat clung to people like a virus, making them volatile, cranky. There was no rain for long stretches of time and the trees were wilted, the grass brown, the earth parched. The masses of bright wild flowers that grew on the hills surrounding Masjid-e-Suleiman had all died, exposing the brown earth underneath.

When school ended, the days ahead stretched before my eyes in a haze of monotony. Too much time to think, to brood, to yearn for everything I desired and didn't have. Jahan stayed out with his friends a lot, often coming home late. I immersed myself in reading everything I could find in English. The central air conditioning in the house rarely functioned for more than half the day because of heavy electricity use during the hottest months. I put a large fan in my room and sat close to it as I read. I had already run through the selection of young adult novels available at the club library and bookstore and I was reading adult books — Ferber, O'Hara, and Hemingway. I read magazines in English I found at the club too. Inside of one, there was a folded poster, an advertisement for a perfume, featuring a young woman wearing a slim jacket and tight pants, taking long strides across a New York City street. Her handbag was swinging over her back, her hair blown by the wind. I cut it out and hung it on the wall of my room next to posters of American actors and actresses. My favorite advertised *A Place in the Sun,* with Elizabeth Taylor and Montgomery Clift.

When tired of reading I listened to the English-language radio station, watched the one English-language channel on TV. One program was about a young girl who strove to be an actress; she wore a mini-skirt, a white sweater, huge artificial eyelashes, and mascara.

In late afternoons I stood by the window and looked out. A bird had made a nest in the branches of the tall palm tree just outside the window and tiny baby birds were sleeping in it. I watched the way light reflected on the tree leaves, changing slightly with every passing moment. I hoped for a momentous event, but there were always only slight variations and the days went on without drama. Only near dusk when the sunlight lost its harshness was there some sign of activity outside. People walked their dogs, women pushed prams, boys bicycled. Vendors from the old city brought their wares out to the streets.

On some afternoons I went to movies with Helen. I was plunged deeper into loneliness when Helen went to spend the rest of the summer in London, where she stayed with her grandmother and got to go out with her boyfriend.

One morning, on Golpar's day off, Maman served us pancakes she'd made from a package and we all ate together for a change. This was one American meal Jahan and Baba liked, judging by the piles on their plates.

But Baba looked preoccupied. "Iranian workers at the refinery are really restless," he said, "Complaining about Americans and English being paid more than they are for the same work."

"That's an old complaint, isn't it? But maybe the heat makes everything worse," Maman said.

"A technician was saying out loud that the Shah is a puppet of the Americans and English. The fact that he dared to say that shows how frustrated workers like him are. We know that the Shah has done some good things—public health programs are better, there's cleaner drinking water, better sanitation in general. But when it comes to the workers' wages and living conditions, he hasn't pushed for reforms. I guess at the hospital things are more equitable for Iranians but conditions have always been appalling at the refineries."

Jahan chimed in, "They certainly are. Bijan says that at the refinery in Abadan the English put up signs on the drinking fountains that say, 'Not for Iranians.' That's horrible."

I was quiet, feeling self-conscious being so close to Jahan with the erotic tension between us so strong, afraid our parents would see right through me and discover my desire.

"Nora, are you still asleep?" Baba said.

I burst out, "Why doesn't the Shah make things better for women?"

"My dear daughter, at home we speak in Farsi," Baba said. I didn't realize I was speaking in English; Baba didn't allow it when we were all together as a family.

"Remember, before the Shah came, women didn't have the right to vote, and he also advanced women's education," Maman said.

"But he divorced Sorraya because she didn't give him a son."

Maman ignored me, and said to Baba, "Cyrus, I wouldn't have met you if not for the Shah. Remember?" She smiled at him, adding ruefully, "It's a self-serving way of thinking, I know."

"You know I'm grateful for that too, Moira," he said, squeezing her hand affectionately. "But seriously, it's hard to see so many Iranians living in poverty."

"You're right," Maman admitted. "All that oil money going into the pockets of the Shah's circle, so much government corruption."

Asghar was honking the car horn outside. Baba got up. "I have to go." He kissed Maman quickly and left.

Maman turned to Jahan and me and said, "My friends from the American Club are all escaping to cool spots. Mary's going to Ireland. Your father and I were talking last night about my taking you to the Meigoon house for a few weeks. He'll join us on weekends. Your aunts and cousins are there right now. Your uncles will come on weekends like your father."

It was his suggestion that she should take us there. Maman had been reluctant to go without him. Not only would they be separated for stretches of time, but she was also not entirely comfortable with Baba's family, particularly if he wasn't around. When the relatives visited us years before, Maman could withdraw into a room, have some time alone. But in Meigoon they wouldn't allow her that privacy. The aunts believed that it was natural for the women in families to want to spend all their time together. They wanted to please Maman, and worried that they were not being hospitable when she withdrew, even for an hour.

"Can't we go to Babolsar instead?" I asked. "It was so much fun with all the tourists there." On the two occasions Maman had taken us to the seaside resort on the Caspian Sea, Jahan and I swam together, and no one stared when I got on the back of his bike and rode around with him.

"It's hard to find something nice there at the last minute. Anyway your father wants to visit with his family when he comes on weekends."

"They're all *chadori*," I complained. Baba's brothers were observant Muslims, and had married Iranian women who were also observant.

"We'll do what we want, no one will force us to cover up," Maman said. Turning to Jahan she said, "I could take Nora and you could stay with your father, if you want, and come on weekends." But then she quickly reconsidered that. "No, you should come. Nora will be bored without you."

"I want to go," he said. "I'll play soccer with Mohsen and Hassan."

Meigoon, a small village in the foothills of the high Alburz range, was less than two hours from Tehran by car or bus. It was famous for its mild climate, its fruit trees and fine honey. Many Tehranis had vacation homes there.

We flew to Tehran and then took the bus to Meigoon and from the station a taxi took us to the villa, passing by fields of bright wildflowers, cows and goats grazing in patches of grass near streams, steep hills and valleys. The jingling of the bells around the goats' necks sounded in the air.

The ruddy-faced maid I remembered from an earlier visit to Meigoon years ago opened the door to us. She was wearing a kerchief and a long dress with a multi-layered skirt. "Come in, come in, they're expecting you," she said. "Can I help with the luggage?"

"Thanks, we can manage," Jahan said. He was carrying his own large bag in addition to Maman's suitcase. The maid took my suitcase from me and led us inside. The villa had pink stucco walls, gray pink marble floors, and was set in a large garden. Rose bushes with huge red, fragrant flowers framed the intricately carved wooden outside door. Sumac bushes and fruit trees—mulberry, white strawberry, cherry—filled the garden. Bright birds sang in the trees. A small round pool, used for ablution in Muslim houses, stood in the center.

As we entered the living room we were greeted by Aunt Khadijeh, married to Baba's oldest brother, Jamshid. "Bah, Bah, how nice that you came." She was wearing a light indoor *chador*.

Her sister, Maryam, who was married to Uncle Kaveh, Jamshid's brother, came in from another room. She had her light *chador* wrapped around her waist but she quickly put it over her head at seeing Jahan. "Look how they've grown," she said, turning to Jahan and then to me. "Not children any more."

Both Aunt Maryam and Aunt Khadijeh were pretty, jolly women with voluptuous figures and long, wavy hair. One by one their daughters and sons came in from different rooms, four girls and two boys, all ranging in age within three or four years from Jahan and me. The two boys were Aunt Khadijeh and Uncle Jamshid's sons and the four girls were Aunt Maryam and Uncle Kaveh's daughters. All the girls wore headscarves. They were supposed to cover up in front of male cousins—who were considered to be like any other man, and in fact could be prospective husbands. Many cousins did marry each other. My two aunts, since they were aunts only by marriage and not by blood, had to cover up in front of Jahan. Maman was wearing a blouse and a medium-length skirt and I was in blue jeans and a T-shirt, but felt as if we were naked in front of Mohsen and Hassan.

Mohsen and Hassan took Jahan out into the courtyard, as their conversation grew lively. Pari, my oldest female cousin, said to Maman and me, "Let me get you some tea, the baby is asleep."

"I'll help you." Zahra, my age and four years younger than Pari, followed her.

The house was sparsely furnished—just kilims on the floors, cushions to lean against. No beds, just mattresses to roll out at night to sleep on. The sparseness was in keeping with observant Muslim homes, demonstrating that you should live simply and give anything extra to the poor. There was a modern kitchen and two modernized bathrooms—that kind of comfort and modernity was acceptable. Baba and his two brothers had inherited the house from their parents, but he let them take control since they lived in Tehran and used the house frequently.

Pari came back holding a tray with tea glasses and rock sugar. A moment later, Zahra returned with fruit and plates and knives. As we drank tea and ate fruit, my two aunts engaged Maman in conversation.

"I marvel at how well you speak Farsi. Most foreigners never learn it," Aunt Maryam said. "No matter how many years they live here."

"I like Farsi, it's soft, musical. My dear friend, Mrs. Farhangi, has been teaching me to speak it correctly for years."

"You're an Iranian by now," Aunt Khadijeh said.

Maman smiled. "I do appreciate this culture so much," she said. "The beauty of things. The kindness of people. I feel protected, the way I didn't in America."

"It's wonderful that you can appreciate such things," Aunt Khadijeh said.

As I sipped my tea I stared at the large framed photograph of my Iranian grandparents on the mantle. My grandfather had on a tall felt hat and a gray suit, my grandmother a dark *chador* that covered her like a shroud, with only her eyes revealed. They were sitting next to each other on hard–backed chairs, not touching. Their expressions were stern and dignified. How different they seemed from Maman's parents.

Pari's baby started to cry and she got up to attend to him. Zahra, Farogh and Fatemeh turned to me.

"Cousin Nora, do you bleach your hair? It's so light," Farogh asked. She herself had jet-black hair and olive skin.

"No," I said.

"It's so pretty, like China dolls' hair," Fatemeh said with a smile.

I suspected she didn't mean the compliment. When they had visited us with their parents I had overheard her say to Zahra, "Nora has no color." It was true I was very pale compared to them, but still it hurt to hear it.

"You have such pretty eyes, like turquoise," Farogh said.

"I wish I had your coloring," I said.

"Do you always wear blue jeans?" Farogh asked.

"Only sometimes," I said.

Zahra, the most thoughtful and quiet of the four sisters, said to Farogh and Fatemeh, "Stop quizzing her. What must cousin Nora think of us." She turned to me. "We're so excited and happy that you're here. We want you to feel welcome. Please forgive our curiosity." Then she reached into a bag and took out embroidery material and a pillowcase. She started embroidering the edge of the pillowcase.

"It's for her hope chest," Farogh explained to me. "She's engaged."

Zahra blushed. "Mahmood works with my father at his jewelry shop. My father thinks of him as the son he doesn't have. Soon your turn will come."

"I want to go to the university first," I said.

"You like studying?" Farogh asked.

Fatemeh giggled. "We'll all end up diapering babies."

Aunt Khadijeh and Aunt Maryam were spreading a *sofreh* in the middle of the room. Maman got up too. "I want to help."

"No, no, sit down, you just arrived, I'm sure you're tired," Aunt Khadijeh said. "Everything is ready, we only have to bring it out."

Maman sat down again, looking a little aimless.

The two sisters went into the kitchen and brought out plates, silverware, and platters of food, arranging them on the *sofreh*. Aunt Khadijeh called the boys in, then she and her sister put their *chadors* back on and my female cousins readjusted their head scarves, which they had let slip over their shoulders. The boys came in and we all sat crossed-legged around the *sofreh*. Pari and her little boy joined us.

Aunt Khadijeh closed her eyes and said, "In the Name of Allah, the Compassionate, the Merciful." Then she began to pass around the platters of food—stew with green beans and dried lemons, saffron rice, minced salad. She was sitting next to me and added an extra portion of *tadigh*, the crusty part of the rice formed at the bottom of the pot, everyone's favorite, to my plate. She said, "You'd be even prettier if you put on some flesh. Eat a little more." My female cousins, like their mothers, had plump figures and round faces.

"Thank you," I said and began to eat quietly.

She turned to Jahan, "Take more, *mashala*, you've grown so tall, I didn't recognize you when you walked in."

Jahan added more food to his plate. "I love your cooking," he said.

Farogh was looking at Jahan with admiring eyes. "My mother makes really good *tadigh*," she said to him.

Then Mohsen and Hassan engaged Jahan in conversation again. Mohsen was a year older than Jahan, and Hassan a year younger. They were both stocky and short, Mohsen with a round fleshy face, Hassan a little trimmer.

On the surface Jahan seemed at ease with the cousins, but the fact that his eyes went to me frequently made me think that he, too, felt vulnerable among the relatives.

After we finished eating we had tea again and honey-filled sweets, and then we withdrew into the rooms my aunts had assigned to us. The three younger girls and I shared a room and Jahan shared a room with the boys. Maman had her own room, so did each of my aunts. Pari shared her room with the baby. Their husbands would join them when they came on the weekends.

# 7

I liked Meigoon; it had a bucolic beauty and aura of serenity in spite of the division between the summer people and the locals, who were generally poorer. I liked the villa too, with its stucco walls, the marble floors and the garden. Even its simple furnishings were more pleasing than the dark wood and heavy furniture that filled most of the rooms of our house. What seemed tedious to me, however, was the round of religious observances—prayers four times a day, my aunts reading the Koran and reciting lines from it, rosaries passed between their fingers. In the course of conversations they'd frequently look heavenward and say, "It's all the will of Allah."

Maman did, more or less, go her own way. The first time when she set out from the house to do some exploring, Aunt Khadijeh called after her, "Do you want to borrow my *chador* or a scarf? This is a small village."

"You know, dear, I'm not used to that," Maman said.

"It's up to your husband to tell you how to dress," Aunt Khadijeh admitted, shaking her head.

"I'll be back soon. I want to look at rugs in the bazaar."

Then later that afternoon Aunt Khadijeh asked Maman, "Would you want to pray with us?"

Trying to keep peace with Aunt Khadijeh, Maman explained gently, "Cyrus believes we can be Muslims without observing the rituals, God should be in our hearts."

My aunts were more determined with me than with Maman in giving guidance, even though they believed that a daughter was obligated to follow her father's rules. Perhaps they thought I was still young, impressionable, and they could more easily influence me.

One afternoon, when the sunlight spread to every corner of the garden and everyone started to withdraw indoors I asked Jahan if he'd like to go out and explore.

Before he could answer, Aunt Khadijeh said, "Nora, it's better if you didn't go out in those pants."

"They're comfortable for walking."

"My *dokhtar joon*, at least cover your hair, for your own sake," she advised.

"I'll wait for you outside," Jahan said.

He left and Aunt Khadijeh retreated into her bedroom and came back holding a navy blue silk scarf. She put it over my head and tied it under my chin. "You look nice this way."

"Thanks, Aunt Khadijeh," I said and went out to join Jahan.

He was standing under a gas lamp, kicking pebbles into the narrow *joob* that ran along the sidewalk.

As soon as we were out of sight, I took off my scarf and put it in my handbag. He laughed, more relaxed with me now that we were out of our usual environment in Masjid-e-Suleiman and away from the relatives.

"They all like you," I said. "They think of you as one of them." I stretched out my hand. "Put your hand next to mine."

He stretched out his hand.

"You are a nicer color, like the cousins," I said.

"You're beautiful! How can you doubt yourself?" he said vehemently, as if the words had flown out of him.

"You mean that?" I asked, in a tremulous voice.

"Do I ever say what I don't mean?" he said in the same urgent tone.

I felt a rush of something like gratitude.

We turned onto a steep, cobble-stoned street. He held my hand, helping me climb.

"Do you like Mohsen and Hassan?" I asked.

"I envy them in some ways. They're so close to their families. They believe in things."

"But they're so traditional."

"Maybe a little of that doesn't hurt, brings people closer to each other. Look at Maman and Baba—I don't understand them. They believe in one thing and then do another."

We walked around until siesta time was over and stores were opening up. Then we went to a little bazaar, looking at clothing shops that carried both Iranian and American merchandise, a shop with chickens kept in cages, a bakery with an open oven lined at the bottom with stones. The narrow, maze-like lanes were crowded and noisy with shoppers. We sat down in a little café and had ice cream with hard pieces of vanilla in it.

We left the bazaar and after a few minutes came to grassy fields sloping down to a stream. Turning up a steep hill, we then passed villas and more modest cottages that stood side-by-side, orchards filled with cherry, pear and plum trees. We picked cherries and ate them. Jahan hung two cherries, joined at the stems, over one of my ears. "Looks good on you."

We came to the town square, crowded with people, and bought fresh pecans from a sidewalk vendor who kept them in pails of water. Later we ate corn on the cob, roasted on a charcoal brazier and then plunged into salt water. We ate as we walked through still more streets stretching out beyond the other side of the square.

As dusk approached, lights flickered inside the houses and along the roads. Through the open doors of houses we could see cooking fires set up in courtyards. Fireflies gleamed in tree branches. We climbed up a rock and stood on top of it, looking at the expanse of the village. Lights from cottages and villas among the woodsy hills winked as brightly as the stars in the vast, high sky. Then our eyes caught a man and a woman lying on a mattress under mosquito netting on the rooftop of a house below, their naked bodies visible in the moonlight. We were riveted on the sight. Then the man climbed onto the woman. Her legs were wrapped around him, and he began thrusting hard. Suddenly he hit the woman, bringing his clenched fist down on her again and again as she gave out intermittent cries. He stopped just as suddenly and they rolled away from each other.

Jahan and I were struck dumb. I realized I was clinging to him. He broke the silence. "I'd never treat a woman I love like that."

A woman I love. One day he will be in love with a woman. The woman wouldn't be me. I was his sister. Being in love with him, and he with me, was a mere fantasy. "I know you wouldn't," I said. But inwardly I went on, one day he will get married, and then I will be only at the periphery of his life. He became quiet and I wondered what was going on in his mind just then. Was he having similar thoughts: that I will get married to someone arranged by Baba? These things were better left unspoken.

Starting back, we came to a wide stream and had to step on one rock after another to get to the other side. I almost fell, but Jahan held my hand until we were safely on the bank.

My right foot was hurting and I limped a little. He leaned over. "Let me see, where is it hurting?"

I took off my sneaker and sock and he rubbed my foot gently. "It's from walking on the hard rocks."

It was as if his touch was magic. The pain just disappeared.

We came across a village wedding celebration in a restaurant garden. Tables and chairs were set alongside a stream in front of the restaurant. Bottles of bright orange soda held down the tablecloths. The bride was wearing a white wedding dress and a gauze veil; the groom wore dark balloon pants and a white caftan. They were surrounded by men, women, and children in colorful village clothes with sequins at the necklines and edges of the sleeves. Three musicians came out and began to play the drum, tambourine, and sitar. A singer, a voluptuous woman with long black wavy hair came out too and started to sing.

> On that moonlit night in the alley, you stole my heart.
> Spring came to town with you holding a bunch of wild violets;
> And when you went back through the doorway there was a
> smile, alive, on your lips

And your eyes spoke memories of our love.
Every time I look at you with my heart's eyes,
the darkness turns into sunshine.

The bride and groom and then some of the guests began to dance with abandon. There was more freedom among these rural mountain people than among my aunts and cousins. They had their own rules as they had their own dialect.

I couldn't stop a powerful impulse that came over me and slipped my hand into Jahan's. He tightened his grip, and I felt a harmony between us, our desires interlocking without restraint.

Still holding hands we walked to a dark corner, hidden behind a large sycamore tree. We stood there and kissed, first tentatively, then with more abandon. Finally he pulled away and whispered, "Noor, this is dangerous."

"I don't care."

"It's going to have consequences we can't predict. It could be even worse for you."

I was burning as if I had flown too high, like a lost bird, into the eye of the sun, but I could only say, "Jahan, I love you."

"I love you too, you know that, don't you? But I'm your older brother. I should be protecting you."

We started to walk back, overwhelmed by the turbulent emotions flooding us. As we approached our house, I put the scarf back on. In the courtyard, cousin Mohsen was picking mulberries and putting them into a large basket. "You were out a long time," he said to Jahan.

"We stopped to watch a wedding in the village."

Mohsen picked up the basket and came inside with us. We sat with our other cousins in the living room. I felt stiff, afraid something would give away our secret, and could sense Jahan struggling, too, to not give his feelings away.

Noticing his eyes focusing on Pari's round, olive breast as she began to nurse her baby, I felt a pang of jealousy. Why was it all right for a mother to expose her breasts in front of a man while nursing a baby? Pari was a lovely woman, with light olive skin, a striking oval face, with dimples that deepened when she smiled. I tried to alleviate my jealousy, thinking, Jahan is imagining my breasts as he looks at hers. As if aware of my feelings and wanting to reassure me he turned to me, looked into my eyes and smiled.

In a few moments we gathered around the *sofreh* to have dinner, which we ate very late that night. Jahan sat between Mohsen and Hassan, and I among the girls. After dinner we all withdrew to bed. As I lay next to my cousins my whole body was vibrating with the sensations that Jahan's kisses had evoked in me. How scandalized they and their parents would be if they knew. But who would approve? No one. Yet I couldn't stop myself from reliving the feeling of Jahan and me in an embrace, kissing. It was like seeing the same scene of a movie over and over again and never tiring of it.

I woke at dawn to the voice of the muezzin and saw my aunts and female cousins going into the courtyard. They washed at the pool and came back inside to pray. Mohsen and Hassan would have already gone to the mosque for prayers. Jahan must have gone with them. After prayers my aunts sat against the wall and passed rosaries between their fingers while reading *suras* from the Koran.

After breakfast, Maman, who didn't accept my aunts' invitations to pray, tried to be accommodating in other ways, by joining them in some of their tasks. She, Maryam, and Khadijeh spread a sheet under the white mulberry tree in the courtyard, shook it and then picked up the berries that fell onto the sheet in a white stream. They put some of the mulberries on platters along with the cherries that they had picked the day before. They laid them next to bowls of pistachio nuts and candies on a small *sofreh* in the corner of the room for snacks. They made jam with the rest of the fruit.

Jahan helped Mohsen and Hassan in the garden, cleaning out the bottom of the small pool, guiding the water from the *joob* into the house reservoirs. My cousins and I chopped the vegetables and cleaned out the rice, getting them ready for my aunts to use in meals.

At the end of the day Baba, Uncle Jamshid, and Uncle Kaveh arrived one by one to spend the weekend. We all ate together and then the men withdrew to talk among themselves. Jamshid and Kaveh were closer to each other than to Baba—not only did they marry sisters but they also owned adjacent jewelry shops in the bazaar. The conversation turned to politics. It was an animated discussion about deteriorating economic conditions and the inflation that had plagued the country after oil prices rose a few years back.

"Over a million people are unemployed, and small merchants are being ruined by all the foreign goods coming in," Jamshid said, "And things are getting worse all the time."

Baba agreed. "Resentment of foreigners is growing too. It looks to people like Americans are manipulating prices and making huge profits. Being married to an American is creating a precarious situation. I worry about my family."

"Everything is getting out of control," Kaveh said.

"People are relying on religious authorities for guidance and help now," Baba said.

"Most of the mullahs want to work with the nationalists and reformers, but Khomeini is uncompromising. That makes him very popular, of course, with some people," Jamshid said.

"Yes, thousands of pilgrims are going to Najaf to see him. Well, he is a leader with deep moral values," Kaveh said.

"Only time will tell about Khomeini," said Baba. "His idea of government by religious authority is too extreme. The mullahs have always been advisers, never rulers. He could be a disaster for Iran."

That put an end to the conversation. Jamshid and Kaveh didn't always agree with Baba, but they thought too highly of him, the only brother with a university education, to be critical of him. Uncle Jamshid said jokingly, "What do Kaveh and I know, two ignorant bazaaris." The rest of the evening they played backgammon with Mohsen, Hassan, and Jahan taking turns.

# 8

Ramadan, the ninth month of the Islamic lunar calendar, fell in July that year. The holiday commemorates God's revelation of the Koran to the Prophet Mohammad. During that month all Muslims are supposed to fast for self-purification, spiritual growth and to remind themselves of the privations of the poor. Our days had a somber tone; my aunts or cousins kept the radio on to listen to religious sermons.

> Allah the Compassionate, the Merciful. He created Man, he created the Sun and the Moon. . . . Those who strive against the Lord's revelations will face doom. He will reward those who believe. Those who sin will be taken to Hell in chains. Those who obey the Lord's rules will go straight to the Garden of Eden, where streams flow with water and fruit hangs from boughs of trees and the air is fragrant with flowers.

Sometimes religious plays were acted out on the radio. The mournful voices of the actors and the melancholy music accompanying the words filled the house. The plays were all about the different Imams' martyrdoms, centuries ago.

I sometimes woke in the middle of the night when Baba's relatives broke their fasts with a big meal, then again at dawn when the muezzin's voice called people to prayers.

Our family didn't observe Ramadan. No one directly criticized us, though I could sense disapproval from Aunt Khadijeh. We ate our meals by ourselves on the porch. As the four of us sat together, an island separate from the others, I didn't feel I could reach to my parents for emotional support or guidance. They were as remote as ever with their contradictory rules and inconsistencies. Here was

Maman, an American woman, independent enough to have come to Iran for a job and marry outside her own culture; yet now she acted as if she had no mind of her own separate from Baba's. She had given up her job to be with us but in fact she was rarely home, spending most of her time shopping or at the American Club. And why did Baba impose all those old-fashioned rules on me? It didn't make any sense. What were they but hypocrites?

In the quiet of siesta time, I listened to small birds twittering, wild parrots' repetitive squabbles, and the jingling of goat bells. I yearned to find a way to go out with Jahan again, but Baba's presence was too forbidding.

After the first weekend of Ramadan, Maman suggested to Baba, "Maybe we should all go back home now."

"It's still unbearably hot in Masjid-e-Suleiman," he reminded her. "If I didn't have work to do I'd stay on here the whole month!"

Maman agreed to stay. She had met an American woman in the bazaar who was apparently as interested in Persian rugs as she was. Now the two of them went looking at rugs together.

On the last day of Ramadan, Baba and his brothers arrived even though it wasn't a weekend, for Id al-Fitr, a feast day with a huge variety of food served. Mohsen and Hassan brought a sheep into the garden to slaughter it in the proper Muslim way so that it would be *halal*. Hassan held down the sheep while Mohsen said, "In the name of Allah, the Compassionate, the Merciful . . . ." As Mohsen raised a knife, I left the window to avoid seeing the rest. But I heard the animal's pained, frightened bleating.

The men helped in the preparation, charcoal-broiling the kebabs, spreading a *sofreh* on the rug in the courtyard and arranging the platters of food on it. As we sat around and began to eat, we could see the lights in the neighboring villas over the walls of the garden, and could hear the faint clatter of dishes and utensils coming from them.

When Mohsen and Jahan got up and went inside to get something, Uncle Jamshid turned to me and said, "Nora, my dear niece, in a blink of an eye you've become a grown woman. You were just a child not long ago. Time has come to find you an appropriate man. Who's better for you than my son Mohsen?"

I blushed. I didn't like Mohsen. He avoided looking at me and never addressed me directly. Uncle Jamshid turned to Baba for his reaction. I had a sense they had already discussed the matter between them. Baba's eyes focused on me.

"I don't want to get married," I stammered.

"You don't have to make up your mind at this moment," Uncle Jamshid said.

"My daughter's head is in the clouds," Baba said.

Aunt Khadijeh looked heavenward and said, "It's all up to Allah."

Most likely she didn't think I was an appropriate wife for her son. She probably preferred one of the other female cousins to be Mohsen's bride. I was surprised that Uncle Jamshid had picked me. Luckily when Mohsen and Jahan came back the subject was dropped.

A little later I heard Maman and Aunt Khadijeh discussing it.

"Of course it's good to marry someone whose blood is a little like our own," Aunt Khadijeh was saying, "Someone who is a part of the family."

"My dear, I've heard that children born to blood-related couples often have problems, some are even born deformed. The further you go from your own blood, the better for your children's health." Maman was probably thinking of herself and Baba, but I was happy she was talking that way.

The day before we left Meigoon, Jahan and I went out exploring. As soon as we were out of the house, I said, "I've been so lonely with you out all the time."

"I wish I could be with you more but you know it's hard." He paused, and then said, without looking at me, "Mohsen told me Uncle Jamshid wants to set you up with him."

Blood rushed to my face again. "It's ridiculous, I don't even know Mohsen. And I'm not attracted to him at all."

"He likes you."

Was Jahan testing me? I tried to discern his feelings. "We wouldn't make a good match. Besides, I don't think he really likes me."

"I guess I can't imagine the two of you together."

"I told Uncle Jamshid I don't want to get married." My heart was pounding talking to Jahan this way.

When we reached the bazaar, we bought sheets of paper and took them to the wide stream that ran through the village. We folded the paper to make boats and then set them afloat on the water. Village women were washing clothes downstream, spreading them on the sun-baked rocks to dry.

Then we went to an open field and flew a kite Jahan had brought along, watching it dance upward. Some boys had gathered there and were flying kites too. Soon all the kites were moving together, trembling, touching, entangling and separating.

After we got tired of that we hiked on the paths through the hills and sat on the soft, mossy ground by another stream. The water rushed by wildly, like the blood flowing in my veins. Its color changed from turquoise to amethyst, to deep green, to foam-flecked blue. Everything around us brimmed with sensuality. Bees sucked at the jasmine blossoms that grew wildly everywhere, a male cat chased a female cat, a bird mounted another bird. Small green grapes hung from a tree. Patches of sunlight dappled the ground, trembled on the tree branches.

Jahan lay down and I next to him, protected from view by the hills. We listened to the sounds of insects, birds, and the flowing water. Then as if it were inevitable that we would come to this intimacy again, Jahan turned, enclosing me in the curve of his body. "Noor, I want you to myself," he whispered. "I want us together, always. I don't want you to go to someone else." He kissed my lips, neck.

The intensity of my desire made me tremble, brought tears into my eyes. His kisses were sweet and sharply thrilling at once. I began to caress him, my hand under his shirt, going downward. All the warnings I had been given were meaningless now. My mind was closing one door after another, as I guided his hand under my shirt, jeans. We were sailing out of reality, sealed off together in a place where there was no concept of the past or the future, no endings, no worries or losses. It was wonderful to be sinful. It was really fine, more than that, it was thrilling. Nothing mattered as much as these sensations.

The jingling of bells brought us back to reality as a shepherd prodded his goats down a hill. We sat up and I saw on my thighs the soft, jelly-like liquid that I had felt coming out of him. He picked up some leaves and wiped it off. Then we quickly put back on the clothes we had taken off; they were damp from the spongy ground. As he tidied my hair with his fingers he said, "I pulled out in time."

I nodded, in a happy daze. We started walking back through a meadow, filled with flowers. Goldenrods, asters, weeds with red and yellow bells were glistening in sunlight.

"We won't tell anyone about this, what we have between us," he said.

"Even Maman and Baba should never know," I said.

"Of course not."

After a moment he said, "My real mother must have been abandoned by a man who seduced her."

I was startled to hear him talk about his birth mother. We hadn't referred to the adoption for a long time.

"I'd never abandon a girl I love."

"Am I that girl?"

"Of course." He turned to me and looked into my eyes as if he wanted me to see the inside of his soul.

"Have you ever done it, with another girl?" I asked.

"Never."

We said little else all the way back. I was overwhelmed with feeling. Something of infinite significance had happened and I had no idea what to do with it, where it was leading.

I was up most of that night. Lying in the dark I let fantasy take over: Jahan and I could run away from home, go to Isfahan or Shiraz, where no one knew us, assume new names and then get married. We would find a way to make money. He could work as a carpenter and I could be a receptionist in a travel agency. But the fantasy was interrupted by thoughts of our parents searching every inch of the country until they found us.

# 9

Back from Meigoon, we were rudely thrown back into reality, as our relative freedom came to a halt. It was hard for Jahan and me to immediately revive what happened by the stream. We were now shy, hesitant with each other. I yearned for what happened between us and was frightened of it too. I wasn't sure what Jahan was feeling. Was he regretful? I wished we could talk about it but the thought of his saying it was wrong was even harder to take than the uncertainty.

In the evenings, Jahan went out with his friends. The world he had with them was mysterious, so distant from our world together, and it felt threatening to me now.

When school started, I hated the classes, except the English ones, and hated the gray uniforms we still had to wear in spite of the new American and English girls. The muggy heat didn't help. The principal's lecture on the second day of school, a repetition of others given before, now seemed aimed right at me. "Do you know what the future is for a girl who disgraces herself? Abandonment. Men are predators."

When Helen returned, a week late, I was glad to see her.

"I didn't want to leave my boyfriend," she told me. "His school started a week later than ours."

She was so excited about everything they had done. "We had a grand time," she said. "I may go back to London for Christmas. Why don't you come to my house this afternoon?"

I couldn't bring myself to confide in her about what happened between Jahan and me. The terror of disapproval drove it to a deep, dark part of myself. She didn't even know Jahan wasn't my blood brother. Still I burned to tell her everything. "I have a crush on someone," I said.

"Who?"

"Someone in my own family."

"Really?"

"My cousin. He was in the house with us in Meigoon."

"Your cousin?"

"We're allowed to marry our cousins."

"What does he look like?"

"Amber eyes, curly hair."

"Just like your brother."

"There's a strong family resemblance there."

"Tell me about it. Did you make love?"

"A little. We kissed. He's a great person."

"Are you going to marry him?"

"I don't think so. Not right away. First, I want to go to the university and then who knows."

We talked like this until I had to go home.

One evening when our parents were away visiting some friends overnight, I was glad to find Jahan at home. As we ate what Golpar had left for us, it was as if he were someone else, he had so much power over me now. The wind was blowing in the palm trees in the courtyard and the street. A bee banged against the mesh screen of a window, buzzing and buzzing. Dragonflies darted back and forth in the air. As dusk deepened, the hills in the distance were swallowed by darkness, broken only by the streetlights and lighted windows.

Jahan smiled at me and said, "I want to show you something I made. I cut classes to finish it."

We cleared the dishes and went into his room. He had removed the door of the large windowed closet and made it into a studio. His art instruments and materials lay on a big table there. Sculptures in different states of completion, some of clay, some of wire—a man walking with a cane, two children holding hands—stood on a shelf. He picked up the piece he wanted to show me—an abstract design made with pieces of stained glass, lined with copper foil and soldered together—and said, "Hold it against the light."

I held it up to the ceiling lamp. The light broke into a myriad of colors and reflected them on the wall. "It's beautiful," I said. From the window, in the streetlight I could see a few late birds going to roost. Finally I asked, "Where do you go at night?"

"We sit in the back of a café and talk, play backgammon."

Were there any women in the dark back area of the café? I didn't dare to ask.

I said, "What if we went together to America, to a university there?"

"America's all right, but I like it here."

As we talked the physical distance between us was painful. Why isn't he coming over to me, holding me in his arms, kissing me? Is he just being sensible, has he already fallen out of love with me? In novels girls always fell in love more helplessly than boys did. Why is it so impossible to talk about it now?

I got up to go to my room. As I was about to leave, I picked up his checkered white and maroon shirt he had thrown on the bed. "Can I keep this?"

"Sure. What do you want it for?"

"To wear instead of a nightgown."

"Give me something too. A lock of your hair. I'll cut off a lock."

I could hear my heart beating.

"I'll be very careful." He got up and took a pair of scissors and a plastic bag from his desk drawer. He came over to me and gently cut a lock from the bottom. That distance between us was narrowing.

"Look in the mirror. It doesn't show, your hair is so thick."

I looked at myself in the oval mirror hanging on the closet door.

"Cut a piece of my hair too. I want to put them together." He gave me the scissors and sat down.

I cut a part of the long curl that fell over his forehead. He put both locks into the bag. "They look good together, don't they, dark and light."

"Yes."

He put the plastic bag into the drawer, and then suddenly, as if again under the spell of that uncontrollable force, he held me to him and kissed me hard. In a moment he was latching the door, we were lying on his bed. "Noor *joonam*," he whispered as our bodies entwined. "I miss you every moment I'm not with you."

"I wish we could run off together, go and live in Isfahan or Shiraz."

"Yes."

Our voices sounded high-pitched to me even though we were whispering. Then we were undressing, both out of control, sailing out to that other space, to that different reality. He was going further and further.

Finally when I sat up, I could see drops of blood were mingled with that jelly-like liquid on the sheet. My mind went painfully to a report in the *Masjid-e-Suleiman Daily* of a girl living in the old town, murdered by her father after her brother caught her with a neighbor boy. The father insisted she be tested by a gynecologist, who attested that she was not a virgin. He had taken out a knife and murdered his daughter, screaming, "You disgraced me." Of course Baba would never do something like that. But horrors for girls were all around me. How different this was from other worlds I knew from American movies and books.

"Noor *joonam*, what's wrong? You aren't upset, are you?" Jahan asked, sitting up too and putting his arm around me.

"Look at the blood."

"That isn't blood, they're designs in the sheet."

I looked more closely. "Oh, you're right!" We couldn't help laughing.

He held me tighter to himself. "Noor, I tried my best to protect you."

We heard some noises and held still. But it was only the sound of leaves thrashing in a breeze that was blowing after days of stagnation. Through the window I could see the bright moon above a tree.

We lay back again and Jahan pulled the patchwork quilt, which Golpar had made for him, up to our chests. In a moment he was asleep, breathing rhythmically. I was wide awake.

After a while I, too, fell asleep on his bed. I was awakened in the morning by a knock on the door and Golpar announcing, "Jahan *agha*, time to get up, you said to wake you."

Jahan gave a start and opened his eyes. "I'll be right down," he said.

Golpar walked away. I got up and tiptoed to my room. I had kept my door shut, so Golpar couldn't have seen that I wasn't there. But did she suspect? Was she aware of the sparks of attraction between us that had finally driven us to that hidden, forbidden space? How shocked and condemning she would be if she knew. But how can this be wrong, this joyous glow?

I dressed and went downstairs and was relieved that Maman and Baba weren't there. Jahan came down in a rush and left without eating breakfast. "I almost forgot soccer practice," he said.

As Golpar served me breakfast she talked in her usual stream. "You should never provoke animals. Some of them are *divs*, spirits who have come back in this form. They may still have a little of the devil in them. You should watch out for *djinns* too. Allah made man out of clay and the *djinns* out of flames. If you ever notice *djinns* hovering around, you should throw water at them and they'll go back underground. If an owl comes to the house, sitting on the roof or on top of a tree, we'll have to start watching out. An owl is bad omen." She was wearing the necklace with eye-shaped stones, which she believed warded off the evil eye, and the turquoise necklace that she said brought her good luck.

She started folding the linen napkins and tablecloth she had washed, bleached, and starched, and put them into the large ornate wooden cabinet in the corner. Then she looked at me in a strange way. "Allah is all knowing, Allah is merciful. He'll forgive the sinners. If they repent, they can still go to heaven."

What if she does know? What if she says something to Maman?

# 10

Jahan and I were inseparable all the next year. As long as I was with him, our parents weren't concerned. We went to the movies more frequently than we used to and sat in the dark back seats and held hands as we watched. Afterwards we went to a café for ice cream or soft drinks, but we were drunk on our love. We held hands under the table. Sometimes his friends came in, waved at him and went to a different table because they didn't think it proper to sit with him while he was with his sister. We went to Ahvaz and took the boat to the other side of the Karoon River as we had for my fifteenth birthday, and stood in a quiet, empty corner of the park and kissed.

When our parents stayed out late or were away overnight, we spent the night in one of our beds. He was careful not to get me pregnant but in my drunken state of mind I sometimes imagined having a baby with him. I kept fantasizing that one day we'd find a way to be together and then we could have a baby. Whenever a dark fear that I was breaking a taboo clutched at my heart, I reminded myself: Jahan isn't related to me by blood. I am in love with him and he with me and that's all there is to it. But those thoughts didn't completely dispel the darkness I sank into sometimes. Every night I drifted into sleep with pictures of Jahan filling my mind, but I woke in the middle of the night, alone and frightened.

I decided I'd feel better if I confessed everything to Helen, so one morning I went to school determined to talk to her about it. I looked for her but she wasn't there. In my literature class I found that some of the other English and American students were absent too. Sonia was there and I asked her if she had seen Helen.

"I saw her last evening leaving the English Club."

Anna joined in. "There's serious trouble out there."

"What do you mean?"

"My dad said warnings were given to the English and Americans at work. We might have to leave the country if things get worse."

Miss Patterson, our young American teacher, walked in. "A small class today," she said. But she lectured as usual, like any ordinary day.

Helen wasn't at school the following day either. I called her from the phone in the school dining room but there was no response. Periodically I kept calling; the fact that there was no answer made me really apprehensive. I couldn't bear being at school. I needed to get out for a while. Impulsively, I left. Without thinking, I wandered around the streets behind the school. Then I suddenly lost my bearings, until gradually I realized I was nearing Pahlavi Square. Something strange was going on there.

A man on a platform bellowed through a microphone: "We have to weed out foreign vices. We have to put an end to nightclubs where foreign women in scanty clothes dance and where liquor flows like water."

A huge crowd, mostly men, but some women too, wearing *chadors* or headscarves, had gathered around the platform. They shouted, "Yankee go home! English go back to where you came from!"

Shopkeepers had come out and were standing by their doors watching. The teahouses and restaurants looked empty. Coca Cola and orange soda bottles set on the outdoor tablecloths in front of restaurants were untouched. Some boys had climbed up the tall palm trees, looking down at everything from above, and yelling.

I stood outside of the circle of people, straining to hear every word.

The man on the platform said, "There are 150,000 Iranians in this town. There are no more than 3,500 Americans and English combined, but they act as if they own Masjid-e-Suleiman. They steal our oil and give us nothing."

A few people shouted, "Go home oil eaters!"

The voice of the man on the platform overwhelmed all the other voices. "Tehran has become a whore town, even worse than Masjid-e-Suleiman. Women wear almost nothing and wander around the streets like that. Western whores calling themselves dancers perform in nightclubs where alcohol is served freely like water. All with the Shah's knowledge."

I was stunned that these men were publicly criticizing the Shah. Where was SAVAK, the Shah's brutal secret police with its force of 65,000, who punished the slightest criticism—or anything construed as criticism—with summary arrest, torture, and execution? To remind people of the Shah's power, his statues were everywhere, several in this very square—one behind the platform. The square was named after him. Statues of him stood on crossroads, in parks, at the tops of hills. His portraits, sometimes along with Queen Farah, hung on walls everywhere. Carpets had his image woven into them. Postage stamps and currency, of course, bore his portrait.

A group of men holding black banners with slogans written on them in purple letters came into the square and gathered around the circle. The banners only intensified the color of anger in the air. In the distance the flames from the refinery refuse burner spiraled upward menacingly.

"We have suffered oppression for too long, it's about time to put an end to it. We must unite," the man on the platform shouted, his voice rising to an even higher pitch. "We will drive out the blue-eyed, blond-haired exploiters."

Blue-eyed, blond-haired. Helen and her mother and father, Maman and me. I felt menaced but I just couldn't move away.

The man on the platform went on, "Many of our people have to crowd into tiny huts or sleep on streets. They have only one set of clothes to wear day in and day out. They are forced to work as sweepers, garbage collectors, factory workers. And they're paid a starvation wage and given no benefits, while foreigners are stealing our money and insulting us too. Do you know what our exploiters, the Americans and the English, call us? Camel culture. Bedouins."

A hard wind began to blow, picking up debris and dead leaves, throwing them around the air. In the sky, thick, dark clouds were racing, merging and dividing. Then a helicopter appeared as if from inside the clouds and circled low in the sky.

Oblivious, the man carried on, "Too many of our own people have become Westoxicated."

I finally tore myself away. What was the best way to get back to school? I tried to orient myself. As I entered a narrow street a snake charmer was playing a melody on a flute and a yellow and black snake was dancing to it. A few people stood by and watched, indifferent to what was going on just blocks away. A little further a few people had collected around a magician who was swallowing fire and letting smoke out of his nostrils.

On a whitewashed wall someone had scribbled, "Weed out evil, death to America. Death to the English." Blind and crippled beggars approached me and held out their hands. They were proving the point that the man on the platform was making. I gave each a few coins until my money was gone. Jahan always gave money to beggars, telling me, "There shouldn't be so many poor people."

I walked down a small winding alleyway. A little naked boy was sitting in a pile of dead leaves, looking into space with vacuous eyes. A voice in the distance was wailing, "Oh, Allah, have mercy, our country is soon going to blow up."

I was half way down that alley when I heard footsteps behind me and then a male voice shouting, *"Faranghi, faranghi!"* The words sent a chill through me. A stone hit me and then another and another. I turned around to face two boys about my age. "Does your cunt have blond hair, too? let's see it."

I ducked inside a produce shop and waited until I didn't see the boys. I resumed walking rapidly, when suddenly someone from behind held my skirt, forcing me to stop.

"Help!" I shouted, "Help!"

A window opened and a man looked out. "What's going on?" he asked. On seeing him the boys began to run. Panicked I started to run too, in the opposite direction through a maze of alleys until I came out onto a familiar crowded avenue. The bell above the Armenian church began to chime. A group of nuns came out, talking among themselves in whispers. I looked at my watch. It was almost four o'clock. Asghar was supposed to pick me up after my last class.

I got back at 4:15, just in time, and got into the car. Asghar stared ahead with a stony face. "There's big trouble out there," he said.

I was shaky and silent. When I got home Jahan was back and in his room, sketching.

"What happened to you?" he asked, looking concerned. "I was early and so went to your school but didn't see you."

"I thought you were at soccer practice," I said, trying to keep my voice calm.

"No one wanted to play today. Everyone wanted to get home early."

I plunged into a chair. "Helen wasn't at school and then someone said that the Americans and the English have been given some kind of warning. I got worried for Helen, and called her but there was no answer. I couldn't bear being at school. I started walking and got lost for a while. Finally I got back to school just in time for Asghar to pick me up."

"You walked alone?"

"Yes, some boys followed me and threatened me. They were very scary." I left out their saying, "Is your cunt blond too?" I couldn't be open with Jahan about that. I wanted our love to have a beauty to it, and not be violated by vulgar words. I wanted it to remain in our special world, free from outside reality.

"Who were they?" he demanded.

"Some boys. I managed to get away."

"I'm going out to find them."

"No point. Anyway there's no way to find them. I didn't even get a good look at them."

"I should have been there to protect you."

We went on talking about the turmoil everywhere. Was this more than the culmination of the normal tensions in Masjid-e-Suleiman? In addition to the Iranian-American-English clashes and the modern-traditional conflicts, the Shiite Muslims, the majority of people in Masjid-e-Suleiman, despised Sunni Muslim Iraqis who came there to look for work. And they had never been more than barely tolerant of the few hundred Iranian Jews and Christians. How depressing the situation in Masjid-e-Suleiman was—and how dangerous.

"Do you think we have to get out of Iran?" I asked Jahan.

"I hope this is a phase and that it will pass soon," he said.

Did he feel less anxiety than I did? A boy wasn't supposed to show any weakness. I tried to blur the pain inside me by looking at familiar objects—the globe on his desk, the patchwork quilt, the palm fronds outside the window.

# 11

And so our idyllic private life was being swept away. All of Iran was in upheaval. Amnesty International had condemned Iran's record of torture and human rights abuses. Demonstrations were going on in the streets in every city and town. Factory workers were demanding higher wages, slum dwellers wanted subsidized housing, and everyone wanted an end to SAVAK's power. Newspapers were openly reporting arrests and torture by SAVAK.

Many factions were struggling for a voice now— democratic reformers, nationalists, popular citizens' movements, student groups, Marxists, anarchists, religious moderates and religious fundamentalists.

One morning as I was eating breakfast alone, the doorbell rang and I went to the door, a little apprehensive. I was startled to see Helen. "I'm so glad to see you. Where have you been? I've been so worried," I said.

"We went away. My father was sent to Shustar and he took us along. I didn't know until we were actually going."

"Come in."

"I can't. My mother's waiting for me in the car. I came to say goodbye. I'm going to London to stay with my grandmother. My parents will follow soon."

"But you're in the middle of school."

"I'll be going to school in London. I can hardly wait. I wish you could come too. Oh, I'm sorry, but I'd better go now."

"I'll miss you so much."

"I'll miss you too. I'll write."

We embraced and she ran to the car. I went back inside, threw myself onto the couch, and began to sob. I would be so lonely without Helen.

"What's going on, Nora?" Maman asked, coming out of her bedroom. "Why are you crying?"

"I hate this life, living here. Helen is leaving the country. We should leave too."

"Don't worry, Nora, it will work out," Maman said, and left the house.

School became more strict. For me, there was also the loss of Helen. In fact, there were very few English and American students left.

One day as we lined up to sing the national anthem, one of the truant officers came into the courtyard from his office and said, "No national anthem today."

We dispersed to different classrooms. In my history class, Mr. Moghadessi, a dry, distant man, asked us, "Do you know what Operation Ajax means?"

No one raised her hand. We were shocked that he dared to bring this subject up. "Back in 1951," he said, "We elected Mohammad Mosaddeq prime minister. He nationalized the oil companies, expelling the English, who had taken huge profits and cheated us out of our fair share. Under Mosaddeq, for the first time, we began to envision a future of prosperity and democracy."

He paused, looking at the portrait of the Shah that still hung on the wall, took a deep breath and dared to add, "He was so popular that in 1953 the Shah fled Iran in fear. But the CIA, through bribery and contacts provided by British intelligence, put together a group of people to restore the Shah. Mosaddeq was forced out, the Americans took control of the oil with the British, and the Shah was restored to his peacock throne."

The bell rang, though the session wasn't over, and he stopped suddenly, looking a little tense. It rang again. "There must be an important announcement," he said and started for the door. We all followed him into the yard. Others from other classrooms poured out.

As we all stood around silently, the principal said urgently, "We have to evacuate, we've been instructed to. Begin leaving in an orderly manner."

But we all rushed out, bumping against each other. I walked speedily towards home. At a distance, near the refinery, a big fire had started, the flames mingling with the refuse burner flames. It was a breezeless day; the smell of petroleum became trapped in the still air. Sirens shrieked.

A sermon rang out through a loudspeaker to the crowd collected in the courtyard of Azimeh Mosque. *Sofrehs* were spread on the ground on two sides of the courtyard, one for men, one for women and children. People listened to the sermon as they ate.

> Angels are deserting our town because of all the vices plaguing it. We have to pluck out the weeds of sin—wine, beer, the infidels. The foreigners have made our cities into nests of sin. Listen to our prophet Mohammad, Allah's messenger. Let not ⟨ the life of the world beguile you.

A little further down the street a long procession was taking place. Men wearing black and carrying green flags, Imam Hussein's color, were beating their bare backs with chains; blood was streaming down from the wounds. I had forgotten this was Ashura, the tenth day of Muharram, the month good Muslims wore black in mourning for the martyred Imams. They mourned as if the Imams had died just then—not hundreds of years ago. Black–clothed women followed the men, crying and repeating after them, "Yaaa Hussein, you gave your life for our religion, may that be a lesson to us."

Through the wide open door of a house I could see a passion play being performed, enacting the martyrdom. Men and women were sitting on rugs spread in the courtyard, watching the performance and weeping loudly, some beating their chests.

"Noor, Noor," I heard Jahan calling. I turned around. He was running toward me. "I went to look for you at your school," he said, reaching me. "I caught up with you as fast as I could."

We walked on together, rapidly.

"We had to evacuate," I said.

"So did we."

"We didn't even sing the national anthem today."

"We didn't either."

As we passed the Jam'e Mosque's large blue dome with golden script, a sermon was pouring through a loudspeaker.

> Men are in charge of women, because Allah has made the one of them excel the other. So good women are obedient, guarding in secret what Allah has wanted. As for those women from whom you fear rebellion, admonish them and banish them to beds apart and scourge them. Oh mankind, remember Allah's grace toward you. Is there any creator other than Allah who provides for you from the sky and the earth? There is no Allah but Allah. Listen to Mohammad, Allah's messenger. The devil is an enemy, so treat him as an enemy.

Jahan shook his head despairingly. "That's all wrong. That's not at all what Islam is."

A little farther, our way was blocked by a demonstration. "The oil eaters must go," they shouted. "Marg be English! Marg be Amrika!"

"Jahan, we must talk Baba and Maman into taking us out of the country."

"I heard them talking about it, but exit visas are hard to get."

"I'm so depressed now."

"Oh, Noor, please, please, don't be sad, you have me. We have each other."

No one was home. We went to his room and lay in bed together, embracing, undressing quickly, letting go. Caution was meaningless now. This time the red spots on the sheet were blood, wet and real.

"Noor, we've entered another stage, we've got to find a way for us."

"No one would marry us. Maybe we should tell Maman and Baba."

"They'd die. Anyway, they'd kill *us*."

"You're right." We got dressed in a somber mood.

Then Jahan spoke passionately, "Let's make our own vows. I take you as my wife. I promise to be always by your side in time of need."

"I take you, Jahan, as my husband."

We were enacting one of our fantasy games, like we used to as children, and that began to make us feel much better.

A shot rang out, then an explosion, people running and yelling. We heard the outside door opening and then Baba from downstairs: "Jahan, Nora, are you here?"

"Yes," Jahan said.

"We were worried about you," Maman, who must have come in with Baba, said. "We had Asghar drive around but we didn't find you. Thank God you're back."

Our schools were closed and opened, closed and opened. In the fall, one morning at school Soheila was talking nervously to a group of other students in the yard. "My father, they came and took him. We don't know where." She began to cry. "My mother and I are going to live with relatives in Tehran, hire a lawyer and try to find him."

Her words were drowned out by demonstrators right outside. "They teach the wrong things," they were shouting. "How long will it take to remove the filth put in people's heads by the wrong books and magazines like *Today's Woman?* We'll have to bring the Koran to the people."

The bell rang and the principal came onto the porch. "From now on we are going to have a religion class the first thing every morning. We will also say prayers instead of singing the national anthem. You will be required to wear a scarf on your head, which you must leave on until you return to the safety of your homes. The English courses are cancelled." She said all that with conviction in her voice as if she believed this was for the best.

"The police are now taking orders from the mullahs," one of the teachers said to another.

"We should just continue as before," my dear composition teacher dared to speak out.

But the trend continued. The English classes were cancelled. All the English and American students stopped coming to Iran Dohkt.

Change was everywhere around us. Tape cassettes with messages from Ayatollah Khomeini, who was living in exile in Iraq, were smuggled into Iran, duplicated and spread all around the country. He criticized the Shah, his "sinful ways," the SAVAK. Now few women dared to walk alone in the streets. Those who did wore scarves and dark, long-sleeved, long-skirted clothes or *chadors*. Men avoided going to cafes, nightclubs.

Underneath the surface, forbidden pleasures seethed. Prostitutes, pornographic videos and alcohol were available in underground markets. At night some men went out to look for love or fixes for their addictions in back alleys. Some left home to avoid sleeping next to their wives whom they didn't love, perhaps never had, and looked for prostitutes. Some merely walked about deliriously. There were reports of these "criminals" being arrested.

There were also reports of people being fired from their jobs because they had been connected to the Shah in some way, and of people being murdered in their homes or offices. Some of our neighbors packed and left for unknown places. In those crazed weeks I witnessed the most courageous teachers—among them my beloved composition teacher—being arrested as they protested that they had done nothing wrong.

The crisis kept accelerating. In November Khomeini's son, Mustafa, died mysteriously in Najaf; it was widely believed that he had been murdered by SAVAK. Whether or not this was true, it swayed the passionate public even more, and thousands of mourners poured into the streets. In the United States, Iranian students staged a noisy demonstration against the Shah during his visit to President Carter, who publicly praised him and called Iran "an island of stability in a turbulent corner of the world." Massive strikes and riots ensued in Iran. The SAVAK was nowhere to be seen.

In our town the Armenian church was closed down. Some of the pet dogs belonging to people in the compounds were taken from streets or backyards and never returned. They were declared *najis*, unclean. The pharmacy in the compound, owned by a Jewish man, was partially destroyed; window panes were shattered and piles of broken glass left in front of the store. The synagogue that stood not far from our school was reportedly closed. A fire destroyed a gift shop belonging to a man with an American wife. Another fire was set in a nightclub that featured foreign dancers and singers. In the American compound, the Maloney Bookstore, which carried English language books, was shut down, as was Kentucky Fried Chicken and McDonald's. The cinemas that showed foreign movies were forced to close, condemned as "nests of vice."

# 12

Christmas approached, but there were no trees for sale, nor were there any of the usual Christmas displays in American or English homes. Still Maman wanted to acknowledge Christmas, and Jahan and I received presents as usual—an ivory backgammon set for him and a book of Shakespeare's sonnets for me. The poetry book was her idea. She must have bought it before the bookstore was closed down.

They invited their best friends, the Sagaamis, over for Christmas dinner. Golpar came in the morning and helped Maman with the cooking—standing rib roast, pearl onions and mushrooms, sweet potatoes, wild rice, and charlotte russe for dessert. Jahan and I had to attend, of course, even though he had wanted to go hiking with Bijan, and it wasn't ever easy for me to be around Dr. Sagaami. Even though he had done his residency in America and had met Mary there, he was very traditional. He was a small man, and soft-spoken, but he had strong views and tried to pound them in. We all dressed up, even though only the Sagaamis were coming and the whole world around us was falling apart.

At dinner Baba said, "My dear Doctor Sagaami, history is repeating itself. It's 1953 all over again." Men were always addressed by their titles, but not women.

"The Shah could rely on the CIA in those days to bring him back. I don't think that will work this time. The anger is so deep."

"Yes, and the mullahs have gained power."

I was sitting next to Jahan at the end of the table. I felt remote from the conversation and so did he, judging by his silence. Years before we had carved our names beneath that part of the table. Next to our names he had carved a bow and arrow and a heart. It had been so uncomplicated in those days. There was no way to turn back to that innocent state, and no way to get out of the narrow space we had created for ourselves and back into the open.

After we finished eating Mary went to the living room and came back with two small gift-wrapped packages. "For you," she said, giving one to me and one to Jahan. We both had gotten gold rings, his with a carnelian stone, mine with a dazzlingly bright ruby.

"This is beautiful," I said, putting on the ring. Pain stabbed my heart as I thought about how one day Jahan would be giving a ring to his fiancée, someone other than me, unless we could leave Masjid-e-Suleiman. It was the same old fantasy, but each time it came to me in a slightly different way, like a new ray of light.

"Such generous gifts," Jahan said, with his winning half-smile.

"I wanted to give you similar presents, you're so close to each other," Mary said.

I smiled self-consciously, lowering my eyes to avoid hers.

Dr. Sagaami said, "Mary always sends identical presents to her niece and nephew too."

Golpar came in and cleared the table. In a few moments she brought out the dessert and tea.

"Jahan *agha*, have you thought of what you're going to do with yourself? Are you going to be a doctor like your father?" Dr. Sagaami asked.

"I don't know yet," Jahan said. "I've applied to Pahlavi College."

"The one in Masjid-e-Suleiman?"

He nodded.

"Well you still have time to think about your future," Dr. Sagaami said. He looked at me and said, "Soon men will be knocking on the door asking for your hand."

I was relieved when Mary changed the subject. "The doctor and I have been talking and talking about how we might leave the country before things become worse."

Dr. Sagaami turned to Baba and said, "Did you hear that they aren't giving exit visas to anyone before first interrogating them? And of course they'll find people like you and me guilty. We were recruited by the Shah and we have American wives. They don't like us but they don't want us to leave either. They want us in jail."

"Have the mullahs taken over the airport too?" Baba asked, shaking his head.

"Yes, they've moved to every corner, and as you know the Shah isn't capable of stopping them any more."

"And if we did leave the country, we'd have other problems. For one thing we won't be able to practice until we're licensed, and they make the exam very hard for foreigners in most countries," Baba said.

A gloomy cloud descended on the room, enveloping us.

Baba tried to brush it aside, saying, "We've had many ups and downs in our history. This phase will pass too."

Dr. Sagaami looked at his watch. "We should get going, I told Engineer Mehdi Siami we'd meet him after dinner." He and Baba got up.

"I won't be long," Baba said to Maman.

In a moment Jahan left too. "I told Bijan I'll meet him," he said.

I went to my room and sat in a chair with the sonnets but I kept looking at the ring, the deep gold band and the large dazzling stone. My whole being was consumed with desire for Jahan, pushing away all other concerns. Then I heard Maman and Mary talking about their childhoods, how they were forced to go to church, how lucky they were now to live in luxury, with all the leisure time they had. This upheaval has to pass, Maman reassured Mary. Then they were laughing hysterically. They must be drinking, I thought. I closed the door, shutting out their voices.

Baba's optimism at Christmas proved to be wrong. Khomeini, still in exile, called for the overthrow of the Shah, ordering the faithful to disobey existing laws. He'd also begun referring to himself as Imam, which for Shiias meant one who embodied divine wisdom and was an infallible guide to the faithful. Coincidentally, Carter paid a surprise visit to the Shah, during which he praised him to the skies. That gave the Shah the courage to allow Khomeini to be ridiculed in newspapers as a medieval reactionary, which led to student demonstrations in Qom. Demonstrations kept growing. Young revolutionaries roamed the streets of cities, seized government buildings, radio stations, and armories. By March, Khomeini was calling for the assassination of the Shah.

Norooz, which started on March 21, usually Iran's biggest holiday, wasn't to be celebrated that year. With festivities lasting two weeks, it was one holiday that Jahan and I both liked. Its roots were in Zoroastrianism and, as implied by its timing in early spring, it symbolized renewal, rebirth, awakening. Its many rituals used to bring the whole city to life. Lights were strung on trees and displayed in all the windows. Streets were vibrant with color. But that year, rituals unconnected with Islam were disrupted by the police, who were taking orders from Khomeini and local mullahs. The "fire lighters" with their faces painted black, and troops of dancers, acrobats and musicians in colorful clothes studded with small bells, who used to parade the streets during this season, weren't anywhere to be seen. Lighting public bonfires and jumping over them on the Tuesday before the holiday, a ritual of purification and renewal, was forbidden lest it draw young people into the streets and lead to "immoral" acts.

On that Tuesday evening Maman and Baba went to visit some friends. Jahan and I, in defiance of all the new rules, collected twigs and dry tree branches from the courtyard; when it grew dark we piled them in a heap on the sidewalk in front of our house. Other children saw us and began making fires in front of their houses. After Jahan poured lighter fluid on our heap and lit it, we held hands, took a running start, and jumped over our fire. The others invited us to jump over theirs. In a moment everyone was chanting, jumping over fire after fire all the way to the end of the block.

We sang, "Fire, fire, my paleness to you, your redness to us."

Thus we exchanged darkness and weakness for the warmth and

healthy glow of fire and began the new year revived through the power of fire.

We went on like that until the fires died out. We were about to start them up again but a police car drew up and we were warned, "Stop this, or we'll have to take you to the station."

"Let's go in, Noor," Jahan said as he took my hand and pulled me inside the house and locked the door.

We sat on a bench in the courtyard, breathing the cool night air and listening to the songs of the cicadas. A full moon was sailing through the wispy clouds. Bright stars were studded against the sky like jewels. Then a hard wind began to blow, howling through the courtyard. We went inside and up to his room. From his desk he picked up a copy of Hafiz's collected poems. On different occasions, particularly during Norooz, people read this fourteenth-century mystic, whose poetry, some thought, could predict the future. Sitting next to me Jahan opened the book to a random page and read the one on the right side:

> I am filled with love tonight
> Come into my eyes, and let's set sail
> my dear, on a long sea voyage.
> Let's conspire to make the moon jealous,
> such radiance leaping from your cheeks.

The words, so harmonious with my mood, brought tears into my eyes. He put his arm around me and looked into my eyes. "Don't let your radiance get clouded with tears," he said. "Hafiz has brought us good news, hasn't he?"

In a few moments we were on his bed, forgetting all our concerns.

On the day of Norooz we had to visit the Sagaamis with our parents, wearing new clothes, as was the custom; now this year, to be cautious, Maman and I wore headscarves. The Sagaamis lived on the furthest corner of the compound from us so Baba drove. When we reached their house, Mary and Dr. Sagaami, having no children themselves, welcomed Jahan and me warmly. Their house was similar to ours and similarly furnished, mainly with old antique furniture. Mary had set up the ceremonial Haft Sinn table, the table of seven "S's," on which seven items beginning with the Persian letter "Sinn," were displayed. Each item symbolized an aspect of earthly life. Among them were *sabzi*, germinated wheat Mary had grown for the occasion; *sekke*, a coin; *serkeh*, vinegar.

Another table was set for lunch. In a few moments Maman helped Mary bring out the food, the usual daily selection but more elaborate—chicken kebab, barg kebab, a variety of rice dishes and salads.

As soon as we started eating, Dr. Sagaami said to Baba, "Police came to my office and asked me millions of personal questions that were none of their business. My salary, for instance, and if Mary and I had been married by an *aghound*, and why did Mary come to Iran to begin with."

"The police have been completely taken over," Baba said with unusual bitterness. "They used to bow to the Shah and now they bow to Khomeini. I too had a visit from them."

"The local radio stations are all repeating Khomeini's words," Dr. Sagaami said. He got up and turned on the large radio on a table to demonstrate his point. The commentator was saying emphatically:

> Gambling casinos are built while our children in villages are dying from malnutrition or from drinking contaminated water. An American army officer gets $100,000 a year plus a car, a servant, and a house; our own officers get one tenth of that and no benefits. What is the American-Iranian relationship? Pouring oil dollars into the pockets of American stockholders in return for their approving of and supporting the Shah's oppressive regime. They have no respect for us. On the sacred day of Ashura, Americans in Tehran threw wild parties with rock music blaring from stereos, disregarding the significance of the occasion.

Dr. Sagaami turned it off. "Enough of this."

We tried to talk about ordinary matters but it was impossible. The conversation died out. Finally we got up and said goodbye.

Later that day, I found Maman alone in the living room, reading the *Iran Times* and smoking a cigarette. She had been smoking since Christmas. She said she used to smoke when she was in college, and now she was consuming two packs of Virginia Slims a day. Ashtrays filled up with the stubs. Her clothes and the air around her smelled of smoke. She didn't hide this habit from us the way she tried to hide her drinking.

"Maman, when are we going to find a way to go to America?" I asked.

"You heard they aren't giving exit visas," she said, exhaling smoke.

"Who was that man talking to Baba yesterday?" A man I had never seen had come home with him and then the two of them sat in the courtyard talking in hushed tones.

"A lawyer. He's giving your father advice about what we might be able to do. Poor Cyrus has so much on his mind now."

Maman and Baba's wedding photograph stood on the side table. She was wearing a long white satin dress and a gauzy veil. Baba was wearing a dark suit and a tie. They were looking at each other with adoration while his mother and aunt, in headscarves, were rubbing cubes of sugar together over their heads, to sweeten their marriage. They are still so adoring of each other, I thought. They didn't need children, and had us only because they thought having children was expected of them.

"Did you fall in love with Baba as soon as you met him?" I asked.

"Nora, you're always thinking about falling in love."

"Please, Maman."

"All right. I was at the hospital only a week when I noticed your father in the corridor. I fell for him then and there. His face was expressive. Not at all like the boys I grew up with. He was so courteous, almost formal, and yet very intense. Before I met your father I couldn't imagine joy in marriage." She smiled. "And Cyrus felt that with me he'd be more free, not so inhibited by his family's expectations."

"Then why is he so strict with me?"

"He loves you, Nora, and his own upbringing makes him believe he has a responsibility as a father to guide his daughter to lasting happiness and security. It's better for you that he should care so much."

She put down her newspaper and went to the window that overlooked the courtyard, and opened it to let out her cigarette smoke.

"If I never go out with boys, how will I know when the right person comes along?" I asked, testing her.

"Love can happen in many ways—maybe it's always a surprise. So many people in this country have arranged marriages. Most of them are happy together, fall in love after they are married. Just because marriage and other things in this country are done in what seems to us an abnormal way, it doesn't mean you can't be happy. Besides, you know your father would never make you marry someone you really hated. But you're only seventeen, there's no need to rush into things."

"Was Baba perfect?"

"When you love someone you overlook their faults."

"He had faults?"

"What's this cross-examination?"

The truth is I was groping to understand the secret of their closeness.

A muezzin's voice, "Allah O Akbar," interrupted us. This new call to prayer in our area was broadcast from an old mosque that had been recently resurrected. The ruined minarets had been restored and newly equipped with loudspeakers.

Maman disappeared into her room. The brief connection between us was broken. She was out of reach. I wanted to shout, "Maman, come back, talk to me." But it was hopeless.

# 13

The weather was hot and sticky. I didn't feel like getting up. Finally I forced myself out of bed and called my school to see if it would be open, something that Jahan and I had to do every morning now. The principal answered. She said, "Not today, check in tomorrow." Just as well. School was lonely without Helen. I wished she would write, but I never received a letter. She might have written and the letter hadn't reached me because of the chaos in Iran.

As I went to the dining room, Golpar was standing by the window, looking down into the courtyard. "Look, there's an owl there," she said. "That's bad omen. All the agitation is due to our own sins." Serving me breakfast, she announced, "The buses aren't running regularly, I don't know how long I'll be able to come and work here."

"Golpar, I hope you won't stop," I said. "You have to stay with us. We need you."

"My dear *khanoom koochoolo* I don't want to quit. But it's all up to Allah."

That was the last time I saw her. A few days later, after she hadn't arrived, Maman explained that she would be working in her family's orchard now. And so Jahan and I lost the person who had been most attentive and kind to us for so many years of our lives. We felt miserable. We didn't even get to say goodbye.

Our other workers stopped coming too. Only the chauffeur, still being paid by the refinery, remained. On the way to school one day, I saw Ahmad standing in a group of demonstrators, shouting, "Marg be Amrika!"

"People like him are paid to go out there and shout," Jahan told me.

Soon milk and the newspaper weren't delivered to the houses in the compound. Garbage wasn't picked up. Everything had to be individually arranged and paid for. Maman hired temporary help. She had started to keep the thick maroon velvet curtains drawn over the windows overlooking the street. "There are spies everywhere," she said. Baba didn't stay at work as late as he usually did. He said things were getting difficult for him at the hospital. He and Maman talked in their bedroom, whispering things. The ringing of our phone or our doorbell, the sound of footsteps, made them jump. People were being arrested every day now, and we all feared that the police would knock on the door, search the house, find Baba guilty arbitrarily, and take him away.

Maman chain-smoked. Baba was volatile and impatient with all of us, even with Maman. If I played music he shouted, "Turn down that teenage American music." He snapped at Jahan, telling him to watch his posture, or not to spend so much time painting and to read science books. He slammed the phone down angrily when he couldn't reach his brothers in Tehran. He didn't resort to alcohol or cigarettes but he let out his rage freely, slamming things, banging doors shut.

One evening coming downstairs to get something to eat, I heard Maman talking to Baba but slurring her words. Losing all control, he picked up a glass and threw it against the wall and shouted, "Look at you, you're drunk."

As much as I had resented their closeness that stood like a fortress, now their fighting upset me more. It was as if our small world was falling apart too.

I was relieved when he held her in his arms and, caressing her hair, said, "I'm sorry Moira."

It was another hot, still day. Schools had opened briefly for final exams and now were open for a few hours so that we could get our grades. But when I reached Iran Dohkt nothing was posted. The janitor, sitting idly on a bench in the courtyard, said, "Everyone left." I went back to the car and Asghar drove me back.

Jahan was home when I returned. He was in the living room with Maman and the two of them were talking. This was his last year but there would be no graduation ceremony. As soon as Maman saw me she said, "Nora, we're leaving, but don't say a word to anyone."

"Really, where?"

"Your father has arranged everything. Someone is driving us to the Gulf and then we'll be put on a boat. Then we'll be bribing our way into Dubai. From there, America. It's costing a fortune, but at least we have the money; we'll be out of here by the end of the week."

"Do we have to leave this way?" Jahan asked.

"Yes," Maman said emphatically. "Someone saw your father's name on lists posted in the Imam Ali Mosque. He's on two lists: the Friends of Americans list and the Shahis list."

"Lists in a mosque can't mean much," Jahan said.

"Where have you been?" she said. "Don't you see how mullahs are running the country? You know about all the arrests."

Jahan nodded somberly.

"In fact we're Kharej Mamnoon. No Exit Allowed," Maman said. "Any day they could be coming for us. We've applied for political asylum in the U.S. A Catholic charity organization will help us when we get to Dubai. We'll be interviewed by American Immigration there. If they approve, we'll be on our way to the U.S."

"What if they don't approve?" I asked, anxiety taking the place of my excitement. "We'll have to come back here?"

"There shouldn't be any problem. You and I are American born, that helps a lot. And Cyrus is a doctor." She looked around the room. "We hope Jamshid can come and take the furniture. The house belongs to the refinery, of course. Cyrus has been transferring our money to a Swiss bank. Both of you need to get your transcripts from school. Tell them your father is being transferred to Tehran."

Jahan and I climbed the stairs and went to his room.

"It's so unfair. We aren't criminals," he said. "Baba's done nothing but help people his whole life."

"Nothing has ever been fair in Iran," I said.

"Whatever happens, Noor, nothing will ever change our love."

"Yes. Imagine all the things we'll be able to do in America. We'll find a way to live on our own. Baba and Maman won't have so much control over us," I said.

He stared at his most recent painting, examining it. It depicted a nude figure with breasts and a mustache. The eyes were blue, the hair dark.

"It's you and me together," he said, looking deep into my eyes.

Not long after that Jahan was painting and I was sitting on a chair near him, reading a book when Maman called to us, "Jahan, Nora, come down at once."

As soon as we got downstairs, she announced, "We're leaving tonight." She had begun to spread sheets over the furniture—the Italian table and leather sofas, and the Viennese etagère. The huge chandeliers Baba had inherited from his parents looked strange above the disorderly scene. The carpets that had been stored in the basement were piled up in a corner, some covered, a few still spread out. "I have to leave those beautiful carpets behind." She sighed. "I spent years finding them." She pointed to two large leather suitcases in a corner. "One suitcase for each of you. Pack only what you value most."

Jahan and I picked up the suitcases and went up to our rooms. With my exultation went a sense of unreality. Am I dreaming? Are we really leaving? I examined all my belongings. I could easily part with the frilly dresses, shiny patent leather shoes that I wore on holidays. I packed a denim skirt, a cotton blouse, some underwear. I wore a pair of gold loop earrings and the ruby ring, all presents from Dr. Sagaami and Mary. On the collar of my blouse I pinned the butterfly brooch Jahan gave to me on my fifteenth birthday, that day so charged with desire and longing. My ornate jewelry, mostly Norooz gifts from my generous uncles and aunts, was too valuable not to take. I also packed some of the family photographs I had collected over the years and put in Jahan's checkered white and maroon shirt that I had taken from him. Our school transcripts and our passports were with Baba, among other important documents.

When I'd finished I went into Jahan's room. He was having a harder time parting with things. He had put a few items in his suitcase and was pondering on the others. He settled on taking some of his small sculptures. He brought out his nude painting of us as an androgyne and unrolled it. He looked at it, undecided about what to do with it.

"Customs will open your suitcase," I said.

"You're right."

"It can't be left here either. Shall I cover it up?"

Jahan looked dismayed, but nodded his assent.

I took it back to the closet, picked up a brush, dipped it into black paint, and covered the whole surface of the painting.

"Done," I said, coming back into the room. "I'm sorry, Jahan," I said, when I saw his dismay. "Imagine if someone saw it. Not that they'd know it's us, but it's those naked breasts."

"All my artwork abandoned," he said, shutting the suitcase. "We have to come back. What's happening has got to be temporary. There'll be a compromise; things will work out in the end." He didn't look as hopeful as he sounded.

He went to the window and looked intently at the courtyard as if trying to memorize it. I stood next to him. I wanted to bring up plans for our future in America but his mood was heavy, forbidding, so I went downstairs. Baba was standing in front of a window; he was looking out at the courtyard too. He turned around, his face taut. "We're being forced to leave," he said. It seemed he hadn't really accepted the idea.

# Part Two

# 14

We left in the middle of a dark hot May night in 1978. We had applied for asylum in the United States but we were escaping Iran illegally, and though there was some risk in getting away safely I still felt exhilarated. A black Lincoln limousine pulled up outside. Baba got in next to the driver and Maman, Jahan, and I sat in the back. We hadn't said goodbye to our friends who would guess that we, like so many others, had left secretly.

The driver was middle-aged, tall, and muscular. None of us exchanged any words with him, not even words of greeting. He drove very carefully, watching for other vehicles, traffic signs, turns in the road. Frogs were croaking and cicadas trilling; ahead the flames from the refinery towers trembled and the stars were shining against a black sky. The usual sights and sounds had a different feel tonight, more vivid, penetrating, as if anxiously celebrating our escape with us.

We rode along on Petrochemical Plant Road, passing the Iranian National Oil Refinery Hospital, where Baba had worked. I looked out quietly, caught in my dreams.

Soon we were out of Masjid-e-Suleiman and on deserted rocky roads. It took several hours to get to Abadan, a refinery town by the Persian Gulf, normally two hours away. The driver was taking us on roads with no checkpoints so that police wouldn't stop us and ask questions. When we reached the Gulf we got out and he took us to a white fishing boat moored along with many others by the shore. He introduced us to a man standing by the boat who, like himself, was tall and strong looking. Before we got onto the boat the driver went to a general store that stood among a string of others on the shore and stocked up food and drinks for our two-day journey. He emerged with another man whose face was hidden behind his raised collar. We weren't introduced to him. The two men took charge of the boat as our family sat in the cabin and stared out at the sea. The lights from other boats—small freighters, tankers, fishing boats—shimmering on the surface of the flowing water, made colored shapes. It was as if we were participating in a magic show rather than fleeing for our lives. In a few moments Maman and I got into one of the two bunk beds and Jahan and Baba into the other and we tried to get some sleep.

The two-day trip to Dubai was uneventful. When we docked at Dubai it was dusk and the deep blue sky was streaked with red. Small white birds were flying in unison high in the sky. Many boats were moored at the pier; passengers were milling about. Most people were speaking Arabic, and the voice of a muezzin calling people to prayer reached us faintly. The captain of our boat went ahead of us to customs while we waited on the pier. When he came back he took us past the people lined up for the customs booth; a man stepped out of the booth and gave us back our passports. A few feet away a truck was waiting. The driver, another tall, tough-looking man, signaled us inside. Jahan whispered in my ear, "These men have to be ready for the police or bandits!"

In about two hours the driver dropped us off at a hotel in the middle of the city.

We went in, groggy and disoriented.

Closing the door to our suite, Maman exclaimed in relief, "We've survived!"

Baba sighed, "It depends on what you mean by survive. This is only step one."

"You're right," she agreed.

We sat down on the sofa and chairs and sank into silence. Yes, we had escaped Iran and, amazingly, gotten here safely, but now what?

Garlands of roses painted on the sides of the sofas and the headboard of the bed enlivened the room's drabness. Posters of minarets and mosques covered one wall. Abu Zayad, the name of the hotel, was written in large calligraphy on another wall.

"We asked for something cheap," Baba said finally. "Hopefully we won't be here more than a few nights."

In a moment he ordered up food. After we ate we lay down to sleep, Maman and Baba in the bedroom, Jahan and I on the living room sofas.

The following day, after breakfast in a café around the corner from the hotel, we started for the American Consulate, with Baba holding the map. Jahan and I walked a little behind our parents, talking to each other, imagining the new life ahead of us, with him more pessimistic and me trying to bring him out of that mood.

Dubai was a much larger city than Masjid-e-Suleiman, with many more modern buildings. Mosques, cinemas, Western and Muslim-style houses stood side by side. Men on camels moved through wide, palm-lined avenues, along with cars, motorcycles and bicycles. Women and men wore traditional or Western clothes. We passed *souks* that carried locally made merchandise and luxury shops with imported items in the windows. The large number of tax-free shops drew many tourists to the city. It was so peaceful there after Masjid-e-Suleiman, and I was glad to be there. Jahan, too, was gradually coming out of his somber mood.

I put my hand on his arm. "Jahan *joon*, let's not let anything separate us, no matter what," I whispered.

"Nothing will," he said. "Ever."

On a narrow street, lined by modern two-story buildings, we found the American Consulate. The reception room was crowded with people sitting on sofas, talking, filling out forms. Baba went to a window and spoke to the clerk. After a moment he came back and said, "It looks like we have a two-hour wait."

"Why don't we walk around and come back," Maman suggested.

"Nora and I will walk around on our own," Jahan said to them.

"Make sure to be back here at eleven," Baba said. Then Jahan and I went in one direction and they in another. We reached a labyrinthine bazaar and went inside. Some of the *souks'* names were written in Farsi as well as the national language, Arabic. Some people passing by were speaking in Farsi.

One *souk* was called Omar Khayyám after the twelfth-century Iranian poet. "Look, they're carrying Iranian stuff here. Let's go in," Jahan said.

"We just came from Iran," I protested.

"I want to see what they have."

We walked in and went over to a table that displayed several different editions of Omar Khayyám's poetry. He looked through them. One was bilingual, in Farsi on one page and in Arabic translation on the opposite page. There were miniature paintings in the margins.

"I want to buy this," he said. "It's beautiful."

The owner, a middle aged, bearded man, wearing a traditional white robe, answered in Farsi, "That's a rare, unusual edition, only twenty *durhams*."

"I'll take it," Jahan said.

"Aren't we going to run out of money?" I asked Jahan in a whisper.

"I've been looking for one of these for a long time."

The man wrapped the book in a bag for him, and we strolled to a park we had seen on the way, filled with palm trees and bright exotic flowers, similar to the ones in Masjid-e-Suleiman. Mothers with children, single men and women, or whole families were walking on shady paths or sitting on benches. We found a bench near a duck pond where children were throwing pieces of bread to the ducks. Jahan opened the book and turned the pages. "I'd love to learn Arabic, to read the Koran in its original language."

"Really? What for?"

"Mohsen told me it's beautiful in the original. When it's translated it's distorted."

"The original could have been distorted too. Wasn't Mohammad illiterate, and someone else wrote the Koran?"

"But Mohammad was there then to dictate the words."

"Jahan, you don't believe in that nonsense, do you?"

He shrugged. "I love the way it's written in calligraphy."

"The Koran condemns what you and I have together."

He reddened a little but said nothing. He opened the poetry book and we looked at the illustrations, mainly of willowy girls and bearded men sitting under trees, eating and drinking. The illustrations were much more sensual than what Islam condoned, from what I knew. So was Khayyám's poetry.

My mind went to Jahan and me. What was really going to become of us? I tried to brush those thoughts aside. I said, "Let me read to you."

He gave me the book and I looked through it. I began to read:

> But leave the Wise to wrangle, and with me
> The Quarrel of the Universe let be
> And, in some corner of the Hubbub couched,
> Make Game of that which makes as much of Thee.

"I'm not capable of such detachment," Jahan said. He looked at his Rolex, which our parents had given to him for his last birthday. "We're late, we'd better hurry."

We walked rapidly back to the consulate. Baba and Maman were waiting for us outside. "The man in charge is away on some emergency. We'll have to come back in the morning," Baba said. "They're no more efficient here than in our Iran."

"We have ninety days here on our visitor visas, so there's plenty of time," Maman said. Both she and Baba seemed to be battling their anxiety and I tried to do the same.

We started for the hotel. She looked at the display of local merchandise — rugs, jewelry, combs, barrettes, and handbags. "This is a shopper's paradise. Too bad we can't buy anything right now," she said. She sighed. "We left so much behind."

The next day we followed the same routine—going from office to office, waiting, stopping to eat lunch, going back to the hotel at siesta time. Then we started again.

In the evening, back in the hotel, we found many Iranians sitting in the lobby talking among themselves and Baba and Maman joined them. As Jahan and I turned toward the stairs leading to the suite, Baba said, "Where are you two going? Why don't you sit with us?"

Everyone's eyes focused on us. It was hard to go off by ourselves, so we sat down with them. There was no one our age there, but there were a few small children lingering around their parents, asking for things, crying, laughing, oblivious of any problems.

The adults talked openly as if they were a large family—some had left illegally like us, others legally. Most were waiting for entrance visas to other countries—France, England, Germany or, like us, America. Just like the movie *Casablanca*, I thought.

"We're trying to get to New York. My wife and daughter are American citizens. It's just my son and me we have to worry about," Baba said.

"I'd never go back to Iran again, what a hellhole," one woman said as she passed around *gaz* and pistachios.

"Let's not think about it until we know what's going on with our visas," her husband said.

"If we don't get visas it's going to be very difficult," another man said. "They don't like Iranians in Dubai, you know the old tensions over the islands in the Gulf, who owns what. And of course they know we look down on them. Doesn't the Shah always make a big deal in his speeches about how we're Aryans, different from Arabs?"

"Now that the Shah is about to lose his throne it may be different," the first man said excitedly.

Others joined in, their voices intense.

"Is it all leading to a revolution?"

"The SAVAK seems to be in hiding."

"Finally they're running scared."

"Well, it's up to America what will happen in Iran."

"I don't know. Mullahs are already practically ruling."

"Yes, the Shah is a dead man already. About time, he's killed so many people."

"There will be a river of blood."

"It's already flowing."

"If what Khomeini is promising comes about, then we'll be gaining something."

"How can you reconcile democracy with Islam?"

"Depends on how you interpret Islam."

"Can you trust Khomeini?"

A young Iranian man came in, interrupting the heated remarks. He was holding a small Koran. "Can any of you spare some money? I'll pay you back. Someone came into my hotel room last night and robbed me."

"You should have stayed in this hotel. It's safe," one of the men said.

"They had no room available here."

"You could go to the Iranian consulate and borrow money."

"I went there. The Consul is out of town. Another man was robbed at the same time as I was, only worse. His entire savings from years of work was in his suitcase and the whole thing was lifted. He's hysterical, in his room crying all the time."

"It's foolish to carry around all that money in cash," Baba said.

"Won't you help me? I'm not a beggar," the man said, looking sheepish.

Baba took out some money from his wallet and put it in the palm of the man's hand. "I can't help in a major way, but this will buy you supper."

"I'm eternally grateful. Allah will pay you back." He waved the Koran at Baba.

Some of the other guests gave him money also. The man stuffed all the money into his trouser pocket and left.

"He's fake, a good actor," one of the men said.

"Holding the Koran! He's trying too hard to appear righteous," Baba said.

Then we all grew quiet. It was as if the pitiful man was a mirror image of ourselves — loss, uncertainty, and fear of the future had gotten to us, even to me.

Jahan turned to Baba and Maman. "I'm exhausted, I'm going inside." He threw a meaningful glance at me.

"So am I," I said.

"If at your young age you get so tired, what will you be like at my age?" Baba said, trying to be good humored.

We hurried up to the room, but our privacy lasted no more than a few minutes, when we heard the key turning in the door. We took turns in the bathroom and got ready for bed. I wanted to talk to Jahan after our parents went to bed, but I was afraid they would hear us even if we whispered. I tossed and turned on the sofa. Finally I fell asleep but woke in the middle of the night to hear Baba and Maman talking in low voices. They were worrying about the future, asking each other what if, what if that happens, then what.

# 15

On the fifth day, after a standard interview, we found to our relief that visas had been granted to Baba and Jahan. An immigration volunteer, a blond American with a lively, cheerful manner, talked to us about our options. He said there were only certain areas we could go to if we wanted help with housing and other financial matters through Catholic Charities while we waited for our money to arrive.

Maman and Baba immediately chose Long Island from the places available. They liked the idea of being in an area where there were many major hospitals, presumably with good job opportunities for both of them. She planned to work as a nurse until he was licensed to practice as a doctor again.

At the hotel Baba booked a flight for the very next day. Then Maman phoned Catholic Charities to give them the time of our arrival. It was amazing how everything was moving so fast and smoothly.

"We'll make an exception and go to a good restaurant tonight, to celebrate," Baba said. "Then for a while we'll have to be very careful with money."

That evening we went to Al-Ahram, a traditional Arabic restaurant recommended by the hotel. It had velvet-covered chairs, brass tables, and Byzantine lanterns hanging on the walls. The menu offered only Arabic food. It was an ordinary meal, but that night it felt like a special celebration.

As we were leaving for the airport, one of the other hotel guests, a middle-aged man sitting in the lobby, turned to us. "Lucky you!"

"I hope you're next," Maman said to him.

We had escaped Masjid-e-Suleiman as if we were criminals but we were going to enter America legally. It was hard to believe.

I quickly fell asleep on the plane, and the next thing I remembered was a steward announcing that we were landing at JFK. Standing in the customs line we noticed a young woman looking around. As soon as she saw us, she smiled and began to come toward us.

"I'm Janis Shackleton, from Catholic Charities, and you must be the Ellahi family," she said, and led us to baggage claim, where we picked up our suitcases and followed her outside. She pointed to an Oldsmobile. "I'll take you to your apartment. Commack isn't too far from here." During the ride she talked continuously, filling us with all sorts of information.

My eyes were glued to the window, taking everything in—houses, shops, malls, hotels, billboards, and neon signs. One billboard advertising shampoo pictured a young woman, her naked breast only partly covered by her long hair. "This certainly is a different world from Masjid-e-Suleiman," I whispered to Jahan.

"Yes," he said neutrally, not sure yet, it seemed, what to think.

When we drove into Commack, we passed a cinema, restaurants, a tattoo parlor, a small department store, a supermarket. We turned into a side street and Janis stopped the car in front of a two-story apartment building. She gave us a little tour of our apartment—two bedrooms, one and a half bathrooms, a small kitchen. As we anticipated, the apartment wasn't in any way luxurious. It was small, had only a tiny window in each room. From the living room, we could see only a cement wall with some wires affixed to it. The furniture consisted of a Formica table, mismatched kitchen chairs, a convertible couch with a drab gray and beige cover, a double bed and a single bed, both with rusted iron frames. The apartment was given to us free for four months, to tide us over until our money was transferred from Switzerland. It could take several months, having originated from Iran with all its chaos.

Janis gave us food stamps and explained that we would have

access to Medicaid until we found jobs or until our money came. She said that if after four months we still didn't have sufficient funds we could seek help from other organizations: International Rescue Committee or Interfaith Community Service. "Call me any time you have any questions," she said, putting her business card on the kitchen table as she left.

"Let's move some of the furniture closer to the walls to make more room to move around," Maman said.

Jahan and I moved the couch all the way to the wall and Maman and Baba moved the dining table and four chairs to a corner.

"Jahan, you can sleep on the couch, and Nora, you can have the smaller bedroom," Maman said. "Is that all right with you, Jahan?" She and Baba put their crocheted bedspread with its design of birds, flowers and trees on their bed; it had been given to Baba by his grandmother and had been on their bed in Iran too. Maman put her jewelry box, hand-worked silver and studded with precious stones, on the bureau. It was the first present Baba had given her. Next to the bed she spread the only rug she had brought with us: a small pale green silk Isfahan, with a pasture in the background and hundreds of tiny birds and flowers scattered on it.

Jahan and I unpacked our suitcases too and then we all went out to look for a restaurant on the main street we had passed on the way.

"We need to find something cheap," Baba said.

"Tomorrow we'll do grocery shopping and start eating in," Maman said.

"Why do Americans always smile," Jahan said, pointing to the all-smiling faces of people in photographs displayed in the window of a photography shop. "Look, every one of them is smiling. They can't all be so happy!"

"Oh, Jahan, maybe they are," I said, feeling a little defensive about how thrilled I was to be here. Everywhere forsythia bushes had burst into yellow. Tulips dotted the lawns. The trees were full of new tender green leaves. A small carnival on a road next to a row of shops glowed from the numerous lights strung around the Ferris wheel and the merry-go-round. The cheerful voices of children playing seemed an extension of all that light.

We spotted a diner and studied the menu displayed in the window.

"This looks good enough," Maman said.

"The prices are so high," Baba said.

"I'm sure this is as reasonable as we'll be able to find."

"Five hundred *toomans* for a piece of chicken!"

"You can't compare the dollar with the *tooman.*"

"But that's what our money will be worth, with the rate of exchange."

"Hopefully we'll find jobs and we'll be paid with dollars then," Maman said.

Inside, displayed in cases, were a variety of pies, puddings, cakes. On the wall behind the counter hung a poster of a young woman in a red and blue dress, holding a mug of beer in one hand.

We sat at a table and a waitress brought menus to us. "Can I get you something to drink?"

"Just water for now," Maman answered for us, a little more assertive than she was in Iran.

"What should we order?" Jahan asked after studying the menu.

"Let's try the chicken," Maman suggested. "It's lemony, a little like Iranian food."

When it came, it had been deep-fried and was tough, accompanied by a few leaves of wilted lettuce.

After taking a bite, Baba joked, "Could use pomegranate sauce."

"Yes, I miss Golpar's cooking," said Jahan.

After a strange pudding, even I had to admit that American food wasn't so great.

Back in the apartment we went to bed early.

The following morning, as soon as I opened my eyes, my mood was upbeat. My first thought was: we are in America now and the world is wide open. Jahan and I will make a new life here; everything will fall into place. I could even see some good things about the apartment. The floor was covered by a soft powder-blue rug, and one of the windows overlooked a little backyard filled with flowers.

The sun was just beginning to rise but everyone was already up and talking in the living room. I joined them there. Maman and Baba must have gone grocery shopping. Baba seemed unable to push out his concern about the prices. "Everything is so expensive," he said. "A carton of eggs is two dollars instead of twenty cents."

Maman said to me, "Nora, breakfast is ready. Get tea and orange juice from the kitchen. We have everything else here on the table."

I brought them in and sat down with the family.

"We've burnt our bridges behind us, now there's no turning around," Baba was saying.

"Depends on who takes power, doesn't it?" Maman said.

"I'm not confident that anything can be resolved soon."

"At least we're alive and healthy," she said. "There's a lot to get done. We should get started today. We need to fill out forms for health insurance, start looking for jobs. You and Jahan will have to fill out application forms for citizenship."

"We have to look into a high school for me, a college for Jahan," I said.

Jahan, who had been quiet, said, "I'd love to go to art school."

Baba shook his head. "What you need is a BS."

Maman turned to me. "You may not need to go to high school and just enter college. You took all those advanced courses; they may take that into consideration, particularly if you do well in your SATs."

"Will Jahan and I live in dormitories then?"

"We can't afford dormitories. You'll have to apply to local colleges."

"I don't like the idea of dormitory living anyway," Baba said. "You'll live at home and go to classes."

Of course that was how Baba would be, I thought. But at some point Jahan and I will strike out for independence. I turned to Jahan. "Wouldn't it be wonderful to go to the same school together?"

He nodded, but his distracted manner upset me.

We got up and took our dishes into the kitchen, then stood around the living room, a little aimless. Maman took a deep puff from the cigarette she was holding.

"You promised you'd quit," Baba said. "You're poisoning yourself."

"I will, give me time."

Later that day I found Jahan in the living room, lying on the sofa, looking through the Omar Khayyám book. "Do you want to go for a walk?" I asked.

"Sure." He sat up and put on his shoes, which he'd flung by the side of the sofa. "We're going to take a walk," he announced.

"Don't stay out long," Baba said.

"We won't," we said simultaneously.

Outside, Jahan said, "We depend so utterly on them now. We have no privacy here."

"After we finish with college, we'll be independent."

"That's a long time from now."

"You know we have no choice right now," I said.

Jahan looked unhappy and that made my heart heavy too.

On a quiet, empty street, I kissed him. But he was tentative, remote.

We had no money to go to the movies or to sit in a café and Baba had urged us to be back soon. So we turned around after a short walk and headed back to the apartment.

Baba and Maman were in the living room. Baba was complaining, "We've certainly come down in life. This is a parody of what we had."

Jahan said, "We're refugees."

I went into my room, not wanting to hear more.

It wasn't easy at all at first. Jahan and Baba's English was inadequate and that made it hard for them to find jobs. But it was more than that. Baba had an aversion to taking just any job; we all suspected he was turning down offers without telling us. Both of them started taking evening courses in English at the local library but seemed a little reluctant to make it their first language. At home they continued using Farsi. I tried to speak with Jahan in English but he kept switching back into Farsi. I had a feeling that he didn't want to speak English with me because he'd always taken care of me, and now circumstances made him feel powerless. And then our erotic relationship had been in Farsi, our love was born and grew in Farsi. Speaking English made us different people, as if our love wasn't translating well.

Maman began working as a floating nurse in a hospital. She was often on late duty and sometimes returned past midnight, and then she'd sleep late in the morning. I got a part time job in the local library, checking books in and out. Jahan finally found a job as a carpenter's assistant with an Iranian contractor who was building tract homes. Baba devoted himself to a remedial course for his licensing exams. In the evenings after dinner, he sat in the armchair in the living room and read newspapers, the *New York Times* and the Iranian journals he subscribed to, then he studied late into the night.

One month we were so low on money that Maman decided to sell some of her jewelry. She called me into her room one morning after Baba and Jahan had left. She was sitting on the bed with a large wooden box in front of her. She lifted the lid and I was startled at what I saw: jewelry piled up in a heap—bracelets, necklaces, and rings, studded with precious stones.

"You brought all that with you from Iran?"

"I took a chance. I bought them over the years as an investment. I'll keep the sapphire set, but the rest I have to part with."

"I can sell all my jewelry too. I never wear it." I went to my room and gave her everything I had.

We took the train to New York City and the bus to 47th Street with its myriad jewelry shops, some divided into cubicles, making shops within shops. The street was crowded with people, mostly men, talking volubly, arguing, and haggling. Some were wearing what I knew to be Jewish skullcaps or dressed in Hasidic clothes, unfamiliar to me then. Here, except for the differences in dress, the scene was very much like the bazaar in Ahvaz. In fact, I caught a snatch of Farsi amidst the babble. Maman showed the jewelry to several shop owners; they all advised us to sell it on consignment.

"If I buy from you I can only melt down these pieces and give you the price of the stones plus the weight of the gold," one of them, an old man, told us.

"All the good workmanship will be wasted," Maman objected. Still she didn't want to wait until we eventually found a buyer. So she sold it all for $6,000.

"Well, Nora, let's at least have a nice lunch." As we walked up Fifth Avenue I was dazzled by the luxurious shops. Maman said that when she was growing up, her parents, on one of the rare occasions they'd ventured out from their farm, had taken her to New York. It was Christmas and they'd be staying with relatives in New Jersey. She was about eight years old but she still remembered the glittering star and snowflake displays and the elaborate toy acrobats dancing in store windows.

"But we shouldn't go into any shops today," she said. "I don't want the temptation. There's so much in this city. Later, when we have money, you and Jahan will come here, go places, enjoy yourselves."

We wandered around looking for an inexpensive restaurant. Maman knew we had to get as far away from Fifth Avenue as possible, so we walked due west until we came to Ninth Avenue with its restaurants from different countries. We chose an Italian one that had a lively decor and a reasonable menu posted in the window.

I was stirred up just being in the city with all its variety, and I enjoyed the food, which I had never tasted before. But then, caught in my thoughts about Jahan, I was overcome by a sudden loneliness, aware of how he and I were flung apart, not on the same wavelength now.

"What's the matter, love? You're quiet." Maman asked, a look of concern in her eyes.

She wasn't as remote from me as she used to be. It was as if she had come out from behind a mask. She was more in her element here in her own country, in spite of our difficulties, than she had realized or acknowledged. Even physically she seemed more of a real person to me, attractive in her casual American style of dressing, more assertive in manner now that she had more responsibility.

"I just wish Jahan was as happy as I am."

"It's harder for him here," she said. "For Cyrus too."

"I know."

# 16

By fall, most of our savings had come from Switzerland, but because of the chaos in Iran and the mounting tension between Iran and America, the value of the *tooman* had plunged further relative to the dollar. Still, we had enough money to buy a small house. Baba, not used to the idea of a mortgage, bought it with cash. We had a used green Toyota that we'd been sharing, and now we were also able to buy a second car, a used Jaguar for Baba. Having an expensive brand car, even a used one, was Baba's way of reminding himself of our former status.

The ranch-style house stood on a quiet, tree-lined street in Potunk, a small suburb with a tiny main street. It had four small bedrooms, two on each side of the living room, two bathrooms and a small backyard. Before moving into the house, we thought about colors to paint each room. We decided on robin's-egg blue for the living room, pistachio green for our parents' bedroom, a pale, flat peach for my room, deep blue for Jahan's. The outside walls were yellow and we kept them that way. We bought the furniture and other household necessities from a Sears store on Long Island. One day Maman went out to buy things for the kitchen and came back a few hours later with stacks of dishes, pots and pans and silverware. "All for $100! I bought them in a garage sale on the way to Port Jefferson." Then she and Baba made several excursions to New York City in search of used Persian rugs. They brought back two, similar to those we had in Masjid-e-Suleiman.

They made the largest room with its own bathroom into their bedroom. Jahan and I had the rooms on the two sides of their bedroom and shared the bathroom in the hall. Baba used the extra room as his study, where he hung up his diplomas—his Bachelor of Science degree with honors from the University of Tehran, his medical degree from the same university. Jahan put up his soccer trophy and on one wall he hung the poster of Rustam.

Maman said, "It's a good thing we have no leaky faucets or plumbing problems. Neither your father nor I are good at fixing things." But she did a lot to improve the house anyway, and to introduce an air of normalcy. She bought trays of plants and put them into the ground in the backyard. She grew flowers in two large urns on either side of the entrance door and hung a bird feeder on a spruce tree in the backyard, which attracted blue jays, cardinals and chickadees.

As soon as we had a phone in the house, it began to ring. Advertisers were calling to sell us various products—to exterminate termites, build a better septic system, refinance our mortgage. After each call Baba made a sarcastic remark, like, "We don't even have a mortgage! They grasp at what they can. No wonder this country is so prosperous."

"In Iran the vendors come right outside of your door shouting," I said jokingly but Baba snapped, "It isn't the same thing."

When a butcher called to offer delivery, Baba was more tolerant. He said, "We'll think about it, call back in a day or two." He turned to Maman and said, "Maybe they have better meat than the supermarket."

"It costs too much to order from a private butcher," Maman said ruefully.

Baba's bits and pieces of anti-American remarks fell on a background of praise. Before saying, "There's no depth to the relationships, their 'hi hi's are meaningless," he had remarked, "It's an amazing country; Americans are so full of energy, so full of optimism."

"You've been married to me for years, and you're now trying to figure out Americans for the first time," Maman said and laughed.

"You're a category all to yourself," he said.

"I wish there was a center to this town, sidewalks, cafes, real shops, not just a strip mall," Jahan said, pouring out his dissatisfaction. "Everything shuts down at five and then everyone just watches TV. There's no real life here. I miss the mountains too."

But I had never had the freedom of movement he'd had in Iran so I didn't share his nostalgia.

Baba tried to bring Iran into the house as much as possible. He walked in one day with armfuls of packages he had bought from an Iranian specialty store in Queens: a samovar and a set of tiny gold-rimmed tea glasses in silver holders, Iranian pastries—*gaz* and *sohoon*—a jar of pomegranate sauce, a package of mixed dried Iranian vegetables. At least once a week he helped Maman make *fesenjoon* and *koresh*.

Then he bought a short wave radio pre-tuned to a Farsi station. He put it on the counter between the kitchen and the dining area, which was an extension of the living room. Now the news came to us directly from Iranian stations, filling our new home with harsh realities of the home we had left behind. The reception was sporadic but we heard enough. In September there was a massacre in Tehran. Thousands of people walking with banners demanding freedom were machine gunned by the Shah's troops. More than half of them were killed. But that didn't put an end to the uprisings. The funerals of the dead became occasions for further and larger demonstrations. Slogans and posters on walls expressed anger at the Shah: "Down with the Shah! Down with SAVAK! End Imperialism and bloody CIA that taught SAVAK how to torture! Marg be Amrika!"

Then in October when Khomeini was expelled from Iraq and sent to Paris, protests in Iran accelerated still further. Things were reaching a point of no return. Taxi drivers, Iran Air, government ministries, postal, railroad, government hospital workers all went on strike, demanding economic and social benefits and showing support of Khomeini who had established himself as a symbol of freedom from the brutal Pahlavi regime. Strikes were spreading to every corner of Iran. Cement and tobacco factory workers, the atomic energy organization employees, teachers, bank and hotel employees all walked out. Oil workers everywhere, including in Ahvaz, Abadan, and Masjid-e-Suleiman, went on strike. The Shah was desperately trying to reverse the situation. He sent troops to work in the oil fields. He tried to appease the people by freeing about 1,000 political prisoners who had been accused by the SAVAK at one time. Then he agreed to put the head of SAVAK on trial for ordering what he now called "illegal imprisonments and tortures." The Shah also made a speech that liberalization of the political system would continue. But too many people had been killed, too many promises had been broken, and no trust was possible. Khomeini sent tapes to Iran from France, telling people not to trust the Shah.

At first Khomeini had been an idol of the conservatives. They hoped he would pull Iran into Islamic values, get rid of all the "vices." But now, more and more, he was gathering support from other segments of society, the liberals, intellectuals, reformists, and students, who hoped that Khomeini would establish the ground for a future democracy and then would be shunted aside.

My family and I tried to cope with daily tensions of our new home as best as we could. We divided the daily chores. I set and cleared the table, loaded the dishwasher. Jahan vacuumed, picked up dry cleaning, and went out and got groceries when we ran out at the last minute and brought them back in the basket of a bicycle Baba had bought for him. Maman washed the clothes in the machine and ironed them. Baba did most of the shopping and helped her with the cooking. Jahan helped Maman with the work in the backyard. Without servants we were living like an average American family but, not used to taking care of such practical matters, they seemed like a big deal.

When Maman worked in the backyard late in the day she talked to the neighbors over the fence but she felt apart from them, having had vastly different experiences living in Iran. Next to us lived a young lawyer, whose wife assisted him in his office. On the other side of our house was a young executive at a phone company; his wife taught in a nursery school. They were all from Long Island and never left it. Baba had met the husbands and complained about them. "All they talk about is the grass in their backyard, prices of real estate and the weather. Even when my English gets better I can't imagine what I'd say to them." Jahan's and my interaction was different, a struggle, in the new environment.

Baba got a job as an assistant to a group of Iranian internists in Setauket. In his free time he continued to study. Maman found a better nursing job. I continued working at the library and Jahan with the contractor. In his free time he painted in a studio he'd carved out for himself in the garage. Now his paintings resembled Persian miniatures, with birds, angels, mythical animals, hovering above romantic scenes. On the margins of some he wrote, in calligraphy, verses from Omar Khayyám. He had inscribed two lines several times:

> There was a door to which I found no key
> There was a veil past which I could not see

When Maman worked the night shift Baba sometimes invited a group of Iranian men he'd met through other doctors at work to our house. Only some of them lived nearby. The rest were scattered as far away as upstate New York and Connecticut. It took them hours to go back and forth, but they valued being together enough to make the long trip. He had become close to one of them—an ex-colonel who had had conflicts with the Shah and escaped Iran a few years before the revolution. He always arrived before everyone else. He wore suits and took off his jacket and hung it up on a hook in the hallway. He had a large pocket watch, clasped to his belt with a chain. He and Baba played backgammon in the living room while waiting for the others. They reminisced about the past—their childhoods which had been truly magical in their eyes, and the changes they had witnessed growing up in Tehran. They had seen

Iran modernized by the Shah's father and had been hopeful during the young Shah's White Revolution of the 1960s, when he appointed a "literacy corps" (high school graduates sent to teach in villages instead of serving in the army), allowed profit sharing by workers in private sector companies and then extended the right to vote to women. The colonel, even more than Baba, dreamed of going back home one day, when things stabilized there—to the point where he kept his watch and the clocks in his house on Iran time. He expected to get on the plane any day. He couldn't drink tea without asking if Baba didn't prefer Iranian tea. He couldn't look out the window without recalling the rose garden of the summerhouse in a village outside Tehran his parents used to take him to.

When they all came they sat in Baba's study with the doors half shut and talked while they drank vodka and beer and ate pistachio nuts. I could hear them every time I came to the living room for something. Mansour, one of the men in the group, would recite poetry to illustrate his points, but his poems, as well as the general conversation, were bitter and nostalgic.

Maman made a close friend, Olga Kaminski, a woman she'd met at work. I had casual friends I could go to lunch or to a coffee shop with. Jahan liked some of the men he met on the job, but missed his friends at home.

Jahan had a bicycle and Baba reluctantly bought one for me too, so that I could ride to work on my own, as there was no adequate public transportation. After I was comfortable on it, I said to Jahan one afternoon, "Let's go out and ride somewhere together."

Everything was shining under the crisp, cool sunlight. Children were running around the backyards, chasing each other, flying to and fro in swings. Mothers were sitting in clusters, watching their children and taking sips from tall glasses, laughing. The mere absence of certain things felt like an addition to me. Absence of collective fear and anger that swirled in the air in Masjid-e Suleiman. Absence of the police. No smell of petroleum everywhere. Instead, a sweet breeze blew from the ocean. No tragic faces confronted you every day—the beggar boys, some lame or blind or both, clinging to you until you gave them something, the unhappy, jobless laborers sitting against the walls, the shoeshine boys leaning down and beginning to work on your shoes, whether you asked them to or not.

We passed through the main street in Potunk, lined by a small supermarket, a post office with a wooden eagle on top that flapped its wings every hour on the hour, a few restaurants. Then we explored the mall just outside of Potunk. There was such an abundance of everything—movie theaters showing three or four movies, so many brands of clothing and food displayed in windows. We stopped in some of the shops: The Gap, The Limited, Lord and Taylor.

"I hate these malls," Jahan said. "They make me feel homesick for the old town, it was so much more colorful."

"Let's check out the beach," I said, changing the subject.

We detoured to the beach and sat on a rock, looking out at the water. The shoreline was weedy, not good for swimming, but further out it was serene, a deep clear blue. Boats glided by slowly. Mothers and children waded. As sun began to set the gulls wheeled in the air and then dove down to the water. Jahan and I were quiet. It was hard for us to share the experience. We had always seen things differently, I thought, why was it so difficult for us now? It was the shift—he had been the happier, freer one in Iran.

When we returned home we stood by the window in the living room and looked out at flocks of small birds, their wings glinting in the red dusk. The street was empty. Here I was, out of hellish Masjid-e-Suleiman and in our new home in America. The mere thought suffused the silent scene before me with joy.

It was jarring when Jahan interrupted my reverie. "Everything's so sterile here." I thought: I can look at the scene and be filled with optimism and energy, whereas Jahan sees it as empty.

He rested his hand on my back. We hadn't made love for months and now, in the state of mind I was in, his touch felt burdensome. I didn't have to move away from him or tell him anything. He sensed how I was feeling. He turned around and went to his room.

Later, through his half open door, I saw him sitting on his bed and writing in a leather-bound notebook. It seemed he was keeping a diary. Was he confiding in those pages what he couldn't now confide in me? He didn't look up when I paused by his door, tempted to go in. I wasn't sure if he didn't see me or if he was avoiding me. It suddenly seemed that what we had together had been just a dream, evaporating like the light of day.

On Halloween, jack-o-lanterns lit from the inside were visible on windowsills as groups of children in costume prowled the neighborhood. Maman had carved a pumpkin for us and had filled a bowl with candies for Jahan and me to give to the children. Then she and Baba had gone to dinner at the house of Dr. Fazeli and his wife, Nasrin, an Iranian couple Baba had met through his work. Every time children knocked I ran to the door and put something in their bags.

"Doesn't this remind you a little of Norooz?" I asked Jahan.

"How can you compare it with Norooz?"

"You're so negative about anything American."

"And you're excited about everything," he said. "No matter how banal or trivial, you're singing the praise of America. Don't you feel any loss?"

"I had little to lose. I had you, but Jahan, I still love you, don't you feel the same any more?"

"Noor, I do." He put his arms around me and held me but there was that barrier between us, hard to brush away.

I tried to console myself. We came to America just when our childhood was coming to an end. I was startled to feel that even if we had stayed in Iran, sooner or later reality would have set in, pushing us in different directions. Our sexual relationship was starting to feel like it belonged to our abnormal Iranian life.

One day, in late December, Jahan and I were looking at snowmen in front yards and at kids carrying sleds; men in mufflers and heavy winter jackets were shoveling snow off driveways and the tops of their cars. I had never seen snow except in movies or photographs.

"Isn't it beautiful here!" I said to Jahan.

"There's snow in Iran too."

True, snow wasn't new to Jahan. Several times he'd gone to Tehran to ski in the Alburz Mountains with Mohsen and Hassan. "You got to see so much more than I did in Iran. You had it better," I said, repeating a refrain. I knew he was right that I over-praised our new home but it was as if I had to counteract all the negative or ambivalent ways the rest of my family was viewing things. I certainly had some problems I didn't want to admit to: I could never have that casual, light-hearted air, bordering on silliness, that other girls had. I was serious by nature, studious, and a little formal. American pop culture wasn't something I could easily wade into.

"Look what's happening to us ever since we came to America. I don't know what you want any more," Jahan said.

"You know I love you. But we have to be sister and brother until we sort things out for ourselves."

"If that's the way you want it," he said.

There were layers and layers of meaning behind everything we said, every interaction, echoing other scenes in another time, another place.

Jahan and I tried to be just brother and sister. When we had any free time from work, we wrote little plays in English and acted them out with each other like we used to when we were in Iran. Mine were about a girl having a career: a lawyer, an investigative reporter, an actress. Jahan's were about things he did in Iran, places and friends he loved. But it was hard to go backward, hard to go forward.

# 17

As my family members and I were each caught in different struggles, the disasters in Iran kept accelerating, making it clear we weren't going to return there—at least not in the near future. The economy was at a standstill. The Shah's imposition of martial law was only leading to more bloodshed and rage. People from all walks of life joined the street actions, shouting "The Shah must leave," "Khomeini is our leader," "Arrest the Murderer, the American King, punish him, kill him," "President Carter is the incarnation of Evil." In the crowds were women covered by *chadors*, male or female students in jeans, merchants in suits, mullahs in long black robes and turbans. They waved *toomans* with the Shah's picture cut out of them. Some of the rebels invaded police stations and Tehran's main arms factory to get weapons. On the Tehran University campus, they pulled down the statue of the Shah and shattered it with sledgehammers. Others forced the employees of the British embassy outside and then set the place on fire.

On January 13th, Khomeini announced from exile that he had formed a ten-member provisional Islamic Revolutionary Council. On January 15th, the parliament accepted it. On January 16th, the Shah fled the country, saying he was going on "vacation." Carrying a small box of Iranian soil in his jacket pocket he left, on his silver and blue Boeing 707, for Egypt. He was not welcome in the United States as he had assumed he would be. The following day there was jubilation on Tehran streets. Soldiers and civilians embraced. To refer to America, they used Khomeini's phrase, "The Great Satan."

On February 1, Khomeini returned home from exile to a welcoming crowd of some two million people. He said that the monarchy was already abolished and promised a new, democratic constitution. He had the head of SAVAK executed, among the first of hundreds of arrests and executions that followed. Few realized that one tyrant had been replaced by another.

One day in February, Baba came home, rushed to turn on the short wave radio, and we all listened as the announcer reported that the central police station in Tehran was on fire and the army had withdrawn to barracks after heavy fighting. After the radio went silent for a moment, a deep-voiced man who introduced himself as a mullah, announced, dramatically, "This is the true voice of the Iranian nation. The ill-omened Pahlavi regime is finished and an Islamic government has been established under the leadership of Ayatollah Khomeini. We hope to receive a message from him now, please keep listening." But all we heard was static. Baba turned on the TV for more news.

After talking heatedly for a while, speculating about this new regime, we finally said goodnight, exhausted. I woke in the middle of the night, uneasy, and noticed Jahan was up too, in the living room. But neither of us reached out to the other.

It was an incredible relief when on a spring day I found out I had gotten into St. Paul's. I reached into the mailbox and found the letter from the college. I tore the envelope open. "We are pleased . . ." I read on eagerly. As I had hoped, I was accepted even though I had not finished my last year of high school because of the advanced courses I had taken and my high SAT scores. Moreover, they were giving me a full-tuition scholarship. My heart was beating with happiness as I went inside. Jahan was in the living room watching the news on TV.

"Jahan, I got in and with a scholarship."

"Yesterday I had a letter from them—I got in with a scholarship too."

"You didn't even tell me. Aren't you excited?"

"What I really want to do is paint."

"You could major in art."

"I guess so."

"Jahan, things will get better for us when we start college, we'll have a real aim." I wanted to say, "Preparing for our future," but I felt it would fall flat. It had been months since we had talked about a future together. It felt strange to live without our former intimacy and yet we couldn't revive it.

Even though we had scholarships paying tuition, our parents insisted that we live at home for the reason Baba had already expressed: that children, particularly girls, should remain at home until they married. Neither Jahan nor I was reckless enough to run away and, more than that, we were inhibited by the new barrier between us. Feeling dejected and finding it hard to be alone together, we ate with our parents, listened to the radio, or watched TV with them in the evenings.

Spring blended into summer. Coming home from work one day, Jahan saw a soccer game going on in the park. He stopped to watch and was invited to join in. It was a diverse group, with many immigrants from soccer-playing countries who got together every Sunday afternoon for a pick-up game. Through new friends he made there, he met girls, began to go out nights. He took the commuter train into Manhattan alone sometimes to go to art museums and galleries, where he discovered Iranian painters' work — Parviz Talavoni, Siah Armajani, and Mohammad Ehsani. He found the city exciting but also rushed, materialistic, cold.

I knew Jahan was dating girls, and I was jealous but at least he didn't bring them around me. I didn't ask him about them; their existence was too painful to think about. But I realized it was to be expected — he was so attractive — and I was the one who had initiated our separation.

I found some girlfriends through work and hung out with them. I learned to play tennis. We swam in the municipal pool, went to the movies. The library had a book club and I enjoyed reading, discussing ideas.

But while Jahan was free to come and go as he pleased, I realized that in some ways I was as trapped in America as I had been in Iran. Because Baba felt he had lost control over the events of his life, he saw me as a locus of the control he still had. Maman intervened more so than she used to in Iran, but didn't insist on her points, wanting Baba to be happy, her first priority as always.

St. Paul's was a small liberal arts college with about 3,000 students. A Catholic church with large stained-glass windows occupied the far corner of the campus and flowers filled large circular beds in the central quad. The buildings were old, Gothic in style and ivy-covered, but modern sculptures sprang up here and there on the grounds. There was a large gym with a swimming pool on one side of the campus; a baseball field and tennis courts flanked the gym building. The classrooms, recently renovated, were equipped with comfortable chairs and central air conditioning. Dormitories in two rows on either side of the quad were separate for boys and girls, but everyone mingled freely, spending time in each other's rooms. The college appeared serene and pleasant to me. With money I'd saved from my salary, I bought clothes similar to those the other students wore—jeans, sport shirts or T-shirts with different pictures or slogans on them, baseball caps or floppy denim hats that covered the forehead and part of an eye. Baba allowed me to wear that kind of clothing but he didn't go as far as shorts or make-up. Jahan, although he had pointed out there were few foreign students in college, planned to wear dress shirts and dark slacks, basically his high school uniform. At home his clothes were covered by paint, but at school he wanted to be what he considered a serious student.

The college was a twenty-minute bicycle ride from our house and on the first day we rode there together. I was keenly aware of our differences. Jahan was wearing clothes that administrators wore. He was dark, didn't speak English fluently, had an accent, was identified as foreign.

True, the college didn't have the highest standards and, judging by the level of the courses, had an easy admission policy but I still loved it. I loved the fact that the teachers encouraged discussion; that we could raise our hands, even challenge them. I liked mingling with boys and girls. Jahan didn't feel quite at ease with the casual atmosphere and he had to struggle to improve his English, especially written English, by taking ESL courses. His poor English made his favorite subject, history, difficult for him.

After school, several afternoons and evenings a week, I went to my job in the campus library, cataloguing books, arranging and rearranging them in the stacks, and Jahan went to his job in the art supply shop nearby. Before going to work we talked for a while as in the old days, comparing our impressions. Yes, Ms. O'Neal isn't dogmatic. Yes, I like my art course. But everything between us took effort.

Then the conflict between our two countries accelerated and that inevitably made Jahan, whose identity as an Iranian was clear, feel even more out of place at school. In October of that year President Carter allowed the Shah into the United States to be treated for lymphoma, diagnosed five years earlier but revealed now for the first time. The revolutionaries in Iran interpreted this as a ploy to restore the Shah to power, as the CIA had done in 1953. Anti-American and anti-Shah demonstrations intensified. In November the anger came to a head when eighty Iranian students, mostly from Tehran's Polytechnic University, gathered at the American Embassy, found an open basement door, and slipped inside. They seized all the Americans in the building. Putting blindfolds over their eyes and holding guns to their heads, they marched them outside. Embassy staff tried to destroy all the secret documents but before they had finished they too were herded outside. With the documents that weren't destroyed still in their hands, the students shouted, "We have all we need from the nest of spies." The crowd around them roared their approval. Other students got busy spray-painting anti-American slogans on the walls of the embassy, both in English and

Farsi: "Nest of Spies," "American Murderers." Then the students took the Americans back inside and locked them up as hostages. As a condition of their release, they demanded the Shah's return to Iran to stand trial.

On this side, Americans were also enraged. The government retaliated by completely severing trade with Iran. Hatred of Iranians flooded the news. They were portrayed as barbarians. Caricatures of them appeared in newspapers, on walls. Some were evicted from their apartments. Iranian high school students were beaten — one was reported to have died.

One evening, after we all watched the news together, Jahan said, "I can't bear living here."

"I wish we could go back," Baba said, "But there's absolutely no way yet." A wave of sadness passed over his face. "I managed to reach Jamshid on the phone. He went to get our furniture but the house was boarded up; even the hospital at the refinery was closed down."

The following day on the way home, I went to the 7-Eleven to get some soda. In the aisle I came across a woman who lived a few houses down from ours.

"Where are you from? Your father and brother look Middle Eastern," she said.

"From Iran," I said.

She looked startled. "Oh, Eye-ran!"

I picked up a six-pack of Pepsi, paid and left quickly.

Then a few days later something worse happened. I came across Jahan standing at the top of the stairs leading to Allan Hall when a student came up and confronted him. "You're Eye-ranian, aren't you!" he accused.

Jahan ignored him.

"You're keeping our men prisoner."

Another boy joined them. The first one, putting his hand on Jahan's back, said to the other boy, "This is Ayatollah Jahan." The two of them burst into mocking laughter.

Jahan blushed but tried to turn it into a joke. He said, "I'll take you hostage if you don't watch out."

The first boy shouted, "Go home, Eye-ranian, go back where you belong."

I was hit by a terrible anguish as if they had accosted me. I joined Jahan and said, "Let's go inside." He hesitated but after the boys wandered away he followed me. "I can't believe they were so rude," I said.

He looked embarrassed but didn't say anything. Then we each went to our separate classrooms.

After my last class, as I was walking along a corridor, I noticed, written on one of the walls, "Iranians go home," and next to it, "Iranians are shit. Bomb the entire country, wipe it off the map." No one was around. I took a magic marker from my backpack and scribbled over the letters.

When I got home I found Jahan in the garage, painting. He didn't look at me. He kept his attention on the canvas before him, putting down strokes of paint. I said, "I'm really upset about what happened today."

"I have nothing in common with them." He put his brush down on the table and went to the sink in the corner to wash his hands.

I was aware of a thick cloud separating us. I went over and put my arms around him but he was moody and distant. Finally I left, my heart aching.

# 18

After the January break, I was happy to return to school. Jahan was coping with anti-Iranianism by immersing himself in his art. He told me he'd made a big breakthrough in his painting. He'd begun doing assemblage, using photographs of Iran—landscapes, street demonstrations, posters of the Shah, of Khomeini, Persian minia-tures, calligraphy, scraps of poems. Other works juxtaposed images of graffiti—Iranian and American. The work was bold and exciting—his teacher admired what he was doing. Some of his paintings were even exhibited in the college library. He seemed invigorated.

That spring the American attempt to rescue the hostages failed, stirring up a new wave of hostility. Khomeini used the hostages to consolidate his vision and policies for Iran. Despair hung over my family, particularly Baba and now again Jahan, both bearing the brunt of pervasive anti-Iranian feeling. Jahan feared that prejudice against Iranians in the U.S. would never end, as TV was relentless in its focus. There was a nightly count of the number of days the hostages were still in captivity, and the days seemed endless. Jahan's art was now being construed as anti-American by some. He said he just didn't care, but of course he did.

The semester ended and another summer began but the political climate didn't change. We all worked and worked. Baba was still studying for his licensing examination, having failed it once. He feared that there was a quota for Iranians. He had an air of vulnera-bility about him. Maman worked long hours and was always exhausted and miserable. In our spare time, Jahan spent hours in his garage studio, and I did some studying for my fall courses. All my life, in my darkest times, I found salvation in hard work. The ritual

of sitting at my desk with a book or notebook open before me, a
pen or pencil in my hand, comforted me when other areas of my
life were slipping out of control. The tremors of my discontent were
calmed when I did well in a course, shone because of an essay I
wrote, answered a question in class.

But the distance from Jahan was hard, made me feel deeply lonely.
Once I went to his room and after talking about this and that I
asked, "Are you going out with girls, someone special?"

"Yes," he said without elaborating.

I felt utterly miserable and began to cry uncontrollably.

"Don't cry, Noor." He pulled out a Kleenex from a box at the side
of his bed and wiped my tears. "Don't worry, I'm not serious about
anyone. I love only you," he said. "Do you want to change your
mind?"

I yearned to yield to him, to end my loneliness. But somehow I
didn't want to face the intense interdependency that I felt had made
me miserable too before. I shook my head, and no conversation
could be revived.

In the fall of that year, when Jahan and I were sophomores, Iraq
declared war on Iran. My family and I were as usual riveted to the
news.

> Iraq is taking advantage of Iran's weak position with America to
> violate the border treaty. Dispute over the control of Shatt al-
> Arab, our seaway to the Persian Gulf, is escalating into full-
> fledged military action. Iraqi forces have crossed our border by
> land, sea and air.

> Boys as young as fifteen are fighting on the front to compensate
> for lack of armaments. Bombing raids on major Iranian cities
> have demolished houses and buildings. Hundreds of people have
> been killed. There are food shortages, medicine shortages. The
> government has ordered rationing. There are not enough beds
> in hospitals because wounded and dying soldiers have filled
> them all. Blackouts are expected to continue. Towns on the

Iraqi border have suffered the greatest damage — Abadan, Ahvaz, Masjid-e-Suleiman.

After the horrendous news report was over Baba, as usual, reached for the phone to call his brothers. He tried several times and finally managed to get through. When he got off the phone, he turned to us and said, "Jamshid and everyone else is worried sick about Mohsen and Hassan being drafted."

Jahan, utterly despondent, got up and went into his room. I followed him. We talked about the old days, our house, swimming together in the pool, lying on the hammock, dear Golpar. But there was tension in our interaction, and the restraint of my resolution not to fall back into physical intimacy.

When I went back to my own room I had a feeling of displacement, being at once connected to and disconnected from Jahan. The gray rectangles of windows and the trees beyond them seemed as far away as the stars. Even the furniture looked ephemeral. I lay in bed and cried — thoughts of how hard it had become to connect with Jahan, how we both had changed, only deepened my sadness about all the disasters in Iran.

I felt a deep longing to be a normal American girl. But what is a normal American girl? She can go out freely on dates with boys, and she isn't in love with her brother. Baba wasn't permitting me to date. He had set a curfew for me to be home at nine on weeknights and at ten on weekends. Letting me bicycle on my own and stay out alone even that late was a big concession on his part. I had a feeling that I had stepped through a door and miraculously found myself in America, only to find another closed door.

In the morning Jahan was gone by the time I got up. I bicycled to school and went to the cafeteria to have breakfast, thinking I would find him there. But I didn't see him. The cafeteria was filled with dormitory students. I was surprised to see Pamela Marburg there — she was among the few students who, like me, lived at home, in Smithtown. She was pretty with her soft brown curls, large gray eyes, and petite figure; boys paid a lot of attention to her. But she was quiet, didn't seem to belong to a clique. Like me she kept to herself.

After I got my coffee, waffles, and orange juice I went over to her table. "Can I join you?"

"Sure, sit down. I couldn't bear being home today." Then she poured out her problems. "My mother is so sad; my dad left her a year ago. He's a landscape architect and fell in love with one of his clients. I keep hoping he'll come back. My mother's a good Catholic, doesn't believe in divorce. And she's so strict. When my boyfriend, Jack, comes from Boston he isn't allowed in my room. My father isn't like that."

"My mother's a Catholic too, my father a Muslim, but neither of them are practicing. My father is very strict with me anyway, not in religion but in other ways."

I told her about our escape to America. Then we got up and went to our classes, our feet crushing the autumn leaves on the path.

"Will you come to my house this afternoon?" she asked.

"Sure," I said, eager to be her friend.

She made corn bread from a package. We sat on the glassed-in porch and ate it with soda. Her mother came downstairs, dressed to go out. Pam introduced us. Her mother reminded me of Helen's mother. I thought of how being with Helen used to intensify my longing to get out of Masjid-e-Suleiman. Now I was out of there, but I wasn't as free as I hoped to be.

"You want to come to Jimmy's tomorrow afternoon? A lot of kids hang out there."

"Sure, where is it?"

"Port Jefferson, in the stretch along Main Street, across from the wharf."

"I have a couple of hours free before I go to work."

Jimmy's was crowded and noisy. Pam was sitting alone, separate from the group of students from St. Paul's who were sitting at a long table. After getting ice cream from the counter I went and joined her.

"Hello, Nora."

I looked up.

"Frank here, Frank Lockwood. Can I sit with you?"

I didn't say anything as he sat down on a chair across from Pam and me. I had noticed him in classes but we had never spoken. He looked like a lot of the other boys at St. Paul's—light hair, blue-eyed, casually dressed.

"I have a request," he said, addressing me. "Will you go to a party with me tomorrow night?"

Not used to anyone asking me out on dates, I was stunned. After a pause I managed to say, "I don't know if I can. No, I can't . . ."

"Another time then."

I looked at him blankly and he got up and left.

Pam turned to me. "He seems nice and he likes you. Why didn't you say yes?"

"I don't know. Even if I wanted to I couldn't. My father doesn't allow me to date."

"Why not?"

"His idea is to introduce me to someone himself, someone with intentions to marry me."

"That's ridiculous."

"In Iran parents, particularly fathers, are in charge of things like that."

"I'd die before marrying someone selected for me. Isn't India like that too, parents arrange marriages?"

"A lot of countries are like that."

"I'm lucky to live in America," she said.

Frank hadn't given up on me. A few days later he stopped me on campus. "There's another party tomorrow night." He was wearing his long hair in a ponytail. He kept shifting from foot to foot.

After a pause I said yes. I knew I could get away with breaking my curfew the following evening, Thursday. My parents went out regularly on Thursday evenings to visit Olga and David, or Dr. Fazeli and Nasrin. And Jahan would be at his ESL course, which he liked because it gave him a chance to be with other foreign students, and he often stayed out after the class.

"Seven-thirty?" Frank asked.

I nodded.

"Where do you live?"

"I'll be in the library then," I said.

"I'll pick you up there," he said and walked away.

The library was quiet on Thursday evening but I was full of turmoil, waiting for my first date. Just before 7:30 I went to the bathroom and put on eye make-up and lipstick. I studied myself in the mirror. I was wearing a bright purple V-neck sweater, black pants and large, thick gold loop earrings. I put on a smile, practiced it.

# 19

Frank was there on time. He had an expensive car, a convertible BMW. We passed the shopping mall that stretched out almost a mile, houses hidden within landscaped grounds. We carried on a random conversation about teachers, other students. He wasn't particularly interested in my past, didn't ask any questions about my life in Iran.

We entered a dark, narrow road and then turned into the driveway of a large house. "This is Roberta Fantino's parents' house but they're away on vacation," he said.

The living room was already crowded with students, some of whom I knew from different classes. They were drinking, dancing to loud music, smoking pot. A few people waved at us. The music was too loud to carry on a conversation.

Frank took me to a table and we got glasses of red wine and some food and sat on a couch in a corner. The wine had a strong effect on me; I had never drunk more than a few sips before. He leaned over and kissed me, took my hands, and we walked to another room, hidden away at the end of a corridor. He locked the door from the inside and led me to the daybed in the corner and undressed me and then himself. I lay there like a statue. I didn't even know Frank. My body, my emotions, were loyal to Jahan. I could almost smell the musky shampoo Jahan used, recall the heat of his body, the gentle way he touched me. I tried to relax, telling myself to let go but it wasn't easy.

Frank was irritated. "You aren't a fucking virgin, are you?"

"No." I thought, this is just the opposite of Iran. Being a virgin is only a handicap here.

"Are you on the pill?" he asked.

"No."

He got up and, fumbling in his pants on the floor, he took out a condom and unrolled it over his erect penis. He lay back next to me. Soon he was breathing hard as he went inside me, aggressive and oblivious of me. He pulled away quickly and lay there with his eyes closed as if he had forgotten about me. I looked at the glow of the digital clock on the side table. It was ten o'clock.

I sat up and put my clothes back on quickly. "I have to go home," I said.

"So early? Are you sure?"

"I'm not feeling well. I need to get home."

He got up. "I'll take you back," he said somewhat resentfully.

The party had become wilder. People were lying around the floor in tight embraces among beer cans, soda and wine bottles, paper plates and cups. One girl was wearing a T-shirt with "I AM BAD" written on it in large black letters.

Frank was trying not to be irritable as he drove me back to my bike by the library. He even joked, "This is what we learn at a Catholic college."

I bicycled back with difficulty, still feeling the effect of the wine, but more, I was shaky from having been with Frank. At home I parked the bike by the side of the garage and opened the door of the house with my key as softly as I could. Then I tiptoed through the corridor.

To my surprise the light in Jahan's room was on. The door was shut but I could faintly hear Iranian music from his room. I knew the song well, he played it so often.

> Did you lose your way in the dark, winding alley
> Did you lose your way in the dark, moonless night
> Leaving me waiting, expectant.

An urge came over me to go to his room, lie beside him and tell him about the party, about Frank, how empty and disappointing it had been to be with him, but I just went to my room.

I had a terrible dream. There was someone whose face was hidden in dark shadows, but I could tell was Jahan. He was examining my body for traces of others' touches. A tremor went through me. "Stay still," he said sharply. I said, "I have something to tell you." Then I woke, sweating, my heart pounding. There was an ashen taste in my mouth.

It was the middle of the night, but I went to my desk and tried to compose a letter to Jahan:

> Jahan, I love you, but it's wrong.

I tore the sheet into pieces. I began another letter:

> More and more I realize that what we did was bad for both of us. Yes, we were on a dead end road. Something terrible would have happened sooner or later.

I tore that up too. I didn't know what I wanted. I just knew that Jahan was too deeply a part of me.

The next day I saw Frank standing by a dormitory building, leaning over a girl, looking at her attentively. She was smiling at him. He pretended not to see me. Other students passed by, talking, laughing.

After Frank there was Donald Gessner. He stopped me on the campus and asked me to go to Shea Stadium to see a baseball game. I had no interest in the game but I thought I'd go, why not. A group of his friends and some of their girl friends also came. It was excruciatingly boring for me. Almost everyone in the stands, including Donald and his friends, drank beer and kept cheering their team. I took a few sips of beer and, not being used it, it tasted like medicine. I felt uneasy with them even though I tried to be carefree. Donald kept saying, "Relax, honey, enjoy yourself, have more beer."

After the game was over he invited me to his apartment. "I'll order food and we'll listen to records." He shared the apartment with two other students, he said, but he had his own room.

When we got to his apartment none of the roommates were home. I looked around his room and saw a futon bed, a coffee table, and a phonograph. The walls were bare. His books were piled on the floor in one corner. The shade was already pulled over a single window. After we ate the pizza he'd ordered we lay on the futon, kissed for a while, and made an attempt at lovemaking, but it just didn't work. I couldn't let go of myself, and he was rushed and impatient.

We heard one of his roommates coming in and it was a good time for me to make my escape.

I got away with breaking the curfew that night. But on another occasion when I returned late, I was startled to see Baba sitting in the living room, poring over a thick medical book.

"Come here," he said in a whisper as I turned to go into my room. I went and stood before him. "Where were you so late?"

"At the library."

"The library closes at nine."

"After work I went home with a friend. No one tells other girls my age what to do."

"I'm already giving you too much freedom. No dating. I know you were out with a boy." He still was playing the role of an Iranian father, but as usual in inconsistent ways.

"Baba, I don't want to live like I'm back in Iran again. I want to lead a normal life like all the girls my age here. I'm in college now. I'm not a child."

Maman must have heard us, our voices had been rising. She came into the living room. "What's going on?"

"She's acting like an American teenager," Baba said.

"I'm sure she's careful," she said.

"I won't stand for her running around with boys. Too many traps and dangers in it. At the end of it is pain, a lot of crying." He turned to me. "If someone wants to take you out, he should come and meet your family first. Then we know he has serious intentions. And I can see if he deserves you, my pretty, smart daughter."

Jahan came in from the outside and as soon as he saw me he became as tense as a wire about to snap. Of course he must have seen me getting into cars with boys, even though I was cautious. After saying an off-hand hello to our parents he went into his room.

We were silent for a moment, hearing the murmur of the traffic, a dog barking. Then Baba said, "From now on I expect you to be home after work, unless you ask me ahead of time about staying out."

"I'm not going to do that," I said, and dashed into my room and slammed the door.

But that wasn't the end of it. The following afternoon I came home and found Maman in the living room, ironing. She was still wearing her nurse's uniform, though she usually took it off the moment she got home. She was always complaining, "I'm not cut out to be a nurse; I hate the hierarchy at the hospital. I once wanted to be a doctor but I wouldn't be happy with that either now." Taking her uniform off promptly made her forget she was a nurse, at least for a while. The uniform, the thick, practical white shoes, violated her self-image.

"You're still in your uniform," I said.

"I didn't have anything to change into." With a long-suffering air about her, she pointed to the basket full of clothes on the floor. "I didn't have time to do the laundry until now." She picked up a cigarette from an ashtray on the board and took a few puffs; she was still smoking heavily, in spite of her promise to quit. A mist of smoke covered her face.

"I can help you with the ironing," I said.

"I'm almost done."

"Maman, I can't go on living like I did in Iran."

She folded the ironing board and put everything away. "I have to go," she said curtly. "You know how your father feels."

I was overwhelmed by loneliness and misery. She and Baba had their own problems. Baba was homesick; he felt he had come down in life. He was working as a medical assistant, not a doctor. He had lost respect. He hated how Iranians were portrayed as caricatures, and he missed his family and friends in Iran and worried about them. He didn't like Jahan's not trying hard enough to succeed and study for a profession. He didn't want Maman to work, particularly at a job she didn't like, but no end of the need for her salary was in sight.

Maman was full of a sense of loss. When she talked to her friends she complained about how tired she was all the time and described her old luxurious life in Iran as a fairy tale, evoking it in glorious detail. The gardens, unimaginably lush, and the markets, the adventure to go to them. True, I saw a lot more of her now, and I had glimpses into her feelings when she came out from behind her mask, but we weren't much closer than before.

# 20

In January, on the day of Ronald Reagan's inauguration, the hostages were finally released from 444 days of captivity in Iran. It was the focus of all the news, the topic of conversation everywhere. Suspicion about a deal between the Reagan campaign and Iran over the hostages started circulating, even at St. Paul's where there was rarely analysis of politics, only reactions. Though anger against Iran was still in the air, the release of the hostages was cause for celebration across the U.S. and in our household too. Over the weekend Baba and Maman took Jahan and me to an Iranian restaurant in Great Neck, a wealthy town on Long Island where many Iranian immigrants had settled.

In the car Baba said, "Some of them were smarter than we were, got out earlier. Look at these magnificent homes." He parked and as we walked to the restaurant we were aware of passersby speaking Farsi. Next to the restaurant there were several shops with Iranian names, a hair salon, a photography shop. The restaurant too was filled with Iranians who were talking excitedly about the hostage release; some of them talked to each other across tables. With the excitement, though, went a certain anxiety that things wouldn't get easier for Iranians living in the U.S. My family too was caught up in the same concerns, and the evening didn't feel as celebratory as we had hoped.

And nothing became much easier for Jahan or Baba. They were still targets of prejudice, as Iranians continued to be portrayed negatively on TV and in slogans on walls. There were still incidents of Iranian children being beaten, Iranians being ridiculed. On the other side, in Iran, demonstrating masses were still chanting, "Marg be Amrika!"

One day, feeling particularly lonely, I bicycled to a pizza place half a mile away from school to have lunch, get away from the student environment. The restaurant, full of families and couples, was cheerful with lots of plants and bright murals on the walls. I noticed a man sitting at the counter glancing at me as he talked to the cashier. He was wearing faded denim pants and a black T-shirt with a large purple eagle on the front. His long, straight light hair was unruly and fell over his forehead. His eyes were a startling blue-green, I could see even from a distance. He exuded an energy that drew me to him.

A little later, as I was paying at the register, he turned to me and said, "This is on me. My father and I own the restaurant."

The woman behind the register smiled at me and said, "Let him pay, he's the boss here!"

I smiled back, but paid and walked out.

He followed me. "Are you a student at St. Paul's?" he asked as we stood on the sidewalk.

"Yes."

"I graduated from there, years ago. Now I manage our restaurant. My name's Carlo Rossi, and yours?"

"Nora Ellahi."

We talked for a few moments. His reaction to my saying I was from Iran surprised me. "Oh Iran, it's a fascinating country. My parents took a trip there once. They loved Isfahan, Tabriz, the mountains and the desert."

I liked him for not having a negative reaction to Iran.

As I was going toward my bicycle, he asked, "Can we see each other again? How about dinner?"

"I wish I could have dinner with you. But I have a lot to do."

As if reading my thoughts he said, "I know Iranian families are strict. We could meet for lunch. How about tomorrow at noon? We'll go somewhere out of the way."

"Okay," I said.

He gave me an address on a bayside path on the way to Port Jefferson.

As I bicycled to meet Carlo, I managed to push away my nervousness and let myself appreciate the scenery, the flowers visible in backyards, the stark beauty of a wooden church, the pleasant scent coming from the pine trees.

He was waiting by the restaurant door when I arrived; he led me inside. We sat at a table near a window overlooking the bay. We both ordered the day's specialty, flounder, wild rice and mushrooms, salads.

"How about wine," Carlo asked.

"I don't drink wine, but I'll have a few sips if you're going to have it."

"Let's get sparkling water, then," Carlo said.

After the waiter left, Carlo said, "Tell me in your language, you're very pretty."

"To kheyli khosh geli."

"Very soft language. Persian, right?"

"Or Farsi."

He repeated, "To kheyli khosh geli," then said, "Sorry about my bad pronunciation." He laughed, an infectious laughter. "I'm not good at languages. I never learned Italian even though my parents spoke it at home. They were both born in Italy."

"That's how my brother is. His English still isn't that good."

"How many brothers and sisters do you have?"

"Just one brother. He goes to St. Paul's too. He lost a year of school in transition from Iran. We're the same year now. He isn't too happy at St. Paul's though. I don't blame him." I told Carlo about how Jahan was attacked by students during the hostage crisis. "He looks very Iranian."

"That's terrible. People are awful sometimes, aren't they?"

"Yes."

"I wish I had a brother or sister. I'm an only child. My mother had two miscarriages after me. She died when I was twelve. Sometimes I feel she died of grief over the children she lost."

"How terrible, how sad."

"She never really adjusted to America. She missed her large family back in Milan terribly. My dad didn't get used to living here either. He went back to Italy. He visits here once in a while."

"My father and brother are homesick too. Even my mother misses certain things."

"How about you, do you like it here?"

"Yes, but my liking it divides me from my brother. In Iran it was so much better for him."

"You're very attached to your brother, aren't you?"

I felt myself blushing. But I went on, "In Iran I really didn't have anyone else. Some transient friendships. Our parents were involved in their own affairs."

The waiter brought our food and drinks. Looking only at Carlo he asked, "Anything else?"

"Do you want anything?" Carlo asked me.

I shook my head.

"Nothing for now," he said to the waiter. When the waiter was far enough away, Carlo turned to me and said, "He thinks you're my daughter! How old are you?"

"I was born on March 8th, 1961."

"I was born on April 11th, 1948. Thirteen years apart."

As we started to eat he asked me questions about Iran, my growing up there. He said, "I'd love to see Iran. It's so ancient, full of history."

We talked the whole time until we were ready to leave. He was different from boys at school. More worldly, not focused so much on sex. I felt at ease with him, the way I didn't with others.

He insisted on paying. Outside he got into his car, and I bicycled back to school. I was surprised, then disappointed, that he hadn't said anything about a future date. I kept thinking about him.

A few days later I was happy to see him coming into the library and then looking around for me. His face lit up as soon as he saw me behind the counter.

He came over and without introduction he said, "Do you want to meet again tomorrow afternoon? We'll have early dinner at my house."

"I'll be missing classes."

"You could borrow notes, couldn't you?" He smiled.

"I guess I could."

"I'll pick you up from here, if you want."

"I'll come to the school parking lot," I said, not wanting to risk Jahan seeing us together on the campus.

I met him the following day and he drove us to his house in Brookhaven, zigzagging through the traffic. The big wood frame house had a large deck in the back. A painted statue of the Virgin stood by the little flower patch near the front door.

"Are you religious?" I asked.

He shook his head no. "I inherited the house from my uncle two years ago and I haven't gotten around to changing anything."

"My grandmother was Catholic but my mother doesn't practice any religion," I said.

"You and your brother are going to a Catholic school though."

"Catholic Charities helped us get out of Iran and we got scholarships through them too for St. Paul's. And it's near home."

"How about your father?"

"He's a Muslim but he's not religious either. He's traditional though, particularly in what he expects from a daughter."

"We don't always turn out the way our parents hope. My mother wanted me to make something big of myself. She pressured me to take all sorts of lessons—piano, singing, swimming, tennis, skiing—bought me educational presents, bird books, science kits, a butterfly collection. Look at me now, I manage a restaurant!" After a pause he said, "At one time I thought I wanted to become a priest, actually went to a seminary for a year. But I wasn't cut out for it. Very dry and hierarchical, nothing like what I expected. I want a personal life—marriage, children."

Shelves filled with books lined two walls of the living room. "So many books."

"In the evenings I read. History and politics."

"My brother is interested in history too."

"Oh, I'd like to meet him."

The phone rang and he went to get it. He came back and said, "They always call with questions from the restaurant, I never get away from it."

A little later he ordered food from his restaurant and we sat on the deck to eat. He didn't bring out any wine.

"You can have wine; I don't mind," I said. "I don't really like it, myself. I'm not used to it."

"I've more or less given it up. Having a restaurant got me into the habit of drinking too much."

"When things were so turbulent in Iran my mother started drinking, sometimes excessively. Now she and my father drink only a glass of wine each at dinner. They don't like Jahan and me to have even a glass." I stared at the blue and yellow flowers in the backyard, my mind going to the wildflower fields in Meigoon. The excitement of that day with Jahan by the stream, our declarations of love for each other. It was so strange that I was with this man and not Jahan. Tangled and contradictory emotions engulfed me.

"Until recently I was seeing a woman with three children." Carlo's voice brought me out of my thoughts. "Her husband persuaded her to take him back. She said it was because of the children, but I knew she was hooked on the man, even though he was no good for her." He looked at me and said, "A pretty girl like you must have had boyfriends, maybe secretly from your family?"

"I went on some dates since we came to America but my father found out and put a stop to it."

"I really enjoy being with you. We get along so well, will you be my girl?"

"I'd like that," I said.

"Wonderful," he said, caressing my arm.

After we finished eating we went inside and, holding my hand, he led me to his bedroom. We lay on his bed and he began to take my clothes off. I tried to overcome the resistance I was feeling. I said, "I'm not on pills."

He went to the bathroom and came back with a condom. If you try one more time, I said to myself, the trace of Jahan on your flesh will be overwritten. Carlo was patient, more skilled than the college boys, attentive to my pleasure. Afterwards we lingered in his house for a while and then I asked him to take me back to school. It was close to the time for my job in the library.

# 21

The next time I spent the afternoon with Carlo, he said he wanted to walk me all the way back to the library.

"You don't have to," I said.

But he started walking with me. Halfway through the campus, I was startled to see Jahan coming toward us. I tensed up and, I could tell, so did Jahan. I introduced him to Carlo.

"Your sister has been telling me all about you," Carlo said. "It's nice meeting you in person."

Jahan smiled but he looked uncomfortable. I had an urge to lean over and whisper in his ear as I used to, ask him what he thought of Carlo.

"I went to St. Paul's too," Carlo said to him. "It's not the greatest college but you can get an education if you seek out the right courses."

Jahan shrugged. "I wish it had a better art department."

Carlo looked at me. "Nora told me you like history, so do I."

"I haven't found a good history course either."

Aware of tension I said, "I'm getting late for my job."

Jahan said good bye and walked on in one direction and Carlo and I continued to the library.

In the evening at home I waited for Jahan's return. When I heard his footsteps in the living room I came out and said, "Jahan, I want to talk to you."

"It's late, I've got to finish a paper," he said in what seemed to be a deliberately neutral tone. But the space between us was brittle and dry as if it could catch fire from a lit match. He went into his room and shut the door and I returned to mine, sadness settling on my heart.

From my window I could see a pale blade of moon hanging in the orange sky. I thought of the moonlit nights on Jahan's bed in Masjid-e-Suleiman, with that patchwork quilt pulled over us. Those moments, hours, were so intense, filled with love. I went to his room and knocked on the door.

"Come in," he said.

He was lying in bed, his hands behind his head, listening to Persian music. "When you reveal your face, a thousand butterflies will burn around you, as I do . . ."

I sat at the edge of the bed. "Jahan, I miss talking to you."

He got up and turned over the LP, which had finished playing. He came back, sat next to me. He looked so unhappy as he said, "Tell me more about that man."

"Carlo Rossi. He's nice, and very open-minded, not like the kids at St. Paul's. You'd like him too."

He started to say something but stopped. After a pause he said, "He's so much older than you."

"But I feel comfortable with him."

"Have you been . . ." He couldn't say it. Having sex, I finished for him inwardly. "Where did you find him anyway?"

"We met at the pizza parlor near school."

"So you pick up men now," he said, smiling but so tensely that it was like a grimace. "All your declarations were false?"

"You know they weren't. Besides, you've been dating too." I tried to lighten the mood. "At school girls flirt with you," I teased. It was true that unlike male students who saw him as one of those threatening Iranians who had taken Americans hostage, the female students referred to him as sexy and charming. They liked the fact that he opened doors for them, offered them his chair in class.

"Nora, do you really want to go on with this brother-sister thing?"

"I don't like it, but I know it has to be this way. I just wish . . ." I didn't know what I wished.

I started to see Carlo regularly. He knew every patch of beach in the area. Sometimes he drove us far enough away that I had no fear of being seen by Baba or Jahan, but not so far that we couldn't return in reasonable time. When it was warm enough we walked on the sand, swam. His hours were flexible and he often worked at home, taking care of restaurant paperwork. The rest of the time he read, gardened.

I threw caution to the wind and spent a day in New York with him. He took me to a Saturday matinee of *The Magic Flute* at the Met. Some parents had brought their children to this lavish and colorful production and at intermission the corridors were full of conversation, laughter. The lavishness of the opera house decor added to the feeling of festivity. While watching the opera with Carlo, I felt a rare closeness to him.

Afterwards, he took me to a restaurant in Greenwich Village, crowded with young people who seemed to be aspiring actors and actresses, artists, designers. Loud jazz played in the background and spots of light danced on dark gray walls. But Carlo looked ill at ease, and we ate quickly and left. Outside he said, "That's not really my kind of place, but I thought you might like it." It reminded me of one night when we'd gone out with Pam and her boyfriend; Carlo had acted paternalistic then, too. I felt the gap in our ages, and there was sedateness at the heart of Carlo's personality in spite of his surface liveliness. He wanted to settle down with a wife and children and lead a quiet, domestic life.

In the car ride back he said, "Do your parents know about us now? Your brother saw us together."

"I'm sure he didn't tell them."

"Why don't I take you to your parents' house and we'll tell them. You aren't a child, you don't need to be so afraid of your father. Besides, I'll protect you."

My heart was heavy at the thought of suddenly bringing him into the open, of answering Baba's questions. "Why don't we wait a little while."

"Nora, I don't like to live like a teenager, hiding from parents."

It upset me that I was divided into different selves, selecting one or another to show to each different person. But the most I could bring myself to say was, "I promise I'll introduce you when it's a littler calmer at my house. Just now my family is coping with so many problems."

He accepted that reluctantly.

Jahan made a close friend at school. Assad Moradi and his family had immigrated to America from Morocco. With his dark curly hair and slightly hooked nose he looked a little like Jahan. He too dressed impeccably. They were dating two students, Molly Breslin and Maria Sanchez. I tried to push down the jealousy that stabbed at me when I saw the four of them getting into Assad's car, Jahan in the back with Maria. I wasn't sure if Jahan had been going out with her for a while, and now, seeing her more openly because he had seen me with Carlo.

I knew Maria a little from classes we were taking together. She was pretty, wore silver earrings, bracelets, long skirts with matching sweaters. She was born in Argentina and then moved with her parents to America. Both of her parents had died two years ago. Now she lived with six cats in the house she inherited from them, and she let students-in-need live with her temporarily until they found something permanent.

Now that Jahan was overtly dating a girl from school, I couldn't sleep until I heard his footsteps in the hallway and then the door to his room opening and shutting. I tormented myself with thoughts like: what if he brings her over and sleeps with her in his room, what if I hear the sounds of their lovemaking? Then I admonished myself: this is ridiculous; you say you want to be independent from him.

One morning after he left the house I went into his room and put his shirt on his bed, the shirt I had taken from him in Iran and still wore sometimes. I also left the butterfly brooch he'd given to me on that significant birthday, when everything changed for us. I thought that maybe returning those mementos of our love would create some real closure of our old relationship.

But in the afternoon, as I waited for Carlo in the lounge, over-looking the parking lot, I was a wreck. Returning Jahan's shirt and brooch was a dumb thing to do, I was thinking now. It was going to hurt him unnecessarily.

I put some coins in the soda machine and then some in the one with cookies. My hands were shaking as I took them. Then, through the window, I saw Carlo pulling into the lot. I ran out and got into his van.

"Nora, are you all right?" he asked as he drove.

"Yes, why?"

"You look upset."

I thought I should tell him, bring everything into the open. But of course I couldn't. That might mean losing him. Instead I lied, "I'm actually happy, my brother has a girlfriend now."

"You worry about your brother too much. He can take care of himself."

"You're right."

He drove us across the island to the beach in Patchogue. We got out and strolled by the water. Then, I'm not sure why, I told him what I hadn't to anyone else. "Jahan was adopted."

"Really? You never mentioned that."

"I wasn't supposed to tell anyone. We didn't know about it until we were older. Our parents kept it a secret from us and everyone else. We found out accidentally when we came across the adoption documents in a cabinet. He looks so much like our father, no one ever suspected anything."

"Parents have different approaches. Some tell the child and some don't."

It was getting windy. We walked on the main street for a while and came upon an unusually large number of bridal shops for one street, six of them, with mannequins in wedding dresses. One, with a slender waist and a bright smile, was wearing a dress with two irises in pearls sewn close to the neckline; a lace veil with iris embroidery covered her face and head.

"That would look great on you," Carlo said, pointing to the dress.

We looked at another window display. All I could think of was walking with Jahan in the old section of Masjid-e-Suleiman and looking at the jewelry shops there. It was after we had come back from Meigoon. As I saw women buying jewelry, probably for girls they had selected to marry their sons, I was thinking to myself, I will never love anyone but Jahan.

Carlo said, "You know Nora, I wish you'd tell your parents about us. Your mother is an American, you're living in America. It's not good to be confined to just a few hours here and there. I really care for you and want to meet your family. Next time my father comes here I want to introduce you to him."

I was quiet, in conflict.

"What if I were to ask you to marry me? I'm in love with you, my dear beautiful Nora. Don't you feel the same?"

"Yes, Carlo I love you," I said, putting my arm around him. I thought, it used to be so exciting to go to places with Jahan. Any excursion — a boat ride, sitting in a café, going to the cinema — had a heightened quality. Did I feel that exultation with Carlo? No. I liked him, liked to be with him, that was all. At the same time the thought of letting him go, of falling back into interdependency with Jahan, sent a shiver through me. Finally I added, "I'm still in college, could we wait until I finish?"

"If that's how you feel, we'll wait."

I looked up and we kissed. Then he drove us to his house, and soon we were on his bed, making love, with me not quite able to be fully immersed in it, thinking about other things. About Jahan.

I leaned my head against his chest. "We could get married the summer after I graduate."

"Good idea. I'd like it to be warm," he said, caressing my hair.

"Then we could have the wedding outdoors, here at the house, with a reception on the deck and the backyard."

"Are we going to live in this house?"

"Why not?" he said. "We can raise our children here. I'd love to have two or three, all girls and looking like you!"

"Can I go to law school and have children too?" More and more I was thinking of getting a law degree. It went with my image of myself as an independent woman.

"Sure, I don't see why not."

"Carlo, we'll be so happy," I said. "But let's let everyone know closer to the time."

"Is that what you want?"

"It's easier."

A little later, as I bicycled home the sky was a steely blue, in tune with my mood. When I got home I was glad Jahan wasn't there and I didn't have to see what his reaction to finding the brooch and the shirt was. I took a long bath and let myself enjoy the Satin Mauve bubbles Carlo had given to me. Then I sat at my desk and started to make a list of things I had to get done the next day. Making a list and fulfilling it always made me feel good, gave me a sense of purpose and accomplishment. I wrote down even the routine things — exercise, a shower, brush hair twenty strokes, a breakfast of toast with no butter and black coffee, an hour of homework, then leave for school.

# 22

One afternoon I came across Assad on the campus standing by the gym. He greeted me in a friendly way. Maybe out of respect for Jahan he was always courteous to me, never flirted.

"Are you waiting for Jahan?" I asked.

He nodded. "He was supposed to be here by now," he said. He was dressed in a plum-colored polo shirt, a beige jacket and dark denim trousers. I noticed an ugly bruise on the side of his face. It looked like he had been in a fight. But that wasn't a question I could ask him, he was so formal with me.

In class, as soon as I sat down next to Pam, she said, "Did you hear, Gail Van Kamp charged Assad with sexual harassment?" She was whispering, though no one else was in the room yet.

"No! Assad has a girlfriend, Molly."

"That doesn't mean anything."

"I don't think Assad would be interested in Gail." I had seen Gail around the campus. She was a pale blonde, wore bright T-shirts and tight fitting stretch pants. People said she slept with everyone, and she had a vaguely hostile manner toward the other female students.

"She claims he was calling her at odd hours and then he assaulted her in the park."

It was as if it were Jahan who had been accused. "I don't believe any of that," I said.

"He got into a fight with another boy who's dating Gail. Didn't your brother say anything about any of this?"

I shook my head. "I just saw Assad, he had a bruise on his face."

"Assad doesn't have much respect for American girls."

"That's not true."

All day I looked for Jahan but didn't see him anywhere. When I got home he was in the garage, the door open. He was whistling a tune from a Hooshang song while putting paint on a canvas with a brush. He was obviously ignoring Baba's and Maman's pleas that he pay more attention to school work. In fact he had been cutting classes. I was burning to talk to him about Assad, but there had been a real strain between us ever since I had put the brooch and the shirt in his room. He never brought the subject up. I was embarrassed and didn't want to talk about it either. I took a deep breath and went in. "I heard about Assad—it's terrible," I said.

"Gail framed him," Jahan said, not looking at me.

"Is he going to fight it?"

"He isn't the type for confrontations."

"Is there any truth to it?"

"It's all lies."

Then Baba and Maman pulled into the driveway. They came in and joined the conversation. They must have already talked to Jahan about Assad. Maman said, "Can you go to the dean and stand up for Assad?"

"No one is going to listen to me. They know I'm his friend." Jahan said.

"They walk around half naked, all they think about is sex and then this accusation," Baba said.

It was true that the air of the campus was suffused with sex; it was in whispers among friends, in the songs they listened to, in the graffiti all over the bathroom walls. The presence of the nuns and the church on campus didn't create inhibitions—maybe it had the opposite effect.

"Baba, didn't I tell you they're suspicious of people like Assad and me? They lump foreigners together, some of them even think Assad is from Iran."

"He should fight the accusation," Baba said.

"Something like that can stick with him for years," Maman said.

"He doesn't want to stay in school," Jahan said. "I don't blame him. The people at that college are so ignorant; they never think, like a herd."

"It's unfortunate that this should happen to Assad, but it's important to take advantage of what's good about college," Baba said.

"Don't worry so much about me. I've always managed, haven't I?"

Assad's case was the main subject of conversation on the campus the next day and many of the following days. Most of the details were conjured up by speculation. Assad, along with other students, often went to the park to play ball or Frisbee but that time he and Gail were alone. A part of the park was always crowded, but there was also a wild section, with paths through tangled bushes, and it was there that Assad had allegedly attacked Gail. She claimed she had gotten away by promising to have sex with him the "right way," in her room. But when they got to the dormitory, she ran into her room and locked the door from the inside. The next day she went to the dean of students and pressed charges against him. Assad vehemently denied all that, and claimed that it was Gail who was pursuing him. He'd rejected her and she was trying to punish him.

One afternoon when I came home, Jahan was sitting in the living room watching the news. I asked him, "What's going to happen to Assad?"

"We went to the dean together. I defended Assad, explained how people are quick to assume that foreigners are guilty. The dean listened, conferred with some of the teachers and administrators and they decided to give Assad the benefit of the doubt."

"Wonderful. So is Assad going to continue at college?"

"I don't think so. He wants to work for a while, do some thinking about what he wants to do with himself."

"Too bad."

Jahan seemed distraught and it was hard to continue the conversation.

Then over the following days I noticed he was cutting many of his classes. When I saw Carlo I told him how worried I was about Jahan, and how unhappy and lonely he was now that Assad had quit school.

"What about his girlfriend you told me about?"

"I haven't seen him with her lately."

"Why don't I try to talk to Jahan. I'd like to help him. I'm good at talking to people."

"I know he'd be embarrassed to talk to you about his problems."

"I'm trying to be helpful. Maybe I could be. It makes me angry for you to be so emotionally involved with his problems all the time."

"I'm sorry." After a moment of heavy silence between us I said, "It's just that I can't face the turmoil it would create if I got you involved with my brother or my parents."

"Nora, do you feel that you and I have a future together?" he asked. He hadn't brought up marriage for a while. "Tell me, what's going on with you? Sometimes you seem so far away."

"It's just that I'm under a lot of stress." I leaned my head against his chest. "Should we give our children Iranian names?" I asked to reassure him, but it was so clear to me at that moment that I didn't want to be Carlo's wife, live in this house, raise children. I couldn't imagine spending the rest of my life with him, and yet there was the intense desire to have his protection.

"Tell me some names," Carlo said, assuming a light tone.

"For girls Leila, Yasamin, Pari; for boys, Darius, Bijan. My father's name is Cyrus," I said." Then there's Jahan."

"Oh, Jahan!" he smiled. "Wonderful names. And if we want to give them Italian names—for girls Livia, Agnese, Grazia, and for boys Salvatore, Paulo, Rocco."

This time we both laughed and I began to feel better.

Jahan was still skipping classes, except for his Third World Studies course, and he wasn't home doing homework. He told me he didn't care about grades, they weren't important, just a meaningless part of school administration. He was reading the history of the Iranian revolution as a Third World struggle, talked about racism, injustice in

America, poverty in the South Bronx. He seemed angry about everything; bias in textbooks, in the news, the mediocrity of the intellectual level at school. He was irritated with me and our parents, thinking we were too complacent.

At home there was always a worried conversation going on about him. "So his grades have dropped. I'm sure it's a temporary thing he's going through since his best friend quit school," Baba was saying to Maman in the living room one morning. "I don't want to pressure him to go to a therapist. That will only make him feel we think something is wrong with him. I don't blame him for being depressed, under the circumstances. This American psychiatry is a racket anyway."

"But what if he doesn't make his grades? He'd never get into graduate school," Maman said.

"We'll deal with that when it happens."

"How can you force a grown boy to do what he doesn't want to?" Maman shook her head.

"If he flunks out, he'll find his way in the world on a different path," Baba said. He went from panic to denial, trying to make sense of what was happening.

They were so involved in talking that they didn't hear me coming in. I went into the kitchen to get my breakfast. When I came back into the living room, Jahan was there. Maman was saying to him, "I'm not criticizing you, I'm just trying to understand."

"Don't worry about me, I'm fine," Jahan said.

"In this country achievement is everything. It's what gives you respect in people's eyes," Baba said.

"You were good at everything at school in Iran," Maman said.

"I don't even know if I want to live in America."

"Where are you going to live?"

"I want to go back to Iran."

"Jahan, you can't go to Iran now," Baba said, his voice rising. "Don't you see boys your age are being sent straight to the front? Thousands are being killed."

"I won't get killed."

"What makes you think that?" Maman said, her voice at a hysterical pitch.

"Well, even if I do, it's better than this slow death here."

"Oh, Jahan, don't talk like that," she said. "We left Iran to be out of danger, and now you want to go back."

"If you want to become a professional, as I've always hoped for you, you have to do well at school now," Baba steered the discussion in a more rational direction. "I want us to be partners one day, have a practice together."

"I don't want to cut up human bodies."

"That's a small fragment of the medical profession. You don't have to be a surgeon. Besides what do you think you'll be doing in war? Killing people, cutting up their bodies," Baba said. "If your grades are good, you'll be able to go to a better school for further education — Harvard, Cornell. My son, we all make some compromises. It's a sign of intelligence to make the best of things."

"Hassan and Mohsen are fighting to defeat the enemy. Why shouldn't I do the same thing?"

Maman's voice was choked as she said, "Because it's suicidal."

"My dear son, you can do well in life if you apply yourself," Baba said emphatically.

"Thank you," Jahan said, picking up his backpack and going towards the door.

"You haven't eaten breakfast," Maman said to him.

"I'll get something later."

After he left, she pointed to an old photograph of him, and me, that she had framed and put on the coffee table. "Look how happy he is here." She and Baba exchanged a look that acknowledged how much the family had suffered. She turned to me and asked, "What's going on with your brother, why isn't he applying himself?"

"Well, he prefers to spend his time in his studio and study what he likes."

"He locks himself up in that cold garage for hours," she said.

"He has a space heater."

"You know that isn't the point," Baba said.

Maman lit a cigarette and took a few deep drags.

"Moira, please, put that cigarette out," Baba said.

She pressed her cigarette into her wet saucer. Turning to me again she said, "Jahan has an F in economics and an incomplete in chemistry. His other grades weren't good either, all Cs. He didn't even hand in his art project."

"We'd better get going, we're both late," Baba said to her. Then to me he asked, "Talk to your brother, will you?"

I didn't see Jahan at school. He didn't seem to be anywhere on the campus.

At the end of my classes I went directly home to see if he was there. I found him in his room lying on his bed with his clothes on, wearing dark sunglasses, the kind with wide rims that Assad wore. His hands lay limp by his side. I remembered once when we were children I had found him lying under a tree in our courtyard in Masjid-e-Suleiman, his body motionless. Frightened, I had shaken him, calling, Jahan, Jahan. He suddenly sat up and said, "Were you scared?" If only he were just playing a game now.

"Jahan, what's wrong?"

"Parviz was killed on the front." He began to sob, his whole body shaking.

"Oh, my god, how terrible, that wonderful, handsome boy." It was devastating news and it had clearly shaken Jahan deeply. I had never seen him cry—he had always held back his tears. "How did you find out?"

He calmed down a little and said, "I met someone in a Soho gallery who was speaking in Farsi with another man and I started talking to them. It turned out he was a friend of Parviz's family. He gave me the news."

"Hard to accept it."

"I'm going to Iran."

"Are you crazy? You can't go there now."

"I want to die fighting."

"Oh, Jahan, don't talk like that."

He sat up, took a tissue from a box on the side table and wiped his eyes. "I have to go," he said and walked out abruptly.

As soon as I heard the outside door slamming shut I started looking for the thick notebook I had seen him writing in. I was desperate to find a wider window into his feelings and thoughts. I searched in his desk drawer, on the shelves, in the closet, but I couldn't find it.

# 23

For months the war news had been poisoning the atmosphere at our house. Mines planted in Abadan, Masjid-e-Suleiman, and Ahvaz had killed thousands of young Iranian soldiers, the anchors reported. There were scenes of explosions, ditches full of crawling soldiers, men and women searching for the dead bodies of loved ones. Parviz had been killed. And Jahan was threatening to go there. Maman was right. It was suicidal. He hadn't threatened suicide but what he had said came close to it.

My first impulse was to call Carlo and tell him. Then I thought that he'd only say what he had already said more than once, that I was too preoccupied with Jahan.

There was a hotline number in the hallway of the library for students in crisis; it was available twenty-four hours a day. Should I copy the number for Jahan and give it to him? But he must know about it. I could call myself and see what advice they would give. I went to the hallway and copied the number, then waited until the library was about to close and almost everyone had left. Two librarians were far from the public phone in the hallway. I went to the booth, shut it tight, and put a quarter in the slot.

"Hello, what can I do for you?" a woman's voice said in a gentle way.

"I'm. . ."

"Your name?"

"I prefer not to say, it's about my brother. He's been abnormally depressed."

"Can you ask him to call us?"

"I don't think he would."

"Is he a student here?"

"Yes."

"How old is he?"

"Twenty-one."

"See if you can get him to talk to one of our counselors."

"Okay, thank you," I said, putting down the receiver, feeling ashamed of my own impulse to call on his behalf. I felt depressed, too, locked in a gray box, full of conflict and uncertainty. I turned back to the phone, called the infirmary, and made an appointment for myself for the very next day.

The waiting room was crowded with students looking through magazines or listening to their Walkmans. A nurse called me promptly and pointed me to Dr. Harris's office. In the office I found the doctor sitting behind a desk. She pointed to a chair across from hers for me to sit. It was dim in the room; the small lamp burning on her desk was the only light. I could make out a family photograph of her, a man, and two children all holding hands on a beach with the ocean stretching behind them. They were smiling, looked happy. That was the kind of family I wished I had.

"Tell me what brings you here," she said.

I was silent. How was I going to tell her what was burdening me? It wasn't any easier to pour out things to a therapist than it was to others.

"Problems at home? With a boyfriend?" She looked friendly and encouraging.

"I can't sort anything out for myself."

"We could start by your telling me about your family life."

"We came here from Iran, when things became turbulent there. Then we had to make a lot of adjustments here." I didn't know what to say next.

"What precisely upsets you right now? You can tell me, it will be kept absolutely confidential."

"Well, I feel bad about my brother. He has a crazy idea of going back to Iran. One of his closest friends was killed in the war, and now he wants to join the army. It seems suicidal to me.

"Ah, war, very upsetting. Is your brother patriotic?"

"No, that isn't it." A long pause. Then, "His wanting to go there is all my fault."

"Why?"

"I should be helping him adjust. Back in Iran we were close, but here, it isn't the same any more. . . It's very hard for him; he stands out as foreign."

"To feel responsibility is natural, but it isn't your fault."

Her tone, the expression on her face, were non-judgmental. But I still couldn't bring myself to be totally open with her. "Can you suggest something practical?" I asked.

"Why don't you bring your brother for a joint session so we can all discuss things together?"

"I'm sure he wouldn't want to come. He just wants to go to Iran."

"See if you can persuade him to see me."

I nodded, though I knew I wouldn't be able to convince him. As I got up to leave she said, "If you need to talk more yourself, feel free to make another appointment."

I went to the receptionist and made another appointment. Then I turned around and cancelled it. What good would it do if I couldn't be honest?

Later, on the way home, cycling on a path I didn't usually take, I came across Jahan standing with Assad and a few other boys I had never seen before. "Nora!" Jahan said, seeming happy to see me. He turned to the boys, "My sister." Some of my worry about him evaporated because he was in such a good mood.

All the boys looked foreign, but they weren't the ones from his English course whom he sometimes brought over to the house. One of them gave me a critical look. He could be Pakistani or Arabic. I said goodbye and went on my way. It was cool but brightly sunny and I just rode around for a while, stopped at different stores to get things I needed.

When I got home Jahan was already there and he had the boys

with him in his room. I went into mine, but I could hear snatches of their conversation. They were criticizing America. Assad was the most vocal.

"Everything is superficial here, no inner life, no values, hypocrisy and hype, more and more money, money is everything."

"They don't have a clue," Jahan was saying.

Then the voice of a muezzin came out from a tape or maybe from the short wave radio that Jahan took to his room. "Allah O Akbar."

The faucet started running in the bathroom in the corridor. The boys seemed to be doing ablution, getting ready for prayers.

"Mohammad, you go first,"

"Ali, you still aren't doing it right," I heard.

Then it grew quiet. They must be praying. After an hour or so their voices saying goodbye filled the corridor.

After they'd left I went to Jahan, who was lingering in the living room.

"Who are those guys?" I asked in a friendly way.

"Assad's friends from the mosque."

"What mosque?"

"Blue Mosque, in Queens."

"Assad is religious?"

"He mainly likes the people who go there, from all different nationalities. I went there once; I liked the people too, and I was surprised that there's so much to learn about Islam."

"It isn't like you to go to a mosque."

"Assad and those guys remind me of Mohsen and Hassan. They care about spiritual things."

"I guess it's good if it makes you happy."

The phone rang. Jahan went to get it. "Hello, yes, that's a good idea."

He was making plans with someone and soon he left.

From the beginning of December our street was filled with the celebratory aura of Christmas. Lights twinkled in windows, wreaths and colored bulbs were strung above doors. Maman had put a large fir wreath with holly berries on our front door.

On a Sunday morning she asked, urgently, "Nora, will you go shopping with me? Stores are open today for the holidays."

"Sure." More and more I was thinking I should tell Maman about Carlo. This would be a good time.

Smithhaven Mall was colorfully decked out with bulbs and ornaments glittering on huge Christmas trees. We stopped in one store and bought angels and globes to add to the tree ornaments we had kept from previous years. We went on to other stores to buy presents for Baba and Jahan. Then we bought presents for each other, not saying what they were, keeping them as a surprise.

After we finished shopping we went to a diner to eat. It was crowded and noisy with voices, music from a jukebox, footsteps, the ringing of the cash register. Potted plants were hanging on walls in a semicircle. We ordered one vegetable lasagna and a large salad to share, as both of us were always watching our weight. Maman and I were looking more and more alike. We had bleached our hair to a slightly lighter shade than our natural blond. We both had short haircuts, we were the same height and weight.

Maman lit a cigarette and inhaled deeply. Then she said, "I'm really upset about Jahan. I look at him; he's so smart, so talented, so good looking. He has that manner, ready to be there for you. I don't know what to think. Last night Cyrus and I were wondering if his unhappiness here makes him think about his birth mother, and that's part of his desire to go to Iran. I don't know. At first I didn't want to adopt a child. I just wanted a child of my own. Well, that's water under the bridge now, but it wasn't an easy time. When I saw that beautiful little boy in the orphanage, I wanted him immediately." Her voice turned wistful as she said, "All those years, I kept the blue blanket he was wrapped in when I brought him home. Then I left it in Iran. I should have brought it with us. It was hard to think clearly then." She paused. "Nora! Something terrible has happened and I have to tell you about it."

"What?" I felt a sudden chill of apprehension.

"The police came to the house yesterday, asking about Jahan, and that Blue Mosque he goes to. There was a fire at a nightclub near it. Did you read about it?"

"No. But what does Jahan have to do with it?"

"Ever since Assad dropped out of school, Jahan cuts classes to be with him. They spend a lot of time at that mosque. The police went over there and found out about comings and goings of different people."

"It isn't a crime to go to the mosque."

"Yes, but they must suspect something is going on there. Apparently Jahan and his friends rent a room there and they get together to talk."

"I can imagine. You know how they carry on in Jahan's room."

"I'm sure that's all it is, but now with the fire, the police are afraid that a fringe group of radicals is plotting extreme actions. It was just like we were back in Iran. They kept asking questions and writing down what we said. Then they asked the same questions in a different way."

"Jahan doesn't have anything to do with a fire at a nightclub." I was pretty sure of that. He and his friends seemed more focused on the inner life, ideas about virtue and meaning.

"You can be honest with me. You tell each other everything."

"He hasn't said anything, but the accusation doesn't make sense."

Maman became wistful again. "From the beginning, when you were children, Jahan loved you so much, instinctively. I always thought you were closer than any other brother and sister in the world."

Maman's words stirred me deeply. Why hadn't she and Baba ever seen the physical love between us? Jahan was right. They didn't want to see it.

"You complemented each other," Maman went on. "You were serious and determined; he was creative and caring. Once, you threw down his clay piggy bank and broke it into pieces. You must have been angry with him or just wanted more attention from him. Do you know what he did? He took you into his arms and comforted you." She put her hand on mine. "I want you to go on vacation with Jahan during the holidays. It will be good for him to be away from Assad and his pals, even for a couple of weeks. Maybe he'll get some perspective on things."

"I don't know how I can."

"Why can't you? We'll pay your expenses. Your father and I are going upstate for a few days ourselves."

"Do you promise you won't tell Baba? I didn't tell you because I didn't want to start arguments at home. But I've been seeing someone for a while now."

"Really? Who is he?"

"He owns an Italian restaurant with his father. He's an ex-Catholic like you."

"I'm so happy you have someone. What's his name?"

"Carlo Rossi. His parents are Italian—well, his mother died but dad lives in Milan. Maman, I don't want to abandon Carlo at Christmas. I'm sure he wants us to be together."

"Darling, I wouldn't dream of ruining things."

"We've talked about getting married after I graduate."

"Married? That serious?" She looked preoccupied as she stared at her plate. "Of course you wouldn't want to tell Carlo about the police's suspicions. But you could tell him your brother needs emotional support, wouldn't he understand?" She tightened her grip on my hand. "Can't you do this for us? Try to help your brother? Your father couldn't sleep all night. He kept me up too."

"But I want to be with Carlo during the holidays." As I said that, I wasn't sure what I wanted.

Maman drove back slowly. Snow had been falling for the last several days and lay lightly on the road. Shadows of trees made blue etchings on the snow. Through the car window I watched houses, limbs of bare trees, clusters of shops, but my mind was on our conversation. I wanted so much to be happy again, like I was when we arrived in America, when I was so elated and optimistic.

Inside, we put the packages down under the tree, next to the ones already there. Then she said, "Let's bake a cake. Olga's coming over. It'll be fun." I suspected that her asking me to help was an attempt to draw me close to her, so I'd do what she wanted. She stared at the photograph of Jahan and me together by our swimming pool in Masjid-e-Suleiman. "Won't you seriously think about what I asked you?"

I was relieved when the doorbell rang. "It must be Olga," she said, and went to open the door. When the two of them came back, Olga greeted me in her flamboyant way. She was outgoing like Mary Sagaami. She was a volunteer at Maman's hospital, but her main work was running a hair salon in Rocky Point. She sometimes cut and set Maman's hair in a stylized way. Her own hair was dyed a bright red and she was wearing glittery clothes. Maman started making coffee to have with the cake. "Will you join us, love?" she asked me.

"Thanks, but I have too much work to do." Looking at Olga I said, "I'll try to join you a little later."

I was too agitated to study. Carlo, Jahan, my parents, kept circling in my mind. Through the half open door, I could hear Maman and Olga talking. Olga was saying that AHA cream decreased wrinkles, that beer prevented hair from falling out. The scent of the cake in the air and the ordinary conversation between Maman and Olga finally calmed me somewhat.

# 24

The following day was anything but ordinary. I was walking to my bike on the campus and heard someone calling me. I turned around and saw it was Sister Ursula, who was standing on the steps of the Administration Building. She signaled to me to join her. I followed anxiously as she led me to her office. "Sit down." She pointed to a chair as she sat behind the desk, adjusting her habit.

The room was almost bare, except for a bunch of roses that stood in a vase on her desk.

Leaning forward a little, she said, "It's about your brother. It isn't just his grades."

I stared at her, clenching my hands in my lap.

"I left messages with your parents but they haven't called back. He's been distributing inappropriate material."

"What kind of material?" I asked, anxiety swirling through me.

"We value religion of any kind in this college, but Jahan created a disruption in the classroom yesterday. He started an argument with a student who criticized his pamphlets preaching Islam. They got into a fight." She picked up a thin blue pamphlet among several scattered on her desk and handed it to me. "That kind of behavior can't be allowed. I've tried to talk to your brother directly but he never shows up for appointments."

I looked at the pamphlet. ISLAM, was printed in black on the blue cover. I opened it to the first page. "There is no fault in Islam. Whatever faults exist are in wrong interpretations." The next page had a table of contents. Under PILLARS OF ISLAM were listed Faith in the Unity of God and acceptance of Mohammad as his prophet, Daily Prayer, Fasting during the month of Ramadan, Almsgiving, and Pilgrimage. Another heading listed MARTYRDOM. There was a chapter devoted to each of these concepts. Nothing inflammatory. Even martyrdom was a Christian concept as well as Muslim one. "It's just describing the Muslim religion," I said.

"But Jahan was trying to push Islam on other students."

"Hard to believe, he's always respectful of others. But he likes to talk about ideas," I mumbled.

"Yes, he's polite, but he was out of control, obviously."

"Out of control?" Every word she said intensified my apprehension.

"He got into a fight with Peter Sullivan."

My throat had become so tight that I was afraid if I said anything else I would shout, so I was silent.

I was relieved when the phone rang and interrupted her. After listening a moment she said, "I'll be there soon." She put down the receiver and said to me, "I have a meeting. You talk to your brother and your parents too."

Outside, I almost stumbled over piles of snow on the ground. I was feeling dizzy. What was Jahan doing? Why was Sister Ursula so judgmental? Could there be a deep prejudice against Islam in the college like Jahan had told me?

When I got home, to my surprise, Baba and Jahan were in the living room, engaged in heated conversation. Jahan was showing him the pamphlets.

"Where did you get them?" Baba asked.

"Assad gave them to me. He printed them himself. The mosque lets him use their printer."

"What's he trying to prove?" Baba asked.

"He wants to correct the image of Islam, educate people. The college is so narrow," Jahan said. "You have no idea."

"What prompted you to rent a room in the mosque? What do you talk about?" Baba asked.

"We talk about how to help people understand Islam, that's all."

"What's the preoccupation with Islam? We didn't raise you in that religion, or any religion. Didn't I always tell you religion has done more harm than good? Look at all the wars fought in the name of religion." Baba was exasperated.

"Islam is used as a tool of prejudice among Americans," Jahan said.

"Jahan, darling, you should be spending your time studying and bringing up your grades," Maman said, coming into the room. She went over to him and kissed him. "These waves of bigotry come and go in America. Today it's Islam, tomorrow another group will be the target. When I was growing up in Ohio, it was the Catholics they didn't like."

Everyone sank into silence. Finally I said, "Jahan, Sister Ursula said you got into a fight with Pete about those pamphlets."

"He hit me and I hit him back. What was I supposed to do?"

"All right, let's not dwell on what's already happened. Let's think constructively," Baba said. As if hoping for magic to set Jahan on the right track, he added, "In my lab they're looking for someone to help out. I mentioned you and they said they'd be happy for you to work there a couple of afternoons a week. You might find you have an interest in the medical profession."

"I'm not cut out for that, Baba, I'm sorry. You know I'm going to be an artist."

Taking Jahan's arm, he said, "My dear son, there's no security in art. You can paint in your free time. Someone in my group is selling a used Alfa Romeo, not too expensive. I'll buy it for you as your Christmas present. You'll need a car to drive to the lab. You're lucky you have a father who encourages you to become a professional. I didn't have that kind of guidance from my own father. I had to put myself through school. Did your mother talk to you about you and Nora taking a vacation?"

Jahan nodded.

"After you and Nora come back, you can start the job." He was committing us to the vacation and Jahan to the job, and we were both intimidated by his authority.

In a moment we all dispersed, without Jahan and me discussing the vacation.

I came home late in the afternoon the following day and heard noises from Jahan's room. I listened intently. He was banging things around. I stood behind the door of his room and called, "Jahan, Jahan."

"Come in," he said. He was standing in the middle of the room, looking angry and upset.

"Jahan, what's wrong?"

"Baba thinks I had something to do with that nightclub fire."

"I'm sure he doesn't."

"He keeps asking me questions. And I think he came in my room when I wasn't here, looking for some evidence. Some of my stuff isn't in the same place."

"That's terrible, if you're sure it was him."

"He makes me furious. I had nothing to do with the fire."

"Jahan, I believe you."

"I have to get out of here, do you want to go on that trip with me?"

"I want to but there's Carlo, he wants me to do something with him at Christmas." It was not at all good timing, but I had to say it.

Jahan went to his desk and began to look through a book, as if trying to tell me to leave the room.

"I wish you weren't angry with me."

Without looking at me he said, "Carlo isn't good enough for you."

"You don't know him, you saw him only once. He's so kind and generous. He really wants to be friends with you. Wouldn't Maria mind if you go away during the holidays?"

"I'm not seeing Maria any more. She took Gail's side."

"Really? Couldn't you convince her?"

"There wasn't anything that serious between us anyway."

"Jahan *joon*, I'm so happy we can talk like this." I noticed a Koran and a *mohr* on his desk. "Have you really become religious?"

He turned to me and said, "I'm curious about Islam, its history, philosophy and political relevance. Is that a crime?"

We talked like that for a while and finally I said, "Give me a day or two to think about the trip," and started to leave.

"Here, Nora, look through this." He picked up a travel guide from the floor next to his bed. *America on $50 a Day, A Budget Traveler's Handbook.* "We could go west and see how far we get, I'll be able to get my license easily. I already have a permit. Assad's been teaching me how to drive. We'll be each other's best friend again, like old times."

I drove to Carlo's house. A party was just starting across the street. Dressed-up college kids were getting out of cars and going up the stairs, holding hands, laughing. I was envious of how carefree they were. Carlo was home and opened the door promptly. "Hey, what a treat," he said, and helped me take my jacket off. He kissed me and led me to the living room. "Let me put these away—accounts for the restaurant." He collected the papers that were spread on the coffee table and put them on his desk in the corner. "We're having a good year, my father is going to be happy."

I plopped myself on the couch and quickly came out with what was on my mind. "My parents want me to go on vacation with my brother during Christmas break."

He looked at me with clouded eyes. "You're going on vacation with him?"

"They want me to take him away from his circle of friends for a while." I turned to the window to avoid his eyes. Frost had formed triangular shapes on the pane. The neon sign on the general store across the street was blinking on and off even though it was still daytime.

"A few days of vacation isn't going to change anything for him," he said, exasperated.

"It could. It's worth a try."

"Would you like me to go with you? I could join you for part of the time anyway. I still think it would be good if your brother and I were friends."

"Carlo, you're so understanding, but it won't work." I cuddled up against him.

He pulled away and said, "You treat him like a child."

"We were once so close."

"You keep saying that."

Feeling a deep division inside me, afraid I might start crying, I said, "I'd better go, I have a lot of work to do for exams coming up."

I got up. He followed me to the door and kissed me, but he looked gloomy.

Bicycling was hard; I slipped a few times. The streets were icy and all the stress I was feeling didn't help. I was glad no one was home and I didn't have to face anyone in the state of mind I was in. As soon as I entered my room my phone started to ring. I picked it up. It was Carlo.

"Nora, let's go out for lunch tomorrow and talk. What about that bayside restaurant we went to on our first date?"

"I'd love that."

At the restaurant he said, "Nora, you aren't yourself."

I put my hand on his. "It's all the problems at home."

"I've been thinking a lot about us. You can't make a commitment. Do you want to take a break from each other for, say, one month? Then one of us will call the other. What do you think of that idea?"

"Carlo, that isn't what I want. I'm sorry about the way I've been. I'm always in the midst of a crisis and your life is so stable."

"I tell you what, you go on your vacation and we'll talk again when you come back."

Right after we finished eating, we got into his car. He drove me back to my bike.

# 25

Christmas was a happy day for our family. We'd read in *Newsday* about arrests in connection with the nightclub fire. Neither Jahan nor Assad had anything to do with it. Baba had passed his exams and soon would be licensed to practice. He was going to continue with the medical group, but now as a doctor rather than an assistant. Jahan gave in to our parents' pressure, crammed, and managed to do well in his exams—or at least he thought so. He had gotten a driver's license. There had been no more complaints from Sister Ursula, no mention of the pamphlets about Islam or fighting with students. Maman, wrapped up in all the good news, was full of life, bouncing around, laughing a lot. She had paid extra attention to her appearance too—highlighting her hair in different flattering shades of blond.

I was the only one caught in gloom, wondering what was going to become of my relationship with Carlo. Would he even want to see me again? He had been so cold at the restaurant. I had told Jahan I'd go with him but I was full of anxiety.

After breakfast we opened our gifts, kissed each other.

"Now your special present," Baba said to Jahan. "The car. I brought it over last night. It's in the garage." The two of them left. Then in a few moments I saw a small red car coming out of the garage with Jahan sitting behind the wheel.

They drove away and came back in half an hour or so, both animated. "It's a beautiful car," Jahan said to me. "So easy to drive. It practically flies."

A little later we all helped set the table and make early Christmas dinner. Olga and her husband and two of Baba's Iranian friends, Dr.

Azizi and the colonel, were going to drop in afterwards. As we sat at the table, Baba started pouring wine in all of our glasses, filling Jahan's and mine only half way. "We'll make an exception today," he said. "I want you to taste this wine. It's Australian but the grapes originally came from Shiraz."

"Let's toast to all the good things this year," Maman said.

We raised our glasses and toasted.

"Baba, I'm really happy for you," Jahan said.

"I can see the two of you in practice together," Maman said.

"So can I," Baba said.

Jahan didn't protest.

"Nora, have you thought more about your major?" Maman asked me.

"English. Then I want to go on to law school."

Baba looked at me questioningly, then said, "If that's what you want." He turned to Jahan again. "Let's start the new year with a new attitude. There are things about America I don't like either, but there are a lot of good things about it too."

Maman patted Jahan on the back and kissed his cheek. "Yes, make it your New Year's resolution."

Jahan smiled. "I'm willing, but I sure wish more people appreciated my art here. I sometimes feel I'm under censorship."

"In Iran it's worse. Artists have no freedom," Baba said. "There was censorship under the Shah and there's censorship now. The Shah wanted art and literature to just glorify Iran."

"Yes, and now the mullahs want everything to conform to religion," Maman said.

Jahan nodded noncommittally.

"Just be happy we're in a safe place," Baba said.

When we were finished eating, we cleared the dishes and changed into better clothes for the guests. From the outside, we seemed like a totally normal family.

The doorbell rang and Maman went to greet the guests. Baba

introduced everyone, opened another bottle of Shiraz, and brought out pistachios and caviar.

"Oh, this wine, a touch of Iran. Grapes from there are the best," the Colonel said, taking swift gulps from his glass. "I wish I were back in my childhood orchard and could reach to those golden grapes." He turned to Jahan, "More and more you're looking like your father."

"He's going to work in the lab," Baba said. He turned to Jahan for his reaction.

Jahan nodded. "I'm going to try it for a while."

After Olga and her husband left, Baba started talking to his Iranian friends in Farsi, with the short-wave radio turned on and tuned to Tehran.

The grim news and their discussion about it was only adding to my own gloom. I was glad when Jahan asked me to go to his room so he could show me the plan he had in mind for our trip.

A map was spread on his desk. "I marked places where we could stay a night or two on our way to California." He had put thick dark blue marks on some cities: Pittsburgh, St. Louis, Santa Fe, San Diego.

"It will be exciting to see more of America," I said.

"I made some phone calls to hotels in Pittsburgh but I couldn't get anything for the 26th. But a few were available for the 27th. I could only get one room but it's a suite. I don't mind sleeping in the living room. It's better to leave on the 27th anyway. We'll avoid the Christmas rush." There was no hint of that other layer in our relationship in his tone.

I stayed in his room for a long time and we began to talk like the old days, comparing our impressions about everything.

"I don't like the way Jared brags about how rich his parents are," I said.

"I hate the way Mr. Vierra pontificates," he said, starting to mimic him.

We both laughed. His laughter was so warm that it startled me. It was like the old laugh, the one I hadn't heard for a long time.

Then he began to talk about his art teacher. "He thinks I have talent, but he says my work is 'too Iranian.' What does he expect? He means well but he's really provincial."

"Are you still going to major in art?" I asked.

"If I don't quit school and go to Iran."

"Jahan, you know that's out of the question." He hadn't again mentioned his friend getting killed, and I didn't want to bring it up. But it terrified me that he was still talking about going to Iran, taking the chance of being drafted.

"I'll never be happy here," he said.

"We'll be separated then. I know I could never live in Iran."

Then our conversation, inevitably, became more intimate. "I wanted my relationship with Maria to work but there was no way."

"Sometimes it's hard for me to talk to Carlo too."

"I thought about you every moment I was with Maria. Your face, your voice. A few times I even called out 'Noor.' She didn't know what that meant, so I got away with it."

"Oh, Jahan. That's how it is for me too when I'm with Carlo. But we both have to get over those feelings for each other."

Then Baba called us into the living room to say goodbye to his friends, who were leaving.

On the 26th, when I came home from the library, my parents had left already for their trip upstate. Through the living room window, I could see Jahan in the backyard, cutting up dead branches of trees into small pieces and stacking them to use in the fireplace. He had voluntarily taken over the work in the backyard. He was wearing loose, paint-stained pants. The curls in his hair were more pronounced from the damp air. He looked healthy and muscular from working in the yard, hours of playing soccer, and all the bicycling he did.

A moment later he came inside and went to the refrigerator. He took out a quart of orange juice and drank directly from the carton. He had been buying orange juice in quarts and used the empty cartons to mix paint in. "I have to see Assad for a couple of hours. All his friends are away this week."

After he left I started to pack. We would be leaving very early in the morning. I realized the canvas bag was too small to fit everything I wanted to take in it. I decided to use the suitcase I'd bought in Dubai. I had stored it in the large walk-in closet in Jahan's room, along with his. I went into his room to get the suitcase. He had already packed and his suitcase stood close to the door.

I looked in the closet, which was filled with all sorts of things — clothes, records — and found the suitcase all the way in the back. As I was taking it out I noticed the leather bound notebook on a shelf. I couldn't resist it. I took it down and looked through it. It was a diary, as I had suspected. I took it, and the suitcase, to my room, thinking I would return it as soon as I heard Jahan coming back. I quickly looked through page after page. There were only brief entries and their dates were far apart, some just after our arrival in the U.S. and a few more recently.

> On the steep slope of life that Noor and I were treading together, I lost her. Or rather she abandoned me half way. Now I'm going downhill, all alone. I watch the world float by. My existence has dried up since we left Iran. Nothing is going to bloom for me. Baba views me now as lazy, shiftless. Maman also is disappointed in me.

> Noor was sitting in front of the mirror in her room, brushing her hair. She only had a pink bra and panties on. Then she put on an ice blue dress with its neck so low, half of her breasts were exposed. She was going out with him.

One entry written a few weeks ago sounded like a poem.

> Oh, Noor, have you forgotten the pasture,
> the hills, the wild flowers, the butterflies
> that we made our own? Away from others' eyes.
> We alone saw the beauty. Just your eyes and mine.

In that private arena we were one in our minds as well as
   our bodies.
We said such tender things to each other.
Now you have gone into a different field, apart from mine.
Your wandering has killed both of our souls.

My hands were shaking as I turned the pages. There was no more
writing, only a few sketches. One drawing was of cows grazing in a
pasture, another of a cherry tree, full of fruit, standing in the middle
of a field. They were serene, a contrast to the anguish revealed in the
entries.

I closed the diary and took it back to his room. As I was putting
it on the closet shelf, I noticed a large metal box sealed with tape. I
took it down and went back to my room. I removed the tape carefully so that I could re-tape it. Every item in the box had some connection to me—the brooch and shirt I'd returned, the transparent
plastic bag with locks of our hair in it. I remembered that day when
we had cut our hair and all the urgency and excitement I was feeling then. I saw us dancing to that song: "Without Love you're only
living an imitation, an imitation of Life," which reminded me vividly
of the desperate desire I'd felt for him. I saw us lying by the stream in
Meigoon, our bodies entwined, water rolling over stones gleaming
darkly like black diamonds, the ground spongy and soft beneath us.

But did I want us to go back to that? Just the day before, our conversation had quickly become intimate. I needed to destroy those
relics of the past.

In a panic, I emptied the box into my backpack and rode my bike
to the wharf in Port Jefferson. Feeble sunlight filtered through the
hazy clouds. A ferry was about to leave. I got on it and, pulling up
the collar of my coat and wrapping my scarf around my neck, I went
to the deck. The sky and the water had turned yellow as if lit from
below. When far enough from the shore, I took out the treasures
from the past and threw them into the water. Then I began to cry
and thought that I would never stop.

# 26

Back home Hooshang's song was playing on Jahan's phonograph. It was scratched and one line was repeated over and over: "Did you lose your way in the dark, winding alley."

I went to his room, gripped by an urge to tell him what I had done.

"When Maman and Baba said we should go on a vacation together I began to have a fantasy," Jahan said, oblivious of what I was going through. He lowered his head, as he did when seized by a strong emotion. "That we would get into the car, keep going, and never return. We'd stop in a city, find some kind of temporary work, enough to pay our expenses and then move on."

"Alone and isolated, that's what we'd be. Jahan, I was so upset earlier that I took the brooch, our hair in the plastic bag, your shirt." I felt a knot in my throat and then began to cry again.

"What did you do with them, Noor?" He looked at me hard.

"I threw them into the ocean."

Jahan was silent, the muscles of his face taut, the expression of his eyes grave, the way he used to look as a child, when he was upset but didn't want to show weakness and cry.

"Jahan, I'm really sorry but it was a desperate act."

It was as if I had flung something at him, his face was so pained. Then he said, "Noor, we belong to each other."

"Jahan, I want a normal life for myself, and you."

"Let's get married, now," he said wildly.

"You know that isn't possible."

"It's illegal in New York for a sister to marry an adopted brother, but in some states it's legal," Jahan said.

"It isn't about it being legal or not. It just won't work. It will iso-
late us. People see things in black and white. You know how they'll
view us."

"I don't care what anyone thinks."

"You will after a while."

"No, not me. I just want you and me back together."

"You aren't really thinking. I'm not going on the trip. . ."

"You don't mean that." As if to buy time, he went into the
kitchen and came back with two glasses and a bottle of the Shiraz
that Baba always kept around. We became more relaxed and open
with each other as we drank.

"It has been so long since Meigoon," I said.

"Yes, we've experienced new things."

"You know Jahan, I can't stand American boys. I tried to convince
myself."

"The girls are strange too. They try to act independent but they
really aren't, so they play some kind of a game all the time. On top of
everything their parents don't like them to be dating me, an Iranian."

"They're bigoted."

We laughed as we talked more about our dating disasters. Jahan
described how empty his relationships had been. I told him how all
the boys bored me, that Carlo was the best but I had to admit I felt
distant from him. "He's much older than me, eager to settle down. I
love him, sort of. At least I like him very much and feel comfortable
with him. Is that enough?"

"Noor, it isn't. Don't settle for that. We know what love is. You
know we belong to each other."

"You'd want to live in Iran, your heart isn't in America. And I
could never go back to a place I wanted to get out of so badly."

"But we'd be adults. You could work to improve the situation for
women there," Jahan said.

"I wouldn't survive a day there," I said. "If I can't function day by
day, how can I do anything important?"

"Then we'll live here. I'll quit school, get a job, set up a place for the two of us to move into."

"This is a fantasy. Let's be realistic, it would kill Maman and Baba. Think of their shame, their humiliation. And I don't want you to quit school; I want to go on and become a lawyer." The more we talked, the closer we grew, and the barriers I'd built began to completely dissolve. He put his arm around me and held me to him. He said passionately, "Noor, Noor, I can't live without you. I tried." I could feel his skin. I looked up right into his eyes, amber, thick dark lashes. I knew that I still loved him deeply and knew too that I didn't want to.

I don't recall when the music stopped, or when all the usual sounds—the refrigerator's hum, the faint bark of the dog from the house across the street, the scraping of bare tree branches against the side of our house—faded. Our voices were sounding loud in the background silence.

"Jahan, I don't want to, I shouldn't."

We had been talking in English but he switched into Farsi. "Noor joonan, man delam barayeh to tang shodeh," My dear Noor, I've missed you. He went on in Farsi, words that meant, "Don't you understand how terrible it has been for me to see you give yourself to other men?"

"I've been missing you too, but . . ." I began in English. The next thing, we were on his bed. I recall the sensation of the room spinning around me. The bed swayed like the hammock we used to lie on. Our boundaries were melting. I struggled to pull myself away. "Stop, stop," I said.

He pulled off my blouse; his mouth was on my breast.

"Let me go, let me go!"

"Noor, tell me you love me."

"No!" But the magic of our love was flooding us both. We split out of the real world, sealed ourselves off from it, as we used to do.

Afterwards, we lay quietly for a while. Then I said, "Jahan, I love you, and I love Carlo too in a way. But I can't stay with either of you right now. I have to find who I am, I have to be free."

"Let's talk about it in the morning."

I search among the jigsaw pieces of my memory for what else Jahan and I did, what else we said. But memory and dream, dream and reality, blend together. What I do recall with certainty is that a few hours later I got up, collected my clothes, and as I was leaving to go to my room, Jahan said sleepily, "Nora, I'm going to let you go."

I woke in the morning, all shaky. I had slept late. The window in my room was a rectangle of light. I dreaded facing Jahan. I listened for sounds from his room but it was silent. I went into the living room and immediately noticed an envelope on the coffee table addressed to Maman and Baba. My heart skipped a beat. The envelope wasn't sealed and I pulled out the letter.

Dear Maman and Baba,

The only way I can be out of the terrible state I've been in is to break away completely and find a new life. I'm returning to Iran. I've a place to stay until my papers are ready. I've found out from the Iranian Interest Section in D.C. that they don't hold me responsible for us escaping from Iran, as they hold you. I can go back there in a legal way. I'm not afraid of being drafted. If I have to, I'll serve like all the men my age. I have the car, which I intend to sell and add to the money you gave me for the vacation, to pay for my immediate expenses. I promise I'll pay you back when I'm in a position to earn money. Please understand.

Your loving son, Jahan.

There was no address or phone number. I read the letter over and over again. I knew that the phrase "To break away completely," was meant for me rather than our parents. Waves of panic attacked me. Horrible images of Jahan fighting in the war passed before my eyes. I had to stop him from going. I went into his room and looked for his address book to look up his friends' phone numbers but I couldn't find it. He must have taken it. The Koran and the travel book were still on his desk. His calendar that lay next to them was still open on December 27th; the suitcase he'd packed for our trip was gone.

I went back to the living room and looked in the phone book under Moradi, Assad's last name. There were two Moradis listed but only one in Rocky Point, where I knew Assad lived with his parents. I called but there was no answer and no machine was on. I realized I didn't know Jahan's other friends' last names. I drank a scalding hot cup of coffee, burning my throat as I swallowed it. I kept looking out of the window at the chilly late December sunlight. Jahan had been working in the yard just the day before. Now he was no longer at home and who knew when, if, he would return. The phone rang, sharp, jarring. I picked up promptly, but then whoever had called hung up. I spent the rest of the day at home, anxious and aimless.

The next day I managed to pull myself together and go to the library. I told the head librarian that my trip had been cancelled and I could work my usual hours if they still needed me. She said they still needed me.

When I returned home after work I looked into Jahan's room to see if he had come back to get the rest of his belongings. But he wasn't there and the room was exactly as it had been. I tried Assad's number again, but there was no answer this time either.

I went to bed early that night and quickly drifted into nightmares. In one, a window in my room was open and a hard wind was blowing in. Stars were twinkling against the vast black sky but then it began to rain. Drops like melting silver splashed against the windowsill. I wanted to get up to shut the window, but couldn't, no matter how hard I tried.

In another I was standing in the doorway of a room with peeling walls and no windows. Several men were sitting on the bare floor. I looked closely at them in the dim light and recognized Jahan among them. "Don't come in, there has been a bomb threat," he shouted at me. Then I heard an explosion. I woke up. My mouth tasted bitter.

"Nora, Nora," Baba was knocking on my door. "Did you read Jahan's letter?"

"I'll be right there." I dressed quickly and went into the living room. He was standing in the middle of the room, holding the letter, and Maman was smoking by the window, which she'd opened a crack.

"What happened to the trip?" Maman asked, turning to me.

"Jahan changed his mind." My voice was tremulous.

"We must find him and stop him from going to Iran," Baba said.

"What was that mosque Jahan went to, the Blue Mosque? He could be staying there," Maman said.

"Let's go there and see if we can find him or Assad or one of the others." Baba called information and got the address. "Let's get going."

Maman put out her cigarette in the sink and we left. I sat in the back seat, tense and quiet.

# 27

In Queens we found the mosque on a busy avenue teeming with people of all nationalities, talking in different languages. The mosque didn't look like mosques in Iran with their ornate mosaic minarets and golden domes. It was a plain, run down, two-story building with a green canopy extending over the entrance. On the canopy was written in Arabic, MASJID AZRUG, and in English, BLUE MOSQUE. In the center of the thick glass pane of a window there was a hole, surrounded by spider-web cracks, possibly caused by a bullet.

We read some of the notices posted in a glass case next to the door. One of them said, "Lodging available in exchange for work at the mosque."

We went into the entranceway and Baba started talking in quiet tones to the attendant, an old, wrinkled man standing behind a counter. Two women wearing long-sleeved dresses and head-scarves, each with a small child at her side, came in. They took off their own and the children's shoes and gave them to the attendant who put them in little wooden cubicles next to the wall behind him. Then they went to the prayer area at the end of the corridor. For a moment the door to the prayer room was opened and we could see a hanging cloth that separated men and women who seemed to be from all nationalities, along with some American blacks. The women were only barely visible from behind the curtain but the men were in full view. Before the door shut I had a wild feeling that Jahan could be there among them, but he wasn't.

Baba led us outside and said; "The old man doesn't know anything about Jahan or Assad or any of the other boys. He says too many people come and go here. The rooms they used to provide for people are under repair, no one is staying in them."

We walked around on the streets near the mosque but there was no sign of Jahan. The burnt out nightclub stood boarded up in the middle of one street.

On the way home we were all quiet. At home Baba said, "Maybe we should call the police. What if he's in some kind of trouble?"

"What are we going to say to them?" Maman said.

"You're right, no point inviting trouble. I thought I was doing everything to make him happy." Then he turned on himself. "I should have spent more time with him."

"He'll turn around and come home," Maman said. "He'll come to his senses."

My throat felt so tight, I couldn't speak.

Baba turned on the TV and we all sat on the sofa. The young anchor on NBC said in an urgent voice:

> Smoke spirals out of damaged refineries in the south and near the Iraq border. The Islam Guards and the Islamic Republic of Iran Army are fiercely resisting and have succeeded in destroying tanks in Abadan belonging to the Baathists. At least 13,000 men are fighting on the front, which extends over 60 miles.

Baba turned off the TV. "I can't bear it," he said.

Maman held his hand in hers. "Oh, Cyrus, I just know Jahan will come back," she said.

A little later Maman went to Assad's address and found his mother in. "She barely knows English. She kept saying: 'Your son is good. My son is good too.' I was surprised at their living conditions—a cramped apartment above a noisy grocery store."

I decided to go and talk to Assad's mother too. I rode through monotonous roads, punctuated here and there by a Taco Bell, a Burger King, a gas station, a hardware store, a row of mobile homes, a church. Then I was at the grocery store below Assad's parents' apartment. I noticed a stairway on the side with a dingy hallway at the top. I rang the bell and waited. No answer. I rang again but nothing. I went into the grocery store. An Indian man wearing a turban stood behind the counter.

"Do you know the family in the apartment upstairs?"

"I haven't seen them lately." Two customers came in and I left.

I got on my bicycle and detoured to the gas station where Assad had started working after he quit school. Surprisingly, he was there and helping customers. He was wearing stained work clothes and his hair was disheveled, in contrast with his usual dapper appearance. I parked my bike, went to the station and waited by the door.

After he finished with his customers he came in my direction. He was startled to see me and seemed a little embarrassed.

"How are you?" he asked in what seemed like a falsely nonchalant manner.

"Please tell me where Jahan is, you must know."

"Don't worry about him. He's getting his papers together to go to Iran."

"He isn't staying in the mosque?"

He shook his head. "There's no place to stay there now. He went to D.C."

"Where is he staying? Do you have a phone number for him?"

He shook his head, then nodded goodbye when the owner called him inside.

When I returned home, Maman and Baba were still there. I said, "I found Assad at the gas station he works at."

"Really?" Maman looked astonished, and they both gave me their full attention.

"He said Jahan is in D.C."

"If Assad's telling the truth," Maman said.

The following evening Baba told us, "I went to the mosque again this morning and talked to Mostafa Mohammadi, the main mullah there; he remembered Jahan and Assad at his sermons. I asked him to contact us if he saw Jahan but he said that that wasn't his job. I saw that same old man I talked to yesterday, gave him a good tip and my phone numbers and Jahan's picture. Then I called the Iran Interest Section but they couldn't tell me anything about him." After a moment he said, "I wonder if he contacted Jamshid or anyone else in Iran. I'll try phoning until I reach someone."

A few days after Jahan left I pulled out of our mailbox a postcard from him, postmarked in Istanbul. Again he had addressed it only to our parents.

> Dear Maman and Baba,
>
> I got my papers together very quickly. I went to D.C. in person and they gave me everything I needed in twenty-four hours. They want to encourage young men to return to Iran. I'm in Istanbul now, staying for a night and then will be going on to Iran. Don't worry about me. The thought of returning there only makes me happy.
>
> Your loving son, Jahan

I gave it to Maman and Baba when they came in.

"He really is going to Iran," Maman said, lowering her head.

"He simply needs to get something out of his system," Baba said in a resigned voice, failing to mask his worry.

But then, for days to come, he made a frenzied effort to find out where Jahan was—was he in the army, had he contacted the relatives. Finally he reached Jamshid, who told him he hadn't heard from Jahan, but he reassured Baba that he would let him know if he had news. Baba's friends contacted everyone who might have some connection with the army, but their efforts were futile.

We listened to the short-wave radio more anxiously than ever now, in case Jahan's name came up among the list of soldiers, missing or dead. We were relieved when his name wasn't mentioned but then we worried that the reports weren't complete or reliable.

Feeling utterly despondent and lonely I called Carlo.

"Nora! How was your trip?"

"We didn't go."

"What happened?"

"I'll tell you when I see you."

We made a date for the following afternoon. I was relieved that he hadn't completely broken up with me. But since I hadn't heard from him, I wasn't sure if he would want to resume the relationship. Neither was I sure if it could work at this point, if we resumed.

He opened the door and led me inside. "I like your new haircut," he said.

"I was tired of it long." The truth was I had just had it cut short because it gave me an older look, not so far apart from Carlo.

He picked up a box from the coffee table and handed it to me. "Christmas present. I've been meaning to call you but hoped to hear from you first."

I removed the gold ribbon and the wrapping paper from the box; inside I found a pair of gold earrings each consisting of two concentric loops. "These are beautiful," I said.

"Let's see how they look on you." He put them on for me. I thought of the linked cherries Jahan put over my ears in Meigoon.

I went into the hall and looked in the mirror. Then I came back and sat next to him on the sofa. He pulled me to him and kissed me hard on the lips. I felt like a robot, going through the motions. I said, "Can we go for a ride? It's so sunny and beautiful out."

"You're like a little ailing kitten," he said.

"Do I look that bad?"

"Like sunlight blocked by clouds."

We both laughed. We put our jackets on and went to his car. We got out by a beach and walked for a while until a wind began to blow making the cold air hard to bear. Then we went to a restaurant not far from the beach.

"Tell me what happened to your trip."

"Jahan decided to go to Iran. We're totally devastated. He's surely going to be drafted, if he hasn't been already."

"I'm so sorry. But he made that choice, didn't he?"

"Baba even found him a job at his lab. He was still encouraging him to become a doctor. He hoped they'd work together. In some ways they're really alike, look exactly alike too."

"Maybe Jahan is his real son."

"What do you mean? I told you they adopted him."

"It's possible for a man to adopt his own illegitimate son."

Tiny little shocks rippled through me. "How could you even think that?"

"It's not that uncommon. In Italy they do it all the time."

"Not in Iran. And Maman would never put up with it."

"You don't know that."

This was all sounding like some kind of hostile attack. In a short while I said, "I should be going back now."

"Nora, I didn't mean to upset you."

"It isn't your fault. Please, just take me back."

Helplessly, Carlo took me back, and at the door I said, "Listen, if things don't work out, it isn't anything you did. At this point I just have to find my own way in life."

He stared at me, confused and hurt, and said, "Nora, I understand that what I said may have upset you, but don't you think you're over-reacting?"

"I'm sorry. I have to go," I said, and evading any further conversation I kissed him quickly and got on my bike. I saw his head drop, saw his frustration as I rode away.

Soon after I arrived home, the phone rang. It was Carlo. "Nora, I feel terrible we parted that way. I know it's hard for you with your brother there in the war and everything I say about him upsets you."

"Carlo, I have strong feelings for you, but I have to figure myself out first." I knew it was irrational anger but I was burning with it, as if his words—that Jahan was Baba's own son—had been shards of glass he had thrown at me.

"Nora, are you sure you want to do this?"

"I just need some time. . . to sort things out for myself."

A heavy silence followed. Finally Carlo said, "This is a terrible way to break up."

"Carlo, let's not think of it that way. We just need to take a break again, that's all."

"I don't understand you," he said. "How many times are we going to need a break, Nora?"

I could hear finality in his voice and I was suddenly filled with apprehension, as if I were standing on precarious ground. Did I want to lose him altogether? Yet I was compelled to do it, take a break, or let the relationship sever altogether.

Then he just hung up. I sat there, feeling like a lost child.

# 28

School started and the campus was full of greetings, kisses, and hugs. I ran into Jahan's art professor, who stopped me as I was going from one classroom to another. "Jahan left his project incomplete," he said.

"He'll finish it, I'm sure," I said, not wanting to accept the idea that Jahan could already be in the army and not planning to come back.

"He's a nice kid, has talent," he said, and wandered away.

Lonely and depressed, I found Pam and told her about Jahan going to Iran and about my breakup with Carlo and cried on her shoulder a while. She said to call Carlo, try to give the relationship another chance, even though she thought he was too old for me.

I did call him. I went over and threw myself into his arms, told him how happy I was to see him. He reacted with hesitation, not trusting anything, perhaps not sure any more what he wanted. On Sunday we went to the City. We walked around Chinatown, Little Italy, and Greenwich Village. We went to Candella, a restaurant he knew in the Village. It was lit by hundreds of candles set on tables, counters, hung on walls.

"It reminds me of church. We shouldn't have come here," Carlo said moodily.

"We could go somewhere else," I said.

"We're here now."

After some wine we both loosened up and talked about this and that. At the next table a young couple about my age were looking into each other's eyes, leaning over and kissing, whispering. It struck me again that I'd never been in love with Carlo; I wondered if he was really in love with me or was just ready to settle down and I had come along at the right time. Stupidly, I asked him that question, which startled and then angered him. The whole evening was ruined.

What had existed between us was gone and there was no way to put the broken pieces together. Then one afternoon as I was bicycling home his van pulled up next to me. "I'm on my way home," he said. "You want to get in?" I put my bike in the back and got into the cab.

"Yes, sure."

Again it was the same pattern. Something went wrong, something was missing. That was the last time we were together.

Days, weeks went by and we heard nothing more from Jahan. Baba was dispirited, Maman quieter. Then one afternoon I found a photograph of Jahan in a soldier's uniform, along with a note, on the coffee table. The letter was creased, the photo a little damaged. It was lucky they had reached us at all. I held the photograph, staring at it. It was only two by three inches, but it felt heavy. He was looking into the camera with a grave expression. The note was brief and again it didn't include me.

> My dear Maman and Baba,
>
> I'll soon be at the front. Two of my friends from Masjid-e-Suleiman, Bijan and Hamid, are with me. Masjid-e-Suleiman has been completely demolished. No buildings, no houses, nothing is left. I miss you very much.
>
> Your loving son, Jahan.

Along with my apprehensions for him went self-pitying questions: why was he totally shutting me out? Was it pride, hurt feelings, anger, his way of forgetting what had happened on that day before he left? The questions settled on my chest like pieces of hard stone. Rain was falling, splashing hard against the window panes. Behind the rain everything blended into grayness, emptiness. At that moment I could see quite clearly how Jahan viewed America. For him America, at least where we lived, was a dull place, everything in hues of gray, sounds muffled, emotions hidden or insincerely expressed. Leaden winters when it rained and drizzled all day long. Deathly quiet descending at night. At the college, on the streets, he felt like a ghost of himself, living on a narrow margin with his real life all in the past. I knew I was right to go my own way without him, but I felt guilty and tried to reason my way out of that feeling. He left because this culture had no place for him. He left because of his spiritual awakening.

Then I was back inside the black hole of guilt. No question, he left mainly because of me. If only I had handled things differently he would still be here; he wouldn't have jeopardized his life.

Once again I turned to counseling. I signed up to tutor a child with learning problems at a high school. I read a few hours a week to an old blind woman and listened to her stories of loss—her husband had died, her children had moved away and forgotten about her.

Baba was on the phone with his relatives in Iran whenever he could get through. Jamshid told Baba that he had checked with the war office and found it would take months to identify Jahan among thousands of young soldiers. Jamshid had called information and post offices in the larger cities to see if he could find an address or phone number for Jahan, but there was no sign of him. He had mailed letters to Jahan in care of the army but had received no response.

Baba also kept trying the Interest Section in Washington to see if there was any way to get himself and Maman off the blacklist, so that he could go to Iran and search for Jahan himself.

What was harder for me to grasp was how Maman was trying to seek solace in religion, which she had renounced for so long. One evening I saw her in a shadowy corner of her room kneeling and whispering prayers, and crossing herself. As I was bicycling to St. Paul's once I saw her going into Our Lady of Good Counsel. A white banner with blue writing on it: "Open Wide The Door To Christ" was hanging in front of the church. Later that day, I asked her about it. She said, "It gives me comfort, that's all there is to it." She added, "I miss my mother."

Then she stopped going to church and joined a women's support group she'd heard about from Olga. They met once a month at the house of one of the women. I heard her telling Baba about a son who had run away from home when he was sixteen and let his parents know of his whereabouts two years later with a letter asking them to donate money to Reverend Moon. Another woman's daughter had become schizophrenic when she was in college. She had been a brilliant student but now she had to be in an institution most of the time. Another woman's son was an addict, had sold drugs and was now in jail for it.

In Baba and Maman's sorrow for Jahan I saw that we were all inconsolable.

One afternoon when I returned home from school Maman was in the yard weeding and she called to me, "Nora, is that you? Come here, I want to talk to you." Was there news from Jahan? Hope and fear mingled in my heart. As I joined her in the yard, she said without introduction, "Nora, we're moving to L.A. We'll be putting the house up for sale right away."

"L.A.!" I exclaimed, perplexed.

"The Sagaamis are living there now. You remember, they were in France, and now Mahmood Sagaami has set up an office in L.A. and he wants your father to join his practice. Thousands of Iranians live in that city, you know."

"How great for Baba. But what about your job?"

"I'll find something else. And you can finish up school there."

"But I'm in the middle of the term."

"You can go to UCLA."

"I will lose all this term's credits. Anyway I can't just go to UCLA. I haven't applied."

"You overcame all sorts of difficulties when we came here from Iran, you'll find a way."

Baba came in and joined us in the yard.

"Baba, I can't go to L.A. with you. I want to finish college here."

"You'll work it all out," he said mechanically as if reciting something written.

"I'll lose at least a semester if I quit now and lose my scholarship too. Can't you wait until I graduate?"

"Dr. Sagaami wants me now."

"Then I can stay on here until I finish. I'll live in a dormitory. After all I'm twenty-one."

"Your mother and I will have to discuss it." His voice was gentle; I knew he'd let me stay.

I turned around and went inside. I tried not to bring up the subject again, hoping I was staying on. They were distracted by their own affairs, selling the house. They had to take care of all the repairs here and there, to make sure it looked its best. Then people began to come with real estate agents who praised the house all the time, not just to the prospective buyers but even to us.

My parents put me in charge of going through Jahan's belongings and keeping what was important. Since he left, I had been in his room only that once. I was terrified of his absence there. As soon as I went in, I felt deep loneliness. His half-finished paintings were leaning against the wall. One was of a luminous door with circular holes cut out of it, each with a finely lettered word suspended in the blue sky behind the door: God, Prayer, Charity, Fasting, Pilgrimage. The pillars of Islam.

I searched for his diary again. After looking everywhere I came across it on the same closet shelf where I had found it before. I took it off the shelf, all excited, as if I had found a lost treasure. There was a new entry with no date—but it had to be on the day he left, since I hadn't seen it before. In the margin he had drawn a picture of a sweet woman wearing a headscarf and holding a young boy on her lap.

> Mother, I dream about you. You come to me as a beautiful woman, wearing a scarf over your head. I see you waiting for

me. I approach and you jump up and say, "Is that you? I've been looking for you . . ."

I took his diary, some of his books, his trophies, and several of his paintings to my room. I went into the garage and took the rest of the paintings and drawings from there and rented a storage locker, where I could keep them until we heard from him.

In a short time Maman announced, "We have a buyer, the couple wants the furniture too. The closing is in April. You can move into a dormitory, your father checked, there's a room available. We're going to miss you, would have liked for you to come with us."

"I'll be lonely, I'll miss you both too, but I will have plenty of work to do."

Before they left for L.A., they helped me move my belongings, along with what I had kept of Jahan's, to my dormitory room. They helped me hang Jahan's paintings on my walls. Baba left me his old Jaguar and told me I should take driving lessons. We parted tearfully. Jahan was no longer with us and now we were going to live far away from each other.

Soon I found that it was a mixed blessing living in a dormitory, both liberating and lonely. At last I was living like most of the other American students—away from home, with a car. But independence didn't give me the exhilarated feeling I had once hoped for. Something inside me was dead.

I kept myself busy. I had two part-time jobs, at the library and in the admissions office doing secretarial work. I continued my friendship with Pam and I struck up friendships with other girls too, with whom I shared meals in the cafeteria or off campus. Sometimes we allowed ourselves a break from work and went to a movie at the art cinema in Port Jefferson, or a concert at the Staller Center in Stony Brook. I went on occasional dates with men, but nothing lasted.

Once, after classes, I went to Port Jefferson and walked on Main Street, looking at window displays. As I was heading in to get some coffee at Grandma's Sweets, I saw Carlo inside sitting with a woman.

I was glued to the spot. She was older than me, closer to his age. He was holding her hand on the table and she was smiling at him. They seemed really absorbed in each other. A few times I had reached for the phone to call him but didn't go through with it. We had tried too many times and it hadn't worked. The only way I can resume with him, I thought, would be if we had an honest conversation about Jahan, with my telling him the whole truth.

On another day, driving through Patchogue, I passed the bridal shops that Carlo and I had looked at and then we had talked about getting married. Impulsively, I went to look at his house. "Erica Wilson" was added to his name on the mailbox. I felt sharp regret at the way things had ended. He had been good to me and I had loved him, though not as deeply as I needed to. I had taken his love for granted in some ways and had acted badly. Maybe his being older had made me think I could act any way I wanted and it wouldn't hurt his feelings. I was tempted to call him, set up a date, try to talk all that out with him. But I knew it would only be awkward and uncomfortable.

# Part Three

# 29

I looked out of the window and, through the shadowy half-light of dawn, saw Jahan sitting on the bench in the backyard. A snowman with a hat on its head and a carrot nose stood in a corner. In the bitterly cold morning, with snow all around, Jahan was wearing only a checkered white and maroon shirt and shorts. "Jahan, aren't you freezing? Anyway that shirt is mine now." He stared down at his hands clasped on his lap and didn't answer. "Jahan," I called out.

I woke in a cold sweat, immediately filled with self-blame. How can I go on with life when I don't even know if Jahan's alive? It was a consolation to have his paintings on the walls. I looked at the clock on the side table. Oh, my God, the alarm didn't go off. I forgot to set it and I'm going to be late to class. Michael Bernstein, my criminal law professor, started right on the dot, not wanting to lose even one minute of his lecture time. I jumped out of bed, dressed, and drove speedily to school, making it in twenty minutes. I filled a cup with coffee, always brewing on a table in Mason Hall, and made it to class on time.

"The case is a young man who asked for money from a passenger on the train. When ignored he decided to use force."

We were all taking notes furiously. I managed to concentrate, was good at focusing that way. Between classes I studied in the library. I spent an hour working out in the gym and swimming, and then ate lunch in the cafeteria.

At the end of the school day I drove back to my apartment, which I had rented after college while working for a year to save money for law school. Though in college I'd majored in English literature, I had found a job as a research assistant to a psychologist at Stony

Brook University. I mainly gave tests to old people who were suffering from memory loss. I liked the university setting and psychology and thought of going to graduate school in that field, but realized I was still more attracted to law. I convinced my parents that I should go to law school on Long Island. I was used to the area, thought of it as home, and had some friends there. Now, with my savings, student loans, and what my parents agreed to pay toward my expenses, I was managing.

I had a sandwich with about a quarter of a glass of wine for dinner, looked through my notes again, and went to sleep.

The weekend came and went. Another week passed by. Summer came. I worked long hours at a law firm in Manhattan. I was single, but I didn't like to think of myself as a single woman looking for a man—I didn't take a share in a house in the Hamptons or hang out in singles bars. If I met someone naturally that was fine. After all these years it was as if my life was on hold, and would start only after Jahan came back, explained his abandonment—not only of me, but of our parents. After those brief notes and photograph at the beginning they hadn't heard anything more from him. He hadn't contacted our relatives in Iran either. The war was still raging in Iran. The holy war against Iraq enabled the mullahs to mobilize popular support and crush the moderate reformers. Khomeini was determined to pursue the war until Saddam Hussein was overthrown. With an infusion of arms from foreign supporters, Iraq escalated the tanker war and used poison gas.

Jahan wasn't reported dead by the army and though Baba said their list wasn't trustworthy, we still hung on to hope. Once, as I was driving to the mall, I saw a boy on a blue bicycle with fat wheels, identical to the one Jahan used to have. He was wearing a navy blue jacket just like Jahan's. For a moment I froze. Cars behind me were honking. When I looked closer I realized there was little resemblance between the boy on the bicycle and Jahan.

Every time Maman and Baba called me, they asked, "Have you

heard anything?" Then, during my second year of law school, I had a different kind of call from them. It was eight in the morning, five their time in L.A. It was as if they had been sleepless, waiting until it was late enough in Long Island to call me. Baba came on first. Hearing his voice, early in the morning, filled me with trepidation but he said, "Nora, we have a Norooz card from Jahan, belatedly."

"Really! That's absolutely the best news I've had, ever. To know that he's alive." I could hear a tremor in my own voice and feel tears welling in my eyes.

"It's a miracle it got here. It was in the mailbox last night when we came home from the Sagaamis. We had been talking about Jahan and then there was the card."

Maman came on the extension. "The card isn't to us, he sent it to Mohsen, then your uncle Jamshid sent it on. That's why it took months to get here. It's postmarked Shiraz, but no return address."

"I reached Jamshid in the middle of the night. He said he'd been looking for Jahan again," Baba said. "He found out from someone he knows in the army that Jahan was discharged more than two years ago but he didn't say where Jahan might be living. Jamshid called the information and post office again, in Shiraz and in nearby cities, to see if he could trace Jahan, but no luck."

"If Jahan wrote to Mohsen, he'll contact him again sooner or later, and he'll contact us too," I said.

"Oh, darling, it's a marvelous card. One of his own paintings is printed on it, signed and everything," Maman said.

"Will you send me the card? I'd love to see it with my own eyes."

"Sure," Maman said.

When we got off the phone I sat there, immobilized by a rush of happiness. It was as if Jahan had been resurrected from the dead.

In a few days I held the card in my hand. His name was there, and his painting was printed on it. It was a simple, elegant image of a rocky stream with trees leaning over the water. All the card said was: "Dear cousin, Happy Norooz! I hope we'll see each other before long."

Baba called again soon. "Your mother and I have been thinking, you should come here and celebrate the wonderful news, Jahan being alive. You can take off a few days, can't you?"

For a split second I considered looking into a flight out, but realized that this would be the worst time for me to take time off.

"I wish I could leave right now but I have a big paper due. I'll come out at Christmas break, and we can celebrate together then. I can't wait to see you both."

Their condominium was in a four-story stucco building on a cul-de-sac in West Hollywood. There was a little yard in front with lemon trees and large rose bushes. The parking area was filled with expensive cars: Mercedes's, BMWs, Cadillacs. Two of them belonged to Maman and Baba. In the lobby a Christmas tree and a menorah were set up. I could smell spices used in Iranian cooking. I asked the concierge, an Iranian man, to ring my parents' intercom.

Both Baba and Maman came to the door and we embraced tightly. Large windows in every room of the apartment displayed a vast view of L.A. Persian rugs, some similar to those we'd had in Iran, the ones Maman had loved, covered the floors. On a living room wall hung two of Jahan's paintings. One was a bold image of two identical women standing by a stream and looking at each other. The other had a blue background with stars scattered on it and in a corner, a boy and girl holding hands and staring up at the stars. That was one I would have taken but Maman and Baba had talked me into letting them have it. Two long-haired, flat-faced Persian cats, one gray, the other orange, were playing together on the ornate sofas and chairs. Maman had set up a Christmas tree and decorated it with bright ornaments; packages lay underneath it.

"I wish Jahan was with us now to celebrate," Maman said.

"We miss him so much; he must be feeling the same," Baba said.

"I hope so," I said.

Maman burst into tears and said, "It was three years ago, around this time, when he left."

"Yes, three years," Baba said, tears streaming down his face.

It shook me up to see them, particularly Baba, crying. I started crying too.

Finally Baba said, "We should be grateful that he's alive."

We wiped our faces with tissues from a box conveniently sitting on a side table as if ready for such tears.

"It's a relief to know he's out of the army," Maman said.

Baba said to me, "Let's have dinner out, I want you to see Little Tehran. It's just a few blocks from here, we can walk there."

In the elevator, then the lobby, almost everyone was talking in Farsi, and almost everyone knew my parents. They said their salaams and Baba introduced me to them.

"The Sagaamis are away on vacation in Ireland, otherwise they'd love to see you again," Baba said as we stepped out onto the street.

"They've been wonderful to us, helped us settle when we first came. Mary and I have a group together—American Wives of Iranian Men."

"They complain about their bad Iranian husbands." Baba looked at me, and we smiled.

"We talk about Iranian things, our experiences in Iran," Maman said.

It was a mellow night with a pleasant breeze blowing through the tall palm trees. As we walked through the neighborhood called Little Tehran, I thought of Little London, the nickname for Masjid-e-Suleiman. It was the same kind of exaggerated comparison. True, Little Tehran was lined with Iranian restaurants and shops, but that was its only resemblance to Tehran from what I had seen of that city.

Baba paused by the Setareh Chelo Kebab Restaurant. "Here we are," he said.

As we walked in, the host, a middle aged Iranian man, came over to us and welcomed us in Farsi, "Khosh Amadid," he said.

"I brought my dear daughter, Nora," Baba said.

The host nodded his head and smiled, then said to me, "Ghabele shoma neest," this restaurant is beneath you. I returned his nod politely, and responded, "Ekhtiar dareen," it has great value. He led us to a table by the window.

The decor imitated that of restaurants in Iran. Copper and bronze pitchers, vases, and a large samovar were displayed on a table at the entrance. Tapestries of Iranian scenes—domes, gardens—hung on the walls. Here, too, as in my parents' building, a Christmas tree and a menorah stood in a corner.

A dignified looking man in a suit who reminded me of the Colonel came over to our table and greeted Baba and Maman.

"What a nice surprise, sit down with us," Baba invited him.

"I have to go to the airport; I'm leaving for London to see my fiancée. Haven't met her yet, all arranged by my brother."

After the man left I asked Baba, "Are you still in touch with the Colonel?"

"I talk to him on the phone and he came for a visit once. He's still setting one clock on Iran time, ready to jump on the plane and go back. It's lonely for him here." Then looking at me intently he said, "What about you Nora, don't you feel lonely all on your own?"

"I'm always busy, don't have time to be lonely."

"You should move here, there are so many young Iranian men who'd love to have you as their wife. A blonde Iranian."

"You're talking like the old days," I said, forcing on a smile. "I'm not their idea of an Iranian woman."

"What are you then?"

"I wish I knew."

He patted my back. "It isn't easy to know who we are. I still don't know who I am."

A waiter came over to arrange our dinner, which Baba had ordered ahead for all of us: *barg kebabs, joojeh kebabs, koofte kebabs,* white fish, saffron rice, yogurt and cucumber and chopped salad.

After the waiter left Baba said to me, "How can you be happy pursuing law? It's a man's field. And Jahan, the artist. Everything is upside down in our family."

"Cyrus, that's nonsense," Maman said in an affectionate tone. "Many women are lawyers and most famous artists in history are men."

"But are those women happy? And most artists don't make it in the public eye. The majority of them are doomed to poverty and all sorts of self-doubts," he said. "Of course, it gives me pleasure to look at what Jahan created, to have his paintings to fill our apartment with life."

"Baba, I love law. And not every artist is doomed to poverty."

"Right now let's all be happy that Jahan is safe," Maman said.

Baba put his hand on hers and said, "I couldn't agree with you more."

# 30

Outside, Baba suggested we go to Persian Nights, so we started walking there, passing the many cinemas near the nightclub. I recalled how magical American movies had been for me, how they used to excite an aching yearning in me to be in America. And now here I was, still full of unfulfilled longings, longings intensified by the conversations about Jahan. I thought of how the mere sight of him used to brighten my gray days, how being with him made me feel paradoxically both free and protected.

"Doesn't L.A. remind you of Masjid-e-Suleiman?" Baba asked.

"Only the palm trees," I said.

"I guess I'm still a bit homesick. When we first moved here I thought maybe Jahan would have been happier if we had come to L.A. instead of Long Island. There are so many Iranian families here."

As soon as we took our seats at the nightclub, the performance started. A man wearing a mullah's costume came onto the platform and started parodying Khomeini. He was followed by another man in a suit and a wig with a pompadour who played President Reagan. After a break, a singer sang popular Iranian songs. The audience, mostly Iranians or Americans married to Iranians, applauded and cheered.

In the morning, after breakfast, we opened our presents. I gave Maman a silver bracelet and matching earrings, and Baba a leather belt and a leather wallet that I had bought at a street fair in Port Jefferson. They gave me a blue cashmere sweater and matching hat and gloves.

"I have something to show you," Baba said to me. He went to his study and came back holding a sheet of paper. He handed it to me. "It's to Jahan."

There was a poem on it in Baba's own curlicued handwriting.

> You heard a voice, sharp and clear,
> calling you, a voice more powerful than mine.
> Only *you* know what that voice said.
> It moved you to leave us,
> disregarding how shaken we would be.
> You knew you had to leave.

"Oh, Baba, it's beautiful," I said, deeply moved.

"Iran is the home of poets. The land's very scent is poetry," Baba said.

Maman got up. "I have a couple of hours of volunteer work to do at Catholic Charities," she said as she grabbed her purse.

"I have to go too," Baba said. "But there's a lot you could do on your own in L.A. See Hollywood first-hand."

He gave me a key. I left soon after they did and walked around the surprisingly seedy streets of Hollywood. Then I came out onto a street with fancy shops owned by Iranians who had been rich to begin with and had multiplied their fortunes here.

On my last morning, Maman and I were alone, Baba having gone out on an errand. She was restless, jittery. She walked around the apartment, watering the plants with a long-necked copper can, straightening the cushions on the sofa, the edge of the rug on the floor. When she finally sat down she said, "Why isn't Jahan writing to us, his mother and his father, and to you who were so close to him? I don't understand. Didn't we love him enough?"

It was the unanswerable question, always on our minds. "I wish I knew," I said, looking at the photograph of Jahan and myself on a side table.

"He sent those few notes at the beginning and then nothing. You know, Nora, it occurred to me that he might have found his biological mother and then just abandoned us. Still, why wouldn't he be in touch with you?"

"The same thoughts go through my mind all the time."

Baba walked in. "We have to leave for the airport. Are you ready Nora?"

I kissed Maman goodbye and left with Baba. It seemed too brief a visit.

The traffic was heavy, but we had left early enough to allow for that. As we crawled through cars and trucks, I said, "Baba, L.A. seems so right for you and Maman. I'm glad. Your marriage always amazes me, you had to get through tough times."

"I must admit, at the beginning of our marriage, we went through a hard period of adjustment. You know, no one in my family had ever married a foreigner; it wasn't easy then, particularly for Moira. And then there was that adoption. . . very hard indeed." He sighed. "Ancient history now, of course."

A car honked at us, Baba had slowed down too much. He speeded up. "We're never one person," he continued distractedly, trying to pass a car, "And every life has its dark places . . . "

What was he trying to say? Was he talking in code, hoping I'd encourage him to tell me more? But it was always hard to ask him direct questions. At the airport, he couldn't find a place to park, so he had to drop me off at the terminal door.

It was August of 1988, and finally a cease-fire between Iran and Iraq was put into effect. The war had been a devastating human tragedy. More than a million people on both sides were killed, and millions more were wounded and made refugees. Both the secular Saddam Hussein and the theocrat Khomeini ruthlessly sacrificed their people while America, along with other Western nations, provided weapons to both sides for the sake of oil and military advantage in the Gulf. And now it was over at last. After intense negotiations between the Secretary-General and two foreign ministers, U.N. Resolution 598 was accepted by both Iran and Iraq.

When I heard the news that the war was finally over I felt such a rush of relief and happiness that it was as if something deeply personal had occurred and I had to share it with someone who understood it. I called my parents.

"All of us here are ecstatic," Baba said.

In a few days he called back and said, "Your mother and I are still on the blacklist. I was hoping that the end of war would bring changes and we could go there for a visit. I'm longing to see my brothers, to look for Jahan."

"But there was only that Norooz card," I said. "It would be hard to find him even if you could get into the country." Then I felt a stab of pain, thinking, as I had at other times in my dark moments: what if he was killed?

"Just looking for him myself would make me feel better." Baba's tone became upbeat suddenly as he added, "My dear, he's alive. I know that because the man at the Interest Section said to me that my son and daughter weren't on the blacklist. I opened my heart to the man, asked him if he knew my son's whereabouts in Iran. He sympathized with me. He told me all he knew, that Jahan's name was on the list of men who had survived and that he was still living in Iran."

"Oh, Baba, how wonderful to be certain of that," I said, my black thought evaporating.

"He didn't tell me anything else. He assured me he would have if he knew more."

The two of us talked for a while longer, elated, and speculating about Jahan, why he hadn't contacted us, where exactly he might be.

After we got off the phone I sang to myself, Jahan is alive, Jahan is alive. I was all stirred up. Then a thought formed in my mind: you aren't on the blacklist, you can go there and find him. I had come to believe that my painful, desperate parting from Jahan was responsible for the subsequent failures of my relationships with men. It was as if I had a bleeding wound that could be healed only if we reconnected, settled things. Just making the effort to find him would help. I had met a man I really liked and was hoping the relationship would work this time. His name was James Wakefield.

There was some risk in my going to Iran. It was chaotic, and resentment against the American government lingered on. But I knew I had to go. This was the time to do it. I was going to have ten days off in late October, between two jobs. After graduating from law school I had started working as an assistant in a small practice in Long Island; on November first I would be starting a new job in a larger firm in Manhattan and moving there, where James already lived.

Having dinner with James in a Manhattan restaurant near his apartment, I told him my plan.

"I think you should do it, absolutely; even if you don't find him you'll feel good about having tried."

"I think so too, but truthfully the odds of finding him are remote, particularly in such a short time I'll be there. I do have a plan. I'll go to the orphanage where he was adopted and see if he's been there to look for his mother. Someone there might have a lead."

"Sounds reasonable."

"Are you sure it will be all right with you, to go away without you in my time off?" Against my will, I found myself feeling anxious about his expectations of me.

"Nora, don't worry about me, you'll have other times off and we'll plan vacations together. Anyway we'll have to get used to stretches of separation like this. My job involves a lot of traveling."

It was liberating to be with a man who gave me support and freedom. It felt miraculous after what I experienced with other men. We loved talking together, exchanging ideas about travel, theater, movies, and books.

"If it weren't for my schedule just now I'd go with you," James was saying in his enthusiastic way. "Great material for a film. You can scout out the terrain for me, and I expect a full report of details when you get back!"

"You'd absolutely love the terrain and the architecture, and the history is so rich," I said, echoing his excitement, "But I'm not sure

Iran would be the most welcoming place for your next film, at least not now. In fact I'm not even sure Iran will be ready for my little visit."

He leaned closer, put his hand on mine, and smiled. "Don't worry so much. It'll be a great adventure. You'll do just fine."

I held his hand, felt his confidence and affection.

James was from England, and he was going to business school at night so that he could have something practical to fall back on while he pursued his real passion, directing films. He had made a documentary on Paul Bowles, the American writer who lived in Morocco. The movie was actually released internationally and he was starting a new project.

Almost immediately after that conversation I began to prepare. I called the Interest Section and confirmed that indeed I wasn't on a blacklist, so I sent on my American passport along with photographs and the required forms. In a few weeks they sent it back along with an Iranian passport (given to me because my father was Iranian born) stamped with a month's visiting visa.

They told me what to do. I wasn't to show my American passport in Iran, only the Iranian one. Even though having two passports was accepted by the United States, it wasn't by Iran. I'd show my Iranian passport entering and leaving Iran, my American passport leaving and entering America. They assured me that so far there had been no reports of arrests or anyone being detained traveling that way. As long as I followed the rules and didn't say anything provocative I would be safe. I had to follow the *hejab*, which meant wearing a long-sleeved, long-skirted garment, or a raincoat, tights opaque enough not to show any leg skin, and a headscarf (an alternative was the *chador*, which covered everything). Also no colorful fabrics — red, orange or purple — no nail polish, no make-up. If I took any books or magazines with me I should make sure there were no photos in them of women with hair or skin showing, no books with titles that sounded political.

Only after I had made all the arrangements did I let my parents know I was going to Iran. I was afraid they'd discourage me. When I told them, they were concerned that I could get into trouble there. Even though I wasn't on that frightening blacklist, I looked American, was an American citizen. They might find out that I had two passports. When I told them that my mind was made up, they urged me to call the uncles as soon as I arrived. I had to explain I that was going straight to Shiraz, that the uncles and aunts wouldn't like my traveling alone and would try to keep me with them in Tehran. Baba's last words to me were, "Nora, you're a grown woman now, living far away from us. I can't always tell you what to do." There was puzzlement, chagrin and regret all mingled in his voice. Then he gave me his brothers' phone numbers, in case I needed them.

# 31

When the day of my departure arrived, James took me to the airport. I boarded a KLM flight to Amsterdam, and then connected with Iran Air to Tehran. From there, another, smaller plane would take me to Shiraz.

Almost all the Iran Air passengers were Iranians. No alcohol was served. The programs on the screens were in Farsi, mostly Iranian propaganda newsreels. But all around me the passengers were talking excitedly about the fact that the war was finally over.

"I thought I'd never see Iran, my neighborhood again," the young woman sitting next to me said.

"My town was completely demolished," I told her. "I grew up in Masjid-e-Suleiman."

"That's very sad, I'm so sorry," she said.

"With reconstruction about to start, Iran is the best place to look for jobs," the young man sitting in front of us was saying to the man next to him.

"The officials are arbitrary there. Don't be surprised if you run into trouble," the other man said.

Restlessly I got up, went to the back and asked the stewardess for a glass of orange juice.

"Are you American?" she asked.

"Half and half."

"It's going to be hard for you in Iran," she warned. "No sources of entertainment. All somber and gray."

The flight attendant was announcing, "Please buckle your seat belts, we are landing in Mehrabad Airport. And cover up please." I went back to my seat and put on my headscarf and raincoat.

As we descended the lights of Tehran appeared in patches. On the tarmac we boarded a bus. A foreign woman wasn't wearing anything on her head. An armed, bearded guard in a green uniform, who was standing by the front door of the bus, came over to her and said, "*Khanoom*, you must follow the *hejab* in our country."

"I'm not a Muslim," she said in broken Farsi mixed with French words.

"While you're in our country you must follow our custom."

An Iranian woman standing next to her took out a headscarf from her handbag and gave it to her. "You can have this, I brought many with me."

The French woman thanked her, and looking dismayed, put it on.

After we got off the bus I followed the crowd into the cavernous lounge and joined a passport checking line. I had a two-hour wait before my connecting flight to Shiraz. Framed calligraphic writing, quotations from the Koran, "In the Name of Allah, The Beneficent, The Merciful," hung on the walls. Next to them stood several framed photographs of Khomeini, his stern face watching over everyone. Armed guards, all with beards and wearing green fatigues, were standing around the terminal; others were sitting in booths, checking passports. They scrutinized the photographs on the passports, and then looked at the faces of the people they belonged to, and then at a list on sheets of paper spread in front of them.

After my passport was checked I joined another line for passports to be checked again. This was repeated five times. When I reached the last booth, the officer looked at my passport, then my face, then his list and said, "Step aside please."

"Can I have my passport back?" I asked in a panic, already unnerved from so much close scrutiny.

"We'll give it to you after we clear your name."

A man standing next to the booth stepped forward. "Come with me." We went to a room at the back. "Wait here, Jalal Goodarzi will be in soon."

"What's this all about?" I had been speaking Farsi on the plane, but now in my sudden nervousness I was having a hard time pronouncing the words right.

"If you haven't done anything wrong you don't need to be afraid," the man said. He walked through the door and shut it behind him.

The room was windowless and bare except for a desk, a few chairs and more portraits of Khomeini on the wall. I sat on a chair and kept looking at my watch. I had only one hour left until my next flight, at four-thirty A.M. How long was I going to be kept here? Every moment was awash with fear. What if I get stuck here? What about my new job? No one at Friedman and Casey was going to be sympathetic. There was no American Embassy in Iran to seek help from. All the law I had learned wouldn't help me here.

Finally a man came in and shut the door behind him. He was almost indistinguishable from the other guards—young, bearded, in uniform—only he didn't have a gun. Instead, he was holding a briefcase. He put it down and sat on a chair across from me.

"*Khanoom*, you shouldn't have come to Iran. Your parents are on our list. They escaped illegally."

"But I was told. . ."

"They say anything they want on the other side, don't you know," he said, not harshly but with clear admonishment in his tone.

"It wasn't my fault if they misled me," I said, trying to keep my voice calm.

"We'll have to check into your record thoroughly." He was firmer, almost threatening now.

Did he expect a bribe? But then, if he didn't, offering him one could get me into more trouble. I wasn't sure what to do so I didn't do anything.

It seemed like an eternity before he asked, "Why are you in Iran?"

"To see my brother."

He took out a folder from his briefcase and looked inside it. "Jahan Ellahi is your brother?"

I gave a start at his knowledge of Jahan's name and his being my brother. "Yes," I said hesitantly, not knowing what to expect.

"He served in the army," he said with a touch of admiration.

"My parents and I lost track, I'm here to search for him."

"You came here all alone?"

"I have family in Tehran. Please give me his address. We had a Norooz card from him, postmarked in Shiraz, but no address."

"After a soldier is discharged he's on his own."

What could I say that would please this man? "My brother loves Iran; he doesn't go back to America, even for visits."

He shook his head slowly, pensively, seemed undecided what to say or do. But then abruptly he reached into his briefcase again, took out my passport, and gave it to me.

I felt a surge of relief. I must have said the right thing. "Thank you," I said, breathlessly, putting the passport into my pocketbook, out of his sight.

"You're lucky it's me here today." He got up and led me out of the room.

Indeed things were arbitrary here, maybe even more than they had been before the Islamic Revolution. It struck me that coming here was sheer insanity.

I went to the baggage claim and looked for my suitcase. My hand was shaky as I reached for my single suitcase that was going around and around the carousel. I picked it up and went to information to find out about the next flight to Shiraz.

The clerk said, "At four-thirty A.M. Tomorrow. Only once a day."

"Do I get reimbursed for the one I missed?"

"It isn't up to me. You have to go to the central office."

It sounded like it would take hours. "Is there any other way to get to Shiraz today?"

"The train. The next one leaves in an hour and a half. Any taxi outside will take you there."

"Thank you." I went to the customs area. I was the only one left.

The man checking said, "Go ahead," without making me open my suitcase. Neither did he search my purse. I felt another surge of relief—I had hidden my American passport in the lining. I had opened the stitches, put the passport in, and then sewn it back.

Outside, I noticed signs on two doors behind me, one saying, For Men, and the other, For Women, segregating the sexes at the entrance to the airport. Another arbitrary rule; on Iran Air and the airport bus men and women hadn't been separated.

I got into a taxi. The driver, a thin young man, raced through the heavy early morning Tehran traffic, zigzagging, honking. The city looked bleak. Even though the war had been mainly fought in the southwestern cities, some damage had been done to Tehran too. The shattered windows and partially wrecked buildings were painful to see.

In many places walls were painted with slogans: "Women Follow Hejab," "Those who Gave their Lives to Fight the Enemy are Now in Heaven," "Death to America," "Death to the English." It reminded me of our last days in Iran.

The driver, looking at me in the mirror, asked, "Where are you coming from?"

"America. But I grew up in Masjid-e-Suleiman. It's heartbreaking to come here and see all the damage."

"Yes, as a nation it's our fate to live with tragedy. My cousins are lucky to live in America." He turned on the car radio and to my surprise a Stevie Wonder song came on. The driver said, "We have a few minutes of foreign music every day."

We entered a street lined by sycamore trees and *joobs* running alongside the sidewalks. At the end of the street was a wide-open area with the train station and tracks beyond it. By the station the driver got out and helped me with my suitcase. "Good trip," he said in English.

I bought my ticket, ran to the train, which was about to leave, and boarded. The passengers weren't segregated. I went into a half-empty compartment and took a seat next to the window. I stared outside at the vast arid land, brown and red with a few patches of green here and there. Then I fell asleep from stress, more than the exhaustion of the long trip.

I was awakened by the voice of a man standing by the compartment door with a cart full of sandwiches, Iranian cola drinks and *doogh.* "The dining car is under repair," he said. I bought a lemon chicken sandwich and a bottle of *doogh.* The three other passengers in the compartment also bought food and drinks. Then they started talking, making negative remarks about America.

"First they put Iraq on their terrorist list, then they turn around and provide them with arms. Just as we had them on the run."

"All America wants is our oil and they'll do anything to get it."

I felt conflicts welling up inside me, and couldn't bring myself to participate in the conversation.

A man in a soldier's uniform sitting across from me looked at me and asked, "Do you come from America?"

I nodded.

"I thought so. I don't like the American government but I love the people. I want to immigrate to America. What's the best way?"

The husband of the couple sitting next to the soldier answered for me. "I have a brother in Texas. He says the easiest way is to find an American woman to marry."

The man with the cart came back, picked up our trash, and left.

"Did you ever meet Jahan Ellahi?" I asked the soldier. "He's my brother."

"If I did, I don't remember. I lost most of my memory. I'm just beginning to remember a little, bit by bit."

"I did some work in Abadan, helping out with soldiers' needs," the other man said. "I didn't meet anyone by that name."

"It's a few years since he was discharged," I said.

"There are things you can never forget. Fountains of blood spouting out of the ground. Legs and arms sticking out of piles of debris," the soldier said, staring into space. "Screams from under the wreck-age, smell of burning flesh."

"Such a terrible tragedy," I managed to say through constricted throat.

Then we stopped talking, everyone overcome by sadness. I turned to the window again. We passed through a town with a stretch of prefabricated houses and then mud-brick hovels. The train hooted as it went through a tunnel.

There was a long delay, and we didn't get to Shiraz until past midnight.

# 32

Outside the station, kiosks selling food and drink were still open, their lights on, and there were many taxis waiting. I took one to a hotel that Maman had recommended after she and Baba couldn't talk me out of going to Iran.

This driver wasn't talkative. He turned on the radio immediately; this time Iranian music came on. A male singer sang in Farsi:

> In the fields we chanted our love
> It was night and a jagged moon was watching us
> and we were still chanting our love.

I thought of the days when my heart had been so full of intense adolescent love for Jahan, the overpowering emotions as we stood under the sycamore tree and kissed. No other man had ever evoked that intensity of desire in me again.

We passed under a large arch with a gigantic illuminated Koran on top of it, and then we were in the center of the city. Here too there were some reminders of war, even though, like Tehran, it hadn't been a direct target. The buildings and houses, modern and traditional standing side by side, were undamaged, but in a park a few sleepless soldiers were sitting on a bench with crutches at their sides. Black flags were draped on the doors of some houses to designate that young men once residing there had been martyred in the war.

Finally the taxi stopped in front of Hotel Sahar, a three-story structure with balconies extending from some of the rooms. Two tall columns flanked the entrance door. The driver helped me inside. Part of the lobby was closed off to be repaired, it seemed, but it was pleasant enough, with a marble floor and pottery and ceramic figures placed here and there. Several foreign-looking men and women were sitting on a sofa, the women wearing the mandatory headscarves and long-sleeved raincoats. Then I told the clerk behind the counter that I had a reservation for the previous night but had been delayed.

He looked in his book. "We gave your room away. But we have another one, although it's a little smaller."

"I'll take it."

He called to a porter who came over and picked up my suitcase. I followed him to my room on the second floor, amazed and pleased that no questions were asked of me, a woman traveling alone. It seemed like a place where tourists stayed, judging by the foreigners in the lobby.

The room was indeed small but it had two windows, one overlooking the street and another, a garden with a fountain. It was simply furnished with modern bed and chair. *Kilims* on the floor and tapestries on the walls provided some color. After unpacking, I took a shower; the bathroom walls and floor were tiled in blue and rust. Before I went to bed I thought I'd call my parents and James to tell them I'd arrived safely. The international lines rang busy for a long time and I finally had to give up. I lay in bed a while, then turned off the lights and escaped into a deep, dark sleep.

I was awakened a few hours later by the voice of the muezzin calling people to prayers.

Allah O Akbar. You pious people stop everything now and pray. Your prayers open the gates of heaven.

Vendors were already on the street, hawking their merchandise, "Sweetest pomegranates, the best raspberries, the freshest chives."

I dressed and went into the hotel dining room for breakfast. A group of Japanese men sat at one table. Other tables were occupied by families and a few single women who looked European but were observing the *hejab* as I was.

After breakfast I asked the clerk for a phone directory to see if Jahan might be listed in it now, though he hadn't been when Jamshid had tried to track him down. "The new directory hasn't been distributed yet," the clerk said. "The wretched war has slowed everything down." He called information for me, but didn't come up with anything.

"Do you know where Bacheh Khaneh orphanage is?"

"Yes, *khanoom*." He looked at me quizzically and then said in a sympathetic voice, "So many orphans, worse now due to the war." He picked up a brochure and turned the pages to a map of the city. He pointed to a street. "You can walk there, it isn't that far."

I could see it was just on the other side of the arch with the Koran sculpture. I took the brochure and left the hotel. The city, lying in a green valley surrounded by high mountains, had a temperate climate and it was pleasantly cool on that October morning. It held historic monuments, tombs of poets, philosophers and kings, and was famous for its orchards, orangeries, and roses. Five miles of rose gardens lined the wide, shady avenue that led from one end of the city all the way to the other. Birds floated like pieces of paper against the vast blue-gold sky. "The city of nightingales and roses," a poet had been moved to call Shiraz long ago.

Vendors were washing down the pavement in front of their stores; some were inside arranging items for sale. People walked about in an unhurried way. I passed under the arch and entered a more run-down, grimy street, with houses made of rough bricks stacked irregularly, the second floors leaning precariously.

Then I came across a mosque, with the name Jamei written on a blue mosaic tile above the entrance door. This was it, the mosque mentioned in the adoption documents; it was on the steps of this mosque that Jahan's mother had left him. I stopped in front and stared at it.

On the same block stood Bacheh Khaneh orphanage, which consisted of an old, large, rambling, one-level structure that at one time must have been a caravansary, where travelers would stop for a night or two to rest on the way to another city. On one side of the structure was a clothing factory with the doors wide open. Inside, in a vast room, young girls and boys were sitting at a long, low table, sewing. Fluffy strands of cotton were scattered through tree branches in the courtyard. On the other side of the factory stood a dingy apartment building, all the units with identical, small windows. A man and then a woman went into the building, both holding long oval loaves of *sangag* bread with little stones, on which they were cooked, still clinging to them.

Finally I knocked on the orphanage door. In a few moments a plain-looking woman in beige, with a beige kerchief on her head, opened the door halfway. "Salam Alaikum. Please, how can I help you?"

"*Bebakhsheen*, pardon me for bothering you, I would like some information. May I speak to you inside?"

"Come in," she said. After looking me over, she opened the door all the way and I joined her in the hallway. She paused there, waiting for me to explain.

"My brother was adopted from this orphanage many years ago by my parents," I stammered. "He's twenty-eight years old now. His name is Jahan Ellahi—Ellahi is our father's last name. He left our home in America and came to Iran. Did he by chance come here?"

She said flatly, "I don't know."

"Is there anyone who can tell me? I've come all the way from America, hoping to find him. We lost track of him once he left home. My coming here is just a stab in the dark."

"Was he in the army? I'm sorry to say many young men were martyred."

"Yes, he served, but we had a card from him postmarked Shiraz, unfortunately with no return address. And then we were told by an official that he wasn't killed. I was hoping that he came here to ask about his birth mother and that you would know where he is."

She warmed up a little. "I'll see if the head mother's available. She might know something." She led me into the courtyard and then to a room on the other side of it. Frogs were jumping around a wet, muddy area next to a small pool. On a rope tied to two trees hung little children's clothes, overalls, dresses, and underwear. In a corner were a rocking horse, two swings, a sandbox. From inside of a row of rooms on one side of the courtyard, I heard children's voices, and through an open door I could see cribs, about twenty, with babies lying in them. Through another I saw several older children, all girls, eating at a table in the middle of the room. They all looked up at me, smiling, frowning, or just staring. Jahan had been lucky to be adopted. What was the destiny of these children, I wondered, that chill coming over me again.

"Boys are adopted quickly, girls remain here for a long time," the woman said as if reading my thoughts. She led me into a small, unadorned room. "Wait here, I'll go and speak to the Mother." I sat on a bench in the room to wait. Some children came into the courtyard and began to play in the sandbox. Then a very old, wrinkled woman, also wearing beige clothes, came in. She introduced herself and after shutting the doors, sat next to me. She said promptly, "So you're here to find something about your brother?"

"Yes," I said.

"He was here, *khanoom*," she said.

"So he came here! I hoped so much that would be the case."

"But I have no idea where he is now." She reached over and held one of my hands in hers, as if to soften the blow.

"Where's his birth mother now? Is she alive?" I asked breathlessly.

She shook her head. "Even if I did know, I'm not allowed to give out that information."

"But I must find my brother. I've come a long way."

"I'm sorry, *khanoom*." She squeezed my hand gently and then let it go.

"Can't you help me find him?"

"If I could help I certainly would," she said.

"It's been so hard for us. My parents are devastated."

"I'm only allowed to provide information to a grown child looking for a biological parent. That's our policy here, I'm sure you can understand."

The younger woman came in with a tray that held two glasses of tea, spoons, and a bowl of rock sugar. She put it on the low table in front of the bench and left. "Have some tea," the Mother said. She put a few pieces of rock sugar in one of the glasses, stirred the tea with a spoon, and began to drink it slowly, lost in her own thoughts.

I took mine black. After a few sips I tried another approach, "My brother came to Iran even though the war was still going on. He wanted to be here so much, he was willing to risk his life."

"Wasn't he happy with his—with your—parents?"

"He missed Iran, and he wanted to find his mother."

"In all these years I've seen so many children, each of them a special child, but I still remember your brother. He was a wonderful baby, so sweet natured. Many couples wanted to adopt him."

"Can't you make an exception and tell me where I can find him?" I asked, still hoping she knew and I could persuade her to lead me to him. "Our circumstances are so unusual."

Instead of answering, she said in a soft voice, "Mothers are so sad when they give up their children."

I kept pleading, but when it was clear she wouldn't give me any more information, I put down my glass and got up to leave. She followed me to the door, laid her hand on my back, and said, "If you're in Shiraz for a few days maybe you'll come across him."

"So he is in Shiraz?" I momentarily came out of the despair I was feeling.

"It's up to Allah to lead you to him," she said. "Allah is merciful."

The courtyard was now quiet and empty. Then two older girls came out of a room and ran over to me.

One of them pleaded, "Take me with you,"

The other looked at me silently, with yearning. Then she held up a plastic doll and said, "This is my doll."

The young woman who had opened the outside door to me came out of a room and walked quickly over to us. Taking the two girls' hands, she led them back inside. I had a wild impulse to run after her and say, "Let me take them with me." Maybe I would come back one day and take a child from here. The thought momentarily comforted me.

All the way to the city center my mind was filled with images of Jahan in that orphanage. His mother would have known that people went into the mosque at all hours. Vivid images passed before my eyes of the mother holding her baby, putting him on the steps of that very mosque. She would have seen someone coming, a man intent on late prayers. He sees the child, picks him up and takes him inside while the mother waits. He comes out a little later and carries the bundle to the orphanage. The mother waits again until he comes out, alone. Every day from then on she lives with the pain of knowing how impossible it is to raise a child born out of wedlock.

# 33

I didn't know what to do next. My hope of finding Jahan through the orphanage was already shattered. I was grateful to the Mother for telling me that I might come across him in Shiraz, but Shiraz wasn't a small town. There were close to a million people here. It was sheer chance that I'd run into him.

Uncertain what to do next, I decided to visit the tombs of the revered thirteenth and fourteenth century poets, Sa'adi and Hafiz, remembering how much Jahan loved them and how their poems had been part of our lives together. They were both natives of Shiraz and buried there. I went to the northeast section of the city and easily found Sa'adi's mausoleum. On the gate leading into the garden surrounding the burial chamber was inscribed:

> The tomb of Sa'adi of Shiraz will carry the scent of love
> Even a thousand years after his death.

A gravel walk led to a portico supported by tall columns of pinkish marble, a traditional Persian architectural feature. Steps led up to a delicately carved tombstone with a turquoise-blue dome. People had surrounded the tomb and, in homage, each of them gently touched the stone walls with two fingers.

I walked on to Hafiz's mausoleum, a short distance away. Again I went through a lovely garden and I climbed a flight of stone steps with a double colonnade at the top. Crossing it I reached the alabaster tomb under a tiled cupola, which looked like a dervish's hat. The cupola was lined inside with wonderful earthenware faience. Here too, many visitors had gathered by the tomb, reading and reciting to each other. I stopped, listening to the murmur of

Hafiz's words while breathing in the soft scent of the garden. I recalled Baba's poem at Christmas, hearing his proud voice saying Iran's "very scent is poetry." With the next breath, a felt a knot in my throat and tears swam in my eyes. I suddenly missed everyone back home, and Jahan more than ever. I even felt a nostalgic longing for Iran itself.

On the other side of the garden, I entered a teahouse shaded by cypress and pine trees. I found a table and ordered tea. Foreign tourists and Iranians were occupying most of the other tables. Some of the men were smoking water pipes. A young boy went from table to table, selling postcards. I bought a few from him and he went on to another table. Hafiz's poems were written on one side of the cards; the other sides had floral or figurative pictures, all reminding me of the last Norooz in Iran when Jahan had recited Hafiz's verses to me. I spread the cards on the white and blue striped tablecloth and read the poems. One indeed seemed to be telling me something:

> I took the riddle into a tavern
> and asked the one who served.
> He said, "Some secrets must be kept,
> not told to the world at large."

I turned the cards over and looked at the pictures. "Panahi Printers" was written at the bottom of all the cards. I had seen that name before. I took out Jahan's Norooz card from an envelope in my pocket book. In small print at the bottom there it was: "Panahi Printers."

At last, something practical I could do. I'd go to the printers at once and find out if any of the employees knew Jahan. The muezzin was calling people to prayers and every shop would shut down for four or five hours, giving people enough time to pray, have lunch, take a nap. I decided to go back to the hotel, find the address of the printer, and go later when the shops opened up again at five.

Panahi Printers was tucked between several other shops on a wide avenue near the city center. It was a photography shop as well as a print shop, and displayed posters on the walls and a variety of frames on shelves. A young man was standing behind the counter. "May I help you?" he asked.

I showed him the Norooz card. "Was this done here?"

He took it and looked at it. "Maybe."

"Do you remember the man who ordered the cards? Jahan, his name, is signed next to the painting. He has curly hair, light brown eyes."

The man smiled. "That fits the description of many of my clients. I know a Jahan Bagi."

"That must be him," I said. Bagi could be his mother's last name, I thought. If he had found her he could have adopted her last name. "Can I have his phone number or address," I asked.

He looked through an index box. "No phone number, just an address. I don't know if he'd want me to give it out."

I didn't know whether I should tell this man I was Jahan's sister. Maybe Jahan didn't want anyone to know about his other life with us. I wasn't here to cause problems for him. I said, "I can get it from information, can't I?"

After studying my face, he said, "I'll give it to you." He wrote the address on a slip of paper he tore off from a pad and gave it to me. "It's about ten blocks from here." He gave me directions.

In a few moments I found myself in a maze of intertwined, nameless lanes and dead ends. Two women in headscarves were leaning out their windows in houses on either side of a street, talking to each other. I asked if they knew where Nejabi Lane was. Neither knew.

A little further, several vendors were sitting against a wall, drinking tea and chatting. They'd arranged their goods on cloths spread on the ground before them—silver rings, belts, and handbags. I asked directions from one of them, an old man in a felt hat. He directed me with elaborate hand gestures.

Finally I was on Nejabi Lane but there were no numbers on the houses. A man with a long white beard was sitting against the wall passing a rosary between his fingers and murmuring prayers.

"Can you tell me where number twenty-five is?"

He pointed to a door. I knocked but there was no answer. I knocked again. This time a little boy opened the door.

"Is Jahan Bagi here?"

"Who?"

"Who is it?" a woman called from the inside.

"Mother, come here," the boy called.

The woman wearing a *chador* came to the door. "What can I do for you, *khanoom?*" Her eyes were the exact shade of brown as Jahan's. She could be his mother.

"I'm looking for Jahan Bagi."

"I don't know anyone by that name, *khanoom.*"

"I have this address for him."

"*Khanoom joon*, I'm sorry but we just moved into this house."

"Do you know any Jahans?"

"Only my cousin. I hope you'll find your Jahan," she said in a kindly tone, then shut the door.

As I tried to find my way back to the wider avenue I kept wondering what I should do next. At this point finding Jahan seemed like a futile hope; he could be around the corner from me but utterly out of reach. I could go back home earlier than I'd planned, or I could explore more. I longed to go to Masjid-e-Suleiman, to see Golpar again. After all these years I still missed her; we'd been cut off so abruptly. Maman had written to her but never got any response. I had to remind myself that nothing was left of that city; even the roads to it were demolished. These thoughts only added to my state of despair.

I came across the shrine of the eighth-century saint, Shah-e-Cheragh, the brother of Imam Reza, one of the twelve Shiite Imams. Shah-e-Cheragh had been martyred in Shiraz and buried here. I decided to go in, suddenly remembering that Jahan had told me this saint's name meant the king of the lamp. In the shrine garden pilgrims were relaxing under broad shade trees. Beyond the walls the arid hills were visible. Before entering the shrine, I took my shoes off and gave them to a bearded man who put them in one of the cubicles on the wall behind him. Inside, a mosaic of tiny mirrors covering the walls reflected the ceiling light. A pair of silver doors led to a raised tomb surrounded by women devotees pushing each other to get near it, as if in a frenzy of love for the long dead saint. Their reflections were broken into bits by the mirrors. It was hallucinatory, like being inside a kaleidoscope.

Later in the garden I noticed a vendor grilling skewers of lamb on a charcoal brazier on the ground. I bought a skewer and a bottle of *doogh* and sat on a bench to eat. I looked at young men passing by, hoping against hope to see Jahan among them.

Finally I went back to the hotel; just outside the door two little girls were sitting and playing with rag dolls, throwing them into the air and catching them, then rocking them in their arms. "She's teething, that's why she cries all the time," one of them was saying. The other said, "She had a bit of fever but now she's well." They seemed aware only of each other and their fantasy world. In the lobby a group of Japanese men and women were watching an English language channel on satellite TV. They were also holding drinks that looked and smelled alcoholic. The hotel management must be bribing the police.

> Iran has borrowed close to ten billion dollars in foreign financial markets to pay for reconstruction. The money has come from Britain, France, Germany, Italy, Japan, and the World Bank. The U.S. government vigorously opposed the loan and furthermore has renewed the economic sanctions that began after the American Embassy was taken in Tehran. Iran, once the second largest producer of OPEC oil, is still in need of oil itself until war damage to oil fields and refineries can be repaired.

How sad that Iran and America couldn't reconcile. My two countries — would they always be at war?

In my room, feeling cut off and lonely, I reached for the phone to see if I could get through to open international lines this time. But again I only got a busy signal and then a recorded male voice announcing, "Due to war damage, access to international phone lines is limited."

Because I wasn't making any headway, I decided to try to call Uncle Jamshid after all. Lines within the country could be okay. Maybe Jahan had contacted him or Mohsen since Baba had last talked to Jamshid. I could arrange to see the relatives on the way back to America.

A woman answered the phone. "This is Nora Ellahi. Can I speak to Jamshid *agha* or Khadijeh *khanoom*?" I asked.

"*Khanoom*, they're away, all the family is in the north for a wedding. Didn't you know? I'm here to take care of the house."

"Who's getting married?"

"Mohsen *agha*, to a girl from the north. Ever since his wife passed away he's been despondent. The family urged him to get married again and now the day has come."

"When are they coming back?"

"They didn't say; they just left yesterday. Jamshid *agha* rented a van and took the whole family away in it."

"Thank you. I'll try to call again."

What would my life have been like if we had remained in Iran? Most likely I would be married to a man my parents found for me. Jahan would have married too. By now we both would have had children. Would we have separated in such a bitter way? Or would our intimacy have evolved into friendship more easily? There was no way to tell.

# 34

In the morning, having decided to stay on in Shiraz just a little longer, I thought about what I'd like to see. I'd always wanted to go to Persepolis, once the ceremonial capital of the ancient kings. When Jahan and I were ten and nine years old, during the Shah's celebration of the 2,500th anniversary of the Persian Empire, our imaginations were stirred by the lavish ceremonies. The Shah's extravagance, millions spent to show off Iran to foreign leaders and royalty, to remind the world of Iran's past grandeur, had angered Iranians who wished the money had gone into improving education, sanitation, and housing for the poor. But in our young minds it was an exciting event and had stimulated Jahan's fascination with ancient history.

Before going into the dining room, I picked up a local newspaper from a pile in a corner of the lobby and looked through it as I had breakfast.

> The aftermath of the bloody war that has depressed Iran's economy is brightened somewhat in Shiraz by the rose water industry and the increasing number of foreign tourists.

On another page my eyes caught an advertisement for a tour to Persepolis leaving from my hotel. Within an hour I had boarded the yellow Fars Tours bus, which picked up passengers on the larger avenue perpendicular to the hotel street.

The tour guide, a young man with a moustache, sat on a seat close to the driver. Most of the tourists were foreign, only a few were Iranian. A middle-aged Iranian woman with a lively manner, and wearing a brighter headscarf and raincoat than most Iranian women wore, sat next to me and introduced herself. As soon as I told her I was visiting from America, she began to ask me question after question. We talked and got acquainted as the guide made comments on significant sights we passed. He spoke in Farsi, though many of the passengers didn't know the language.

The woman said, "Once I dreamed of living in America. I was accepted at the University of Michigan but I ended up marrying and having children and never left Iran. What brings you here after all these years?"

"To look for my brother. He came here, served in the army, and now we have no address for him."

The woman became quiet, perhaps not wanting to suggest that he could have been killed. I told her about the card and the man at the Interest Section telling Baba Jahan was alive, and how I'd gone to the Panahi Printers and had been disappointed.

"But there are many Panahi Printers, at least six."

"Information only gave me one address."

"The rest are in the outskirts, not right in the city."

"How do I find them?" I asked, a ray of hope shining in front of me.

"Look in *Hameh Chee*." She reached into her overnight bag on the floor, pulled out a thick newspaper, and gave it to me. The bus stopped and the woman got up. "I'm getting off here. I'm not on the tour. Good luck. You can keep the paper." I looked through it.

> The Committee of Moral Enforcement has unanimously voted to keep women in veils . . . .
> A woman was stoned by villagers in Ardebil. She was caught in adultery.

Two women in black *chadors*, in the seats in front of me started talking. "He sleeps all day long, has no motivation to make money. I'm taking the children and going to live with my parents," one of them said.

The other said, "At least he hasn't taken a second wife." After a pause she added, "My poor daughter is miserable, her husband took a second wife."

The news and the conversation brought back Golpar's bitter talk. Suddenly I felt the same oppressiveness I used to feel in Iran and thought how amazing it was that I had managed to get out and live in America. As I turned the pages I came to a full-page ad for Panahi Printers. Seven locations, including the one I had gone to, were listed. I looked for the addresses on my city map. They were scattered in different directions. But I had the time; I would search for all of them.

Persepolis was only an hour from Shiraz, but the driver had gone very slowly and paused for comments. Now he stopped the bus and we got out at a restaurant for lunch. Two Iranian couples, the driver, and the guide, went to rooms in the back to pray. After we all ate, we boarded the bus and went straight to Persepolis. Remnants of palaces emerged from the plain against a high, jagged mountain. Flashes of original grandeur were captured in an intricate carving on a stone wall, in a pink marble floor, and a row of columns leading nowhere. And there, too, stood the remnants of giant winged bulls that Jahan had described to me when we were children.

The guide gave us two hours to explore the ruins on our own. I climbed the ceremonial stairway made of massive blocks of stone but shallow enough so that the most important guests of the kings could have ridden up on their horses. The immense structure—once the site of palaces, audience halls, stables, and a treasury—had taken 150 years to complete, before being destroyed by Alexander the Great. The ruins reminded me of the recent war, and I had a heavy feeling in my chest.

A young Iranian man with a European wife and two blond children asked me to take photographs of them with his camera. I had noticed he was talking to his wife in Farsi, correcting her when she mispronounced words. When Maman and Baba came to Shiraz to adopt Jahan they had been about this couple's age. They had visited this very spot, before going to get Jahan.

The following morning I thought of calling the printers first. Then I decided I would get better results if I went in person. I covered three of them in two days, taking taxis and buses and then walking part of the way. But no one was able to tell me anything about Jahan.

I was still determined to check out the other three. The next address was confusing. A wooden sign next to a stairway directed people up to a house above, which eight hundred years ago had been a poet-philosopher's residence. The landing above the stairs was a stopping place for visitors to the house and people were milling about. I thought I'd come to the wrong place, but on the landing I discovered a Panahi Printers between two other small shops. I went inside but no one seemed to be there. Prints of bold-eyed women in colorful village clothes adorned the walls. As I looked around for signs of life, a bearded man slowly emerged from the back and greeted me. I showed him the Norooz card and repeated the same questions.

"You know Jahan?" he asked, a little puzzled.

I had the same hesitation as before, telling this man who I was. "I saw the card in a friend's house. I want to look at more of the artist's work, perhaps buy something."

He surprised me by saying, "I have the original of that painting at home. I liked it so much that I bought it from Jahan."

This must be the right printer, the right Jahan, I thought, full of new hope. "Does he have a studio?"

"He works at home as far as I know. Sit down, I'll look for his address."

I sat in an armchair and he disappeared behind a curtain. He came back shortly holding a piece of paper. "I have this address," he said. But instead of giving it to me he said, "You don't look Iranian."

"My father is Iranian but my mother is American and I take after her."

He hesitated a little but then he gave me the piece of paper with the address under the name of Shirin Sohrabi. Could this be the one? I hardly dared hope.

"They don't have a phone. Phone lines haven't been set up in that part of the city yet," the man said.

Other customers drifted in. In return for the man's help I bought a small, framed print and left.

The address was just on this side of the arch, not far from the orphanage. Orangery Street was narrow and cobble-stoned with orange trees along the sidewalks. Number fifteen was written on a blue tile on the wall next to the thick wooden door of an old mud and straw house. I knocked and a woman opened the door.

"Is this Shirin Sohrabi's residence?" I asked.

"Yes."

"I'm Nora, Jahan's sister," I said, injecting confidence into my voice. "Is he in?"

She gave a start. "His sister?" My heart leapt in my chest.

"Yes, his sister Nora. I'm here from America." I held my breath.

"All the way from America? How did you find this address?" I could detect nervousness in her voice and the way she touched her headscarf. I tried not to alarm her.

"I got it from Panahi Printers. You see, Jahan sent a Norooz card with one of his own paintings on it to our cousin Mohsen. The card had the printer's name on it."

"Jahan isn't home yet," she said curtly. There was a resemblance all right. She and Jahan had the same large, luminous eyes, that crinkled at the corners when they talked.

"Is he going to be back soon? I've been looking for him for days," I said, still incredulous that I was standing face to face with Jahan's mother.

She hesitated, then said, "He probably got caught up with the students. The students at Mostafahi High School are very smart and inquisitive."

"He's teaching?"

She nodded. I could see she was confused and I was afraid she might shut the door. I quickly asked, "If you give me the school address, I'll go and see him there."

"Why don't you let him call you first. Where are you staying?"

I gave her the hotel card I had with me and walked away. Everything was painted lemon by late afternoon sunlight and the streets were filled with shoppers as if it were an ordinary day. But to me it was all so unreal; I had actually seen Jahan's mother. She was different from what I had imagined, with the speech of an educated woman. As I continued to stroll through a crowded square, filled with tourists, vendors, and soldiers, the sky turned robin's egg blue, streaked by soft pink.

When I returned to the hotel I expected a message from Jahan but there was nothing. I got the address of Mostafahi High School from the desk clerk, thinking I would go there the following morning if I didn't hear from Jahan by then. The clerk knew the school, which he said was divided by the sexes—Mostafahi School for Girls, Mostafahi School for Boys. They were on the same block.

# 35

I was elated as I walked to Mostafahi High School. It was like those dreams I had as a child in which I floated across the sky. I was just a few blocks, a few minutes away from seeing Jahan.

The wooden entrance doors of the two high school buildings stood on either side of a stationery store. Boys in blue shirts and black pants and girls wearing gray headscarves and *rupushes* were going in and out of the store. I watched them gather in front as they waited for the school doors to open. A moment later I tensed up with anticipation as I saw, or thought I saw, Jahan approaching. The young man had a beard and was wearing a blue jacket and beige pants. Then I noticed he was limping. Could that be Jahan? I called out his name.

The man looked at me but didn't respond. I went closer to him and said, "Jahan . . . "

"Nora *joon*," he said gently. "You've come so far!"

I had a dizzying sensation that he was at once familiar and strange. I whispered, "Jahan, we've been so worried about you. Maman and Baba and me. You stopped writing."

"I'm sorry. It's a long story. We'll have to talk."

I wanted to ask him about his limp. Instead I said, "You're looking good." He did look good. A few gray strands strewn through his hair and beard gave him a manly, mature look.

"You look ridiculous in that headscarf," he said, jokingly, trying to lighten the air between us. "I have to go in now but I'll be at my mother's house at four. Wait for me there."

It was strange to hear him say "my mother," meaning Shirin rather than Maman. Bells rang inside both schools.

"We'll see each other this afternoon," he said, starting to go into the girls' school, limping. He must have been injured in the war. I thought of us playing hide and seek when we were children. I used to search for him in every corner until I found him. Now I had found him, and yet I hadn't.

Close to four o'clock I started for Shirin's house. On the way I came across a stand with a sign in the shape of a rose lit from the inside. I bought a bouquet of flowers already in a vase and then took a taxi the rest of the way. I knocked and Shirin opened the door. She said, "I'm sorry Jahan isn't here yet."

"He told me to come here at four. I talked to him at his high school."

"Please come in and wait for him then," she said politely.

I followed her through a courtyard. Four flowerbeds planted with purple asters and marigolds in a variety of colors stood around a small pool. A stairway led to a basement. We entered a hallway with a sink in it and then a rectangular room, furnished with only a striking rug, some cushions, a lamp, and a wooden chest. The walls were whitewashed, and a colorful pear, apple, and pomegranate frieze decorated the mantle above a fireplace.

I gave Shirin the vase with the flowers and she put it on the mantle, then pointed to a cushion and said, "Sit down, won't you. You shouldn't have gone to the trouble of getting flowers." Before I could say anything she left the room.

I sat leaning against the cushion and looked around. The rug was dappled with light filtering through the leaves of an orange tree outside the window. I noticed a row of photographs on the mantle — one of Shirin, and one of Jahan and her together with their arms around each other.

Shirin came back with a tray of fruit, plates and silverware, and put it on the floor before me. She startled me when she said, "Please, don't take Jahan away from me."

"Oh! We couldn't, even if we tried. He came here to find you, and he's stayed with you."

"What do you want then?" she asked, avoiding looking at me.

"Just to see him. We worried about him every single day; for a long time we didn't even know if he was alive." To reassure her, I added, "I'm happy you and Jahan are united." As I said that I realized I truly was happy for both of them.

"Jahan showed up here," Shirin was saying, "when he was discharged from the army."

"Did he injure his knee in the war?"

She nodded and sighed. "They operated on it in the army hospital in Ahvaz. It's amazing that he ended up here in Shiraz. I didn't run into him when I worked at the Ahvaz hospital during the war, but of course there were many wounded soldiers there. They had converted a school into a residence for the employees and I stayed there. We could easily have met at that time, but we didn't. Life is a mystery."

"Are you a nurse? My mother was at one time."

"I was trained as a technician, although during the war we all helped in whatever we could. I can't bear the sight of a hospital now; since the war ended I've been making a living as a seamstress."

Footsteps sounded in the courtyard and, through the French doors, I saw Jahan and a young woman walking toward us.

"Oh, here they are. He brought his fiancée with him. I have to go out now but please stay and talk to them."

"He's engaged?" I asked, totally taken by surprise.

"Yes, Ziba is a wonderful girl. She is the daughter of Reza Kiani whose family lives in Tehran."

Jahan and Ziba walked into the room. They both kissed Shirin and then Shirin proudly said, "Nora, this is Ziba, Jahan's wife-to-be."

Ziba stepped toward me and with a warm smile said, "Salaam, I'm glad to meet you," and looking up at Jahan, "I'm so happy to be able to meet your sister."

"I'm so glad to meet you as well," I replied. I was overwhelmed with gratitude just to see Jahan alive and well, standing in the same room with me. And meeting Ziba made me even happier. At that moment, I realized I was surrendering some part of Jahan in order to gain something greater.

Shirin set up a samovar with a blue ceramic teapot in a corner and arranged silver-rimmed glasses, a silver bowl of rock sugar and spoons on a tray, then she quietly left the room.

The three of us sat down. I took off my scarf, the one I had bought at a shop in Persepolis, and laid it on my lap. The colorful bird designs on it shimmered in the sunlight that was now pouring into the room. But my attention was focused on Ziba. She was pretty with a round face, dimples in her cheeks, heart-shaped mouth, and doe eyes. She was years younger than Jahan, no more than nineteen or twenty, but there was nothing flighty or childish about her manner.

"Tell me about Baba and Maman," Jahan said in a strained voice as if he were forcing himself to speak.

"They live in L.A. now and Baba has a good practice. Maman quit nursing."

Jahan nodded. "How about you?"

"I still live on Long Island, but I'll be moving to New York City soon. I'll be working in a law firm there."

"Congratulations, a lawyer, what you always wanted."

"After I've paid all my debts, I want to go into a different kind of law, Legal Aid maybe. I want to help out at Amnesty International too. Try to help out women in Iran or places like it." I was sounding too earnest, trying to prove something to Jahan.

But he said, "I see you're trying to put meaning into your life. So am I. I'm going to be helping a bit with reconstruction in Ahvaz during the summer break. The municipal building there is just a pile of stones; and those fishermen's huts by the Karoon were flattened to the ground. The government is rebuilding war-damaged places and they need volunteers."

"And you're teaching. Are you keeping up with your art too?"

"Yes, I'm making a real breakthrough in my painting." He was becoming more animated now, but then he stopped suddenly and smiled, both of us remembering how he'd so often announced a new breakthrough.

The samovar was hissing. Ziba got up and went to get us tea. She poured tea from the pot into the glasses, added water from the samovar, and carried the tray over to us.

"It would be great if the two of you came to America, at least for a visit," I said as I took a glass of tea from the tray she held before me.

"Thank you, that's a very kind invitation. But right now I'm going to Shiraz University. Good school. Jahan went there too."

I must have looked startled. "I took a degree in art there," Jahan explained. "My goal is to study architecture. I'm taking courses at night. I like teaching, but it's not what I want to do forever."

I was surprised by Jahan's energy and ambition. I turned to Ziba and asked her, "And what are you majoring in?"

"Ecology. I'm interested in resource management and sustainable systems. You know what a severe water problem we have here. I'm exploring the uses of solar energy."

"They let a woman do that?" I asked, surprised.

"We have a long way to go, but we do have women scientists, doctors, professors in Iran," Jahan answered. "You may be surprised to know that most university students right now are girls."

"We're really determined," Ziba said. "Americans think Iran is just like Saudi Arabia but it's not." She changed the subject. "After we get married, at Norooz, we'll live here with Shirin. We don't want her to be alone again."

"She's lucky to have you and Jahan," I replied.

Silence enveloped us. Suddenly we had nothing more to say to each other. A cat came in and stretched out on the windowsill. It kept looking at us and mewed gently. The room and the house were serene, but I was full of a vague dread because of the formality that had fallen between Jahan and me.

I got up. "I should be getting back to my hotel."

"Before you leave would you like to see some of Jahan's paintings?" Ziba asked.

"I'd love to," I said, glad that Ziba was trying to break the tension.

"I'll show them to you," Ziba said, and led me to the second floor, into a spacious room with a high ceiling and good north light. A large table with art materials stood in a corner. Jahan's collages were displayed on the walls; some unfinished ones leaned against the wall. They were darker, more complex than his earlier work. Some of them had war scenes, images of explosions; wounded, bloody bodies. He had signed all of them "Jahan"—no last name.

"These are great," I said.

"He's been selling some." She pointed to a room across the hall. "That's his bedroom. He gets up early in the morning and comes here to paint."

We left and, as we started to go down the stairs, I looked inside the bedroom, hoping to see photographs of Jahan and me together, or of Maman and Baba. But there was none of that. Downstairs, Ziba said, "Will you come back tomorrow? On Fridays Jahan is home."

"Thank you. I'll see if I can," I said. "Tomorrow is my last day here."

Jahan followed me into the courtyard and we walked to the outside door together. The air between us reverberated with myriad meanings, hard to sort out. I took in the whole moment—Jahan standing there, the scented courtyard stretching behind him and, in the room on the other side, an adoring woman awaiting him. I wished I could talk to him more intimately, get his feelings about his life, but he was still formal—courteous but distant.

Then he reached out to me and we embraced. As I disengaged myself, a flash of memory made me expect him to say, "You shouldn't be walking alone, let me take you back." But he said, "Have you been going everywhere alone?"

"Yes, but no one has bothered me. Goodbye, Jahan, I don't know until when, but hope not too long," I said brightly, trying to cover up my unease with him.

"Goodbye, Nora."

I was keenly aware of the fact that he hadn't called me Noor once. As I walked to the hotel, the streetlights were going on one by one and the first stars were emerging. A mass of small birds flew up into the sky. A mist shrouded the mountains, almost obliterating them. The hotel was comforting after the tension of being with Jahan and his new family. I went to the dining room, ate quickly, and went up to my room for another solitary evening. As I was falling asleep the phone rang.

"Nora." It was Jahan's voice. "Can we, you and I, have dinner together tomorrow?"

"Yes, of course."

"I'll take you to Shirazi, one of the old restaurants here, did you go there yet?"

"No."

"I'll pick you up from your hotel at six, if that's a good time," he said.

"Okay," I said, happy to have another chance to see him.

"See you tomorrow then."

I couldn't go back to sleep.

# 36

The next day I went to more gardens, visited more monuments, and came back to the hotel in time to meet Jahan. When I entered the lobby he was already there. We started for the restaurant.

"Should we take a taxi?" I asked.

"It's only ten blocks," he said.

"Does it hurt, I mean. . . "

"You mean my knee? It's just a dull ache. I can't play soccer any more. Even hiking's difficult."

I fought to stop myself from crying.

"I was on the front only a few weeks when our unit came under fire. After I was operated on in the army hospital, they made me an officer for six months, but I could barely function. Right after the war ended, I went to Abadan, where the major fighting had been. All I saw were people looking through the ruins. For what? An unbroken pot, a trophy, a brooch."

He sank into silence. I changed the subject. "You found Shirin through the orphanage?"

"They knew my mother's last name, so I tracked her down that way. The house she lives in now is where she grew up. She stayed there after her parents died."

"We always thought you look just like Baba but I see a resemblance between you and Shirin too."

"You want to know a strange thing? I was coming into the alley to check out the address, and I saw this woman standing by a door looking up and down the street. I went and stood in front of her. I asked her if she was Shirin Sohrabi. She stared at me and said, 'Jahan'?"

"She must have always been waiting for you."

We had come to a busy intersection. Paykans, bicycles, and motor scooters raced by. We waited for an opening in the traffic and then crossed. After a block we came to a small military cemetery, about half an acre in size. At the head of each grave was a wooden post with a glass case mounted on top. Each case contained a photograph of a young man killed in the war. Their names were at the bottom of the photographs: Martyr Hossein Partovi, Martyr Ahmad Jamaly, Martyr Karim Bozorg. Dates of birth and death were inscribed under the names.

"Almost every family lost someone in the war," Jahan said. "The few weeks I fought on the front was the worst period of my life." He was stammering a little as if the trauma was returning to him.

"I can imagine, Jahan. Did you ever go to Masjid-e-Suleiman?"

"By the time I got to Iran the town was already completely demolished. The most I saw of it was from an army plane. Just tents." He stopped by a restaurant. "Here we are," he said, and led me inside.

A mosaic-tiled pool, with a fountain illuminated by colored lights, stood in the middle of the restaurant courtyard. Tables and chairs were set outdoors and indoors. Waiters carried trays with platters of food, pastry, and soft drinks. We went inside and sat at a corner table.

A waiter gave us menus with a fixed price for dinner. It listed several courses at an amazingly low price, considering the grandeur of the atmosphere.

Jahan asked, "Why don't you live in L.A. too?"

"Maman and Baba went to live there before I graduated and I stayed on. Then I got into a law school in Hempstead."

The waiter brought our food and arranged it on the table. Radishes, bread, *kotlets*, Shirazi salad, Caspian fish, cherry rice, *barg* and *joojeh kebabs*, bubbly *doogh*.

"Is Carlo Rossi still in your life?" Jahan asked as the waiter walked away.

"That ended long ago."

"Anyone else?"

"There is someone. His name is James Wakefield. His family's English. He's a filmmaker, documentaries. His next one is going to be about African immigrants in Manchester. You know how much I love movies. He wants to visit Iran."

"I hope he works out." An expression of protective affection had come into his face.

"Maybe this one will. It's been hard." I tried to change the subject, aware of a familiar tension coming over me talking about boyfriends with Jahan. "Do you ever hear from Assad?"

"He actually came here to visit, after he went to Mecca. He calls himself Haji Assad now." He laughed, like the Jahan I knew so well. "It's ridiculous. I personally still like the calligraphy in Korans, the rest is just religion."

The restaurant was getting crowded. People's voices mingled with songs, accompanied by drums, lute, and *santur* broadcast from a tape. The voice of the singer rose above all others as it reached a high pitch:

> There is a poem in my heart
> A poem that is only a desire, a sigh, fire
> It's a burning poem, engulfing me.

A few children ran around the tables; others were staring down into a fish tank set against a wall. At one table a festive birthday party was taking place.

"How did you meet Ziba? Did Shirin arrange it between you?"

"No. She was a student at Mostafahi High School, I met her teaching there, though she wasn't my student. She's very smart, like you. It's very competitive to get into Shiraz University."

"She's lived in Shiraz all her life?"

"She and her mother and her two sisters came here from Tehran after their father died. Ziba's the only person Shirin and I told about my being adopted."

A child's crying stopped us from talking for a moment. Then I said, "You wrote Mohsen. Did you ever see him?"

"No. I sent him the card on impulse."

"Don't you want to see him and the rest?"

"It's complicated. I'd have to explain a lot of things." Now he seemed to want to change the subject. "Tell me more about your Englishman."

"He's exuberant and articulate, but thoughtful and tender at the same time. We're good together. He respects what I do. Jahan, don't you love Maman and Baba, even a little? They were so broken up over you leaving. It was like they had lost a part of themselves. When Jamshid sent us the Norooz card they asked me to go to L.A. to celebrate your being alive."

"There are things you don't know, Nora."

"Really, what?"

"Amazing things." A wave of strong emotion passed over his face. Still I wasn't prepared for what he said next. He leaned over and whispered, "Baba is my real, blood father."

"What! How can that be?" I asked, shaken up by what he'd said; yet I'd had intimations of the possibility before, although I'd dismissed the idea.

I could barely hear him as he whispered, "Baba spent a night with Shirin. She became pregnant with me."

So Carlo was right after all, I thought. That line from Hafiz jumped into my head: some secrets must be kept, not told to the world at large.

"You're my sister after all, well, half-sister." He looked around the room, then said, "Let's get out of here."

He paid and we left. He led me into a quiet, tree-lined street. No one was going by but we talked in whispers anyway.

"Is Baba so cold-blooded?" I asked. I couldn't imagine his abandoning a woman like that.

"It wasn't all his fault. Remember, Baba once worked for a period at a hospital in Shiraz? My mother was a technician there. She knew Baba was going to marry Maman, but she was infatuated with him. When she found out she was pregnant, she was totally confused and bewildered. She didn't want to force Baba to marry her but she couldn't raise a child alone here either."

"Yes, of course."

"She never told Baba about the pregnancy. She left home and went to live in a rooming house by the tomb of Baba Kuhi where other women were staying to be near the poet-saint, and they didn't ask questions. A midwife delivered me. My mother couldn't return home to her parents with a baby, so she stayed there for a while before leaving me at the mosque. Then she thought it was only fair to let Baba know that his child was in an orphanage. She told a close friend at the hospital, and her friend told Baba."

"Do you think Maman knows?"

"She must. It's ironic how the secret they kept between them had so many consequences. Baba should have told me. I still feel it was an unnecessary deception. Damaging. Knowing would have helped me so much."

"Yes, but you can see how that would have been difficult for him. He thought he had to set such high moral standards for us. Imagine, he must have had doubts about marrying Maman, from another culture, then was swayed toward Shirin, then back again. When he found out about you, he must have decided to adopt you, then told Maman everything. How hurt she must have been!"

"So they kept the whole thing a secret, a secret that bound them together so tightly. Excluding us."

"We were certainly a dysfunctional family, to put it in American terms." It was now becoming easy for Jahan and me to talk. "But Jahan, I don't regret those magical years we had together."

"If only they hadn't brought so many years of pain."

We became quiet. Then I said, "I'm so sorry about hurting you in America."

"I have an apology to make, too, for leaving without a trace!"

We managed to laugh in the midst of our somber conversation. We turned to the present again.

"I'm very happy to be here now, to try and have some influence in my own small way," he said. "I want Iran to grow, to become a better place for everyone. I feel at home here, where there was once a great civilization."

"I've been thinking about you everywhere I've been visiting around Shiraz."

Then we went back to our parents again, how strange and exclusive their relationship was and the secret they kept. I said, "For Maman to accept Baba's one night with Shirin and then to bring you home. That was admirable, good. Don't you think so?"

"Yes, I do. I appreciate what she did, and what Baba did too." Then he went on to tell me more about Shirin and Baba.

As I listened, scenes he was drawing appeared before my eyes, my mind amplifying them, filling in blanks. One night, when her parents were away visiting relatives, Shirin invited our father to the very house she lived in now. I imagined them walking there together on the empty back streets of Shiraz. She was only eighteen years old then, going to school and working part time as a lab technician. I imagined our father waking the next morning, sunlight streaming into the room through the branches of the orange tree. Imagined him gently pushing away a curl of hair that had fallen on her forehead and then leaning over and kissing her.

"Did you ever suspect that Baba was your real father?"

"No, not once."

"Carlo said to me once that you might be Baba's real son. I got angry at him."

"Still we love them. I want you to tell them that. But I can't have two mothers. I can't lead two lives. At least, not now. Noor, I've finally found a balance in my life, I can say I'm happy. I wish so much for you to be happy too." He had finally called me Noor.

We turned into another back street. Leaves cast fluid, lattice-like shadows on the wide *joob*. He used to hold my hand and help me jump over *joobs*.

"I have your diary. I took it from your room. It's in the hotel. I can give it to you."

"I meant to go back and get it but never did. Now I have no use for it." Again he said, "Forgive me for not contacting you, but there was the war, and then you must know how I felt after I found out."

"Jahan *joon*, here we are, just sister and brother. It's so much simpler."

He accompanied me into the lobby, we embraced tightly and kissed goodbye. I went to my room and looked out the window, watching him limp down the street. I suddenly recalled that walk, with him in Meigoon when I'd hurt my foot and he'd massaged it gently. It was as if his touch was magic, the way the pain went away. If only it were possible for me to do that for him.

Still, having found Jahan at last, I was feeling lighter. He had said, "I've finally found a balance in my life. I can say I'm happy. I wish so much for you to be happy too."

It sounded like an order and a release.

# READING GROUP GUIDE

1. *Jumping Over Fire* tells the story of an Iranian family with two eth- nicities, two cultures. The mother, Moira, is American, and the father, Cyrus, is Iranian. Nora, the blonde teenage daughter resembles her mother, while her adopted brother Jahan is a typical Iranian boy. The family must leave Iran just before the fall of the Shah and try to make new lives in America. In this predicament, how does each of these characters respond to conflicting identities and loyalties?

2. The schism between cultures, the loss of home, possessions, friends, and family, along with confusing new possibilities, create common ground for people forced to immigrate to a new country. Cyrus and Moira must find work, and Jahan and Nora are about to enter college. How do the personal qualities her characters bring with them affect this adjustment?

3. Rachlin sees the relationship between the parents as a counterpoint to that of their children. What comparisons and contrasts are drawn between them?

4. Friendships are essential and can influence the course of a life. How do friendships move the narrative, and what do they reveal about the characters?

5. Many families have secrets. Where the secrets between Moira and Cyrus justified? What was the impact of these secrets on their children? Discuss the secret kept by Nora and Jahan? How might more open communication in this family have changed the course of events? Might family secrets be necessary in certain cases, or even good?

6. Incest is extremely uncommon between adopted siblings. Why do you think Rachlin chose to incorporate this theme? Discuss the factors that led to Nora and Jahan's intimacy. What is the signifi- cance of the fracture in the relationship when they come to America? Is Nora or Jahan the more sympathetic character?

7. What is the role of religion in the characters' lives? Moira is a Christian, Cyrus a Muslim, although neither of them is active in

their faiths. How does Rachlin highlight religious questions during the family's stay with traditional Muslim relatives in Meigoon? What is it in Islam that attracts Jahan and his friends? Why does Moira become active in her church?

8. Nora and Jahan's endeavor to find love, self-esteem, and satisfying work is the main thrust of the narrative. What stands in their way? Do these characters make the right choices for themselves? What price do they pay for these choices? Discuss the themes of identity that appear and reappear in the novel.

9. Nora is deeply motivated to become an independent woman. What impediments does she encounter? Nora is strong-willed and in most ways very realistic. Why are her relationships with the men in her life — her father, her brother, her boyfriends — so difficult?

10. Do you think the first-person narration by Nora creates more emotional impact than if the novel were written in the third person or from a multiple point of view?

11. Why does Jahan want to return to his roots? What are the attractions for him of life in Iran? Jahan is an idealist and something of a dreamer. Do you think he could find fulfillment there?

12. There is much interest today in the role of women in Islamic society. Rachlin, who was born in Iran and still has family there, explores this issue in some detail. What insights does she offer?

13. After the hostage crisis, Jahan begins to change, and we see intimations of terrorism. Is Rachlin drawing a parallel with the situation of disaffected young men who come here as immigrants? Is she equally sympathetic with all of her characters?

14. The action of the book takes place over a decade, the years the aftermath of the Iran-Iraq war. How does Rachlin make use of these historic events? How does she interweave the political and the personal? What course might the lives of the Elahi family taken if there had been no revolution?

# ABOUT NAHID RACHLIN

Nahid Rachlin was born in Iran, one of ten children. Shortly after she was born, her mother allowed her older sister, a childless widow, to adopt her. Her aunt was a devoted mother to her, and Nahid was very happy. She rarely saw her parents—her aunt lived in Tehran and her parents in Ahvaz, miles away. Then, when she was nine years old, her father forcefully and without consultation with her aunt, took her back. Her aunt had no legal rights to her, and had to relinquish her.

Rachlin found it difficult to adjust to a new family of virtual strangers. Because of this traumatic displacement, she turned to reading and writing very early, and found solace in creating fictional characters whose lives she could shape. The feeling of displacement is a recurring theme in her fiction.

As a teenager, aware of the limiting role of women in Iranian culture, she began to dream of a different way of life. She saw American movies and read books in translation, which were readily available in Ahvaz, an oil refinery town with many American employees. She strove to come to America and study. Although her father was an educated lawyer, he believed that his daughters should marry someone he would arrange for them and, like her mother, settle into a life of domesticity. But finally, aware of his daughter's unhappiness and restlessness, he allowed her emigrate. In America she found her way. Among Rachlin's publications are three novels, *Foreigner* (W.W. Norton), *Married to a Stranger* (E.P. Dutton/City Lights), *The Heart's Desire* (City Lights), a collection of short stories, *Veils* (City Lights), and a memoir, *Persian Girls,* (Penguin U.S.A., 2006). *Jumping Over Fire* (City Lights) is her fourth novel. She teaches at the New School University and the Unterberg Poetry Center at the 92nd Street Y. She has taught at Yale University and Barnard College. Presently she is a fellow at Yale.

For more about Nahid Rachlin check her website: http://www.nahidrachlin.com